st

THE THIRD VICTIM

Center Point
Large Print

**This Large Print Book carries the
Seal of Approval of N.A.V.H.**

THE
THIRD
VICTIM

Phillip Margolin

CENTER POINT LARGE PRINT
THORNDIKE, MAINE

Library of Congress Cataloging-in-Publication Data

Names: Margolin, Phillip, author.
Title: The third victim / Phillip Margolin.
Description: Center Point Large Print edition. | Thorndike, Maine :
    Center Point Large Print, 2018.
Identifiers: LCCN 2018004528 | ISBN 9781683247685
    (hardcover : alk. paper)
Subjects: LCSH: Large type books. | GSAFD: Suspense fiction. |
    Mystery fiction.
Classification: LCC PS3563.A649 T48 2018b | DDC 813/.54—dc23
LC record available at https://lccn.loc.gov/2018004528

For Melanie,
who has brought joy back into my life

PART ONE
THE THIRD VICTIM

CHAPTER ONE

Caleb White slowed his pickup as soon as he spotted the deer crossing sign at the side of the two-lane country road. Caleb had lived his whole life in Whisper Lake and he always slowed down when he saw it. The city dwellers, who only came out a few weeks a year, usually ignored the sign and sped on, but there were no lights on this heavily forested stretch, and when Caleb was eight years old, a three-hundred-pound buck had bounded out of the forest and totaled the family car.

A burst of static from the radio momentarily distracted Caleb just as something staggered out of the forest and into the road. He jammed on his brakes and the pickup fishtailed. If he hadn't slowed down, he might not have been able to stop in time. As it was, the truck ended up sideways and Caleb found himself slumped over the steering wheel, his heart in overdrive. He closed his eyes for a second to calm down. Then he peered out of the passenger window. It was pitch-black and he couldn't see a thing.

Caleb backed the truck onto the shoulder. As he turned, the headlights panned over a body sprawled on the road. He put on his warning lights and jumped out of the cab. A woman was laying on her stomach, her legs bare and the tail of her blouse barely covering her panties.

"Miss, are you okay?" Caleb asked as he walked toward her.

The woman stirred, then weakly pushed herself up onto her hands and knees. She lifted her head and stared at Caleb through strands of long, unwashed, uncombed brown hair.

"Help me," she begged.

"It's okay," Caleb said as he drew closer and got his first clear view. There was duct tape around the woman's wrists and ankles, her face was caked with blood, and her legs were scratched and bruised. The blouse was torn in several places and it hung open. Caleb took off his jacket. He was almost to her when the stench of urine, feces, and body odor stopped him in his tracks.

"Please," she pleaded. Caleb moved.

"I'll get you to a hospital," he assured the woman as he draped the coat across her shoulders. Then he grabbed her under her arms and helped her stand. As she rose, the blouse parted, revealing burn marks and cuts on the woman's ribs and breasts.

Caleb pulled his eyes away and eased the woman into the passenger seat. As soon as he shut her door, she slumped against it. Caleb headed for town and speed-dialed his cousin.

"Yeah?" Harry said.

"It's Caleb. I'm on the way to the hospital with a girl."

"What happened?!"

"It's not like that. You should meet me at the hospital. This girl . . . She came out of the forest and she's hurt. I think someone did something to her. Something real bad."

Whisper Lake, population 2,074, was the county seat of Hammond County, population 17,039. The population was artificially inflated during the summer, when the rich city folk who owned the cabins that ringed the lake and the tourists who stayed at the Whisper Lake Resort came to town. But as soon as school started, the population plummeted and the only tourists who remained were the avid fly fishermen who sloshed through the Bear Run River and the hunters who stalked the woods during deer season.

The cops in Hammond County didn't have much to do most of the year. If it wasn't for the universal staples of lawlessness—speeding, domestic violence, and bar fights—the deputies in the Hammond County Sheriff's Office would be sitting around all day playing video games or talking sports. That is why Caleb White's call induced an adrenaline rush in his cousin.

Harry White, a former high school quarterback and marine, was thirty-one years old. He had curly black hair, a straight nose, blue eyes, and

11

a dark complexion. When Harry arrived at the hospital, the EMTs were lifting the young woman onto a gurney. He went over to Caleb.

"What happened?"

Caleb was upset, and it took a few minutes for Harry to understand what had occurred on the country road.

"You stay in the waiting room," Harry told his cousin. "Stan's on the way and he'll take your statement. Okay?"

"Yeah."

"You all right?"

"Not really."

Harry laid a hand on Caleb's shoulder and gave it a squeeze.

"You done a good deed tonight," he said before following the gurney into the hospital. The EMTs rolled the woman into an examining room. Harry started to follow, but Dr. Nicholas Hayes, a hunting buddy, told Harry to wait outside while he examined the girl.

Harry paced the hall for twenty minutes before Hayes came out. The doctor looked grim.

"How is she, Nick?" Harry asked.

"She's been beaten, tortured, and starved, so not good."

"Will she recover? Is there any permanent damage?"

"With time, she'll heal physically. It's her mental state I'm worried about."

"Did she tell you her name?"

"It's Meredith Fenner."

"Did she say who did this to her?"

"I didn't ask. I figured that was your department."

"Can I talk to her?"

"Yes, but make it short. As soon as you're done, I'm going to give her a sedative so she can get some rest."

Harry opened the door. Meredith's eyes fixed on him. She looked terrified. Her black eyes, broken nose, and split lip were evidence of a savage beating, and it took an effort for Harry to keep from showing emotion.

Harry held up his shield. "Miss Fenner, my name is Harry White and I'm a detective with the Hammond County Sheriff's Office. Do you feel up to answering a few questions? I'll make this short, but I want to start tracking down the person who did this to you."

"I . . . I don't want to talk about it. Please."

Harry walked over to the bed. "I can understand that. But we need to find the person who assaulted you."

Meredith turned her face away. "I can't."

"Can you at least tell me if it was a man or a woman? Was there one person or more than one?"

"A . . . a man. One man."

"Can you describe him?"

13

"Not now, please. I . . . I don't want to think about what . . . what he did to me."

Harry wanted to push a little more, but he held himself in check. He tried to imagine what Meredith had gone through, and he decided that the best gift he could give her was peace and quiet.

CHAPTER TWO

Regina Barrister entered stage left and every eye turned toward her. Even though Regina was actually striding into a ballroom in the Hilton, the description was accurate. A former lover had once told Regina that her regal bearing and charisma transformed any place she appeared into a theater.

In her youth, Regina's ivory complexion, crystal clear blue eyes, and dazzling smile had caused men to catch their breath. Regina, now fifty-eight, was still beautiful, her crown of hair kept golden by Portland's best salon and her figure kept trim by her personal trainer, but she was a presence now and not merely an object of desire.

Regina's father, Abraham Batiashivili, had emigrated from Russia to the United States in 1947. Abraham had learned English by reading British mystery novels. When he realized that Americans had a hard time pronouncing his last name, he changed it to Barrister. The names her parents bestowed upon their daughter turned out to be prophetic. *Webster's New World Dictionary* defines *regina* as "the official title of a reigning queen" and *barrister* as a "member of the legal profession who presents and pleads cases in court." Regina reigned over every courtroom in which she appeared and her record of victories attested to her skill as a trial attorney.

The Oregon State Bar had put on a one-day seminar on recent developments in criminal law. The last lecture had concluded half an hour ago and the participants were gathering for drinks in the Hilton ballroom. Regina scanned the crowd, then walked over to a group that included Stanley Cloud, the chief justice of Oregon's Supreme Court, and Robin Lockwood, one of the justice's law clerks.

Robin was five eight, with a wiry build, blue eyes, a straight nose, high cheekbones, and blond hair that was cut short and molded to her oval face. Regina had seen Lockwood earlier in the day when Robin lectured about recent developments in federal criminal law. She'd been impressed by Robin's grasp of her subject and her sense of humor during the Q &A that followed her talk.

Justice Cloud had shared the program with his clerk and he'd focused on new developments in the state's criminal law. The chief justice was in excellent shape for a sixty-three-year-old, and his broad shoulders and narrow waist made him look ten years younger. He had a full head of snowy white hair, pale green eyes, a slightly crooked nose, and a mouth that often displayed a winsome grin but could straighten with displeasure when he was confronted by a fool during oral argument.

When Regina reached the group, she found that they were in the middle of a heated debate about the death penalty.

"Executing an inmate with a lethal injection is cruel and unusual punishment," Robin insisted.

"Come on, Robin," said Kyle Bergland, a Multnomah County district attorney. "It's certainly more humane than hanging, the electric chair, or a firing squad."

"Not true," Robin said. "There have been numerous reports of prisoners gasping for air, heaving, and clenching their teeth in obvious pain during an execution by injection."

Alex Mason, a senior partner in one of Portland's biggest firms, laughed derisively. He was an ugly man of medium height with a small paunch and rounded shoulders.

"Killers can't complain if they suffer," Mason said. "They don't mind if their victims suffer. What's sauce for the goose should be sauce for the gander. And your argument is moot anyway. The U.S. Supreme Court already decided that Oklahoma could use . . ."

Mason frowned as he tried to remember the name of the drug Oklahoma used in lethal injections.

"Midazolam," Allison Mason interjected hesitantly. Alex Mason's wife was a stunning redhead who was easily twenty years her husband's junior.

"Thank you, dear," Alex snapped as he stared angrily at his wife.

Allison cast her eyes down and hunched her shoulders.

While he was talking, Alex had looked over Regina's shoulder and across the room. "There are the Potters, Allison," he said abruptly. "I've got to talk to Neil about a case. Come on."

Allison followed obediently, and Regina frowned as she watched the couple walk off.

"What do you think about lethal injections, Regina?" Bergland asked.

"I try not to think about them," she replied with a smile. Then she turned to Robin.

"I enjoyed your presentation."

"Thank you."

Regina noticed that Robin did not appear to be intimidated by her, which was often not the case with young attorneys.

"Stanley says you're leaving the court soon and you've started job hunting," Regina continued.

"That's right," Robin said.

"One of my associates is moving back east. Does criminal law interest you?"

"That's my main interest," Robin replied, keeping her voice even.

Regina turned to the chief justice. "Would you mind if I spirited your clerk away?"

"Not in the least," Cloud replied with a smile.

"Would you like to join me in the bar?" Regina asked Robin.

"Justice Cloud set this up, didn't he?" Robin asked after they'd settled in a corner of the bar.

"Of course," Regina replied. "He knew I was in the market for fresh blood and he told me I'd be a fool if I didn't talk to you. He says you're one of the best clerks he's ever had and," she added with a smile, "the clerk with the most interesting résumé."

Robin threw her head back and laughed.

"I understand you worked your way through Yale Law School by fighting in mixed martial arts bouts under the name 'Rockin' Robin' Lockwood," Regina said.

"I did, but I'm not the only Yale Law grad to play a sport professionally. Supreme Court justice Byron 'Whizzer' White worked his way through the law school by playing professional football. He was the leading rusher in the National Football League."

"Is that so? And was his GPA as high as yours?"

Robin blushed. "I don't know."

"You're not going to get modest on me now, are you?"

Robin grinned. "I'll try not to."

"Martial arts training will certainly stand you in good stead when you go to trial," Regina said. "I've often thought of criminal law as the intellectual equivalent of a back-alley brawl. How did you get into MMA?"

"I grew up on a farm in Iowa, one of five children and the only girl, so I had to be tough. My dad was a conference wrestling champ in high school and my brothers all wrestled, so I wanted to, but my high school didn't have a girls team. That meant I had to wrestle with the boys."

"How did that go over?" Regina asked.

"Not well at first, but my coach was supportive and two of my brothers were on the team. They stood up for me and the other boys came around when they saw that I didn't want them to cut me any slack."

"How did you do?"

"I made varsity my senior year as a one-hundred-and-ten-pounder and placed third in the district meet," Robin said proudly. "That was the best any girl had ever done in the state."

"Did you wrestle in college?"

"No. I went to the state university, and that's a top Division I program. There was no way I could make the wrestling team, so I started training in mixed martial arts at a local gym. By the time I started law school, I was ranked nationally. Women's MMA doesn't pay a lot, but I was making enough, coupled with my scholarship, to pay my law school tuition."

"Why did you decide to go to law school?"

"In the small town where I grew up, I was the first girl to try out for the wrestling team. Some of the parents went ballistic when they found out

20

their little darlings would have daily intimate contact with someone of the female persuasion. They complained to the principal and the school board, and the board said I couldn't wrestle on the boys team. So my dad hired a lawyer; we sued the bastards and won. That's when I knew I wanted to be a lawyer, so I could help other people who were being pushed around."

"You're lucky your dad is so supportive."

"Was," Robin said as her happy expression melted. "Dad passed away just after I was accepted at Yale."

"I'm sorry."

"Me, too. He was a great dad."

"He sounds like it. When did you decide to stop fighting professionally?" Regina asked, changing the subject because Robin was upset.

"When I started worrying about getting punch-drunk. By my second semester at Yale, I was ranked ninth in the lightweight division. The number-two-ranked contender was supposed to fight an elimination bout, but her opponent was injured while she was training. They asked me if I'd fill in. I started thinking that I had a shot at a championship, so I took the fight, even though my coach advised me not to." Robin smiled sheepishly. "I should have listened, because I really got my bell rung. Kerrigan was way faster than I was and no one had ever hit me as hard. Just before she knocked me out, it dawned on me that I had no business being in the Octagon with her. After that fight, I had short-term memory loss, headaches, the whole nine yards. My doctor advised me to concentrate on law school, but I'd already made up my mind that I was better off getting beaten up by my professors."

"Smart girl," Regina said with a smile. Then she stopped smiling and looked Lockwood in the eye. "If I offered you a job with my firm, would you take it?"

"You bet," Robin replied without hesitation.

"Then consider yourself hired."

"I'm not sure when I can start," Robin said.

Regina smiled. "Oh, that's easy. I already cleared it with Stanley. You start next week."

Regina and Robin talked while they finished their drinks; then Robin excused herself because she had an hour's drive to Salem, Oregon's capital, where the Oregon Supreme Court and her apartment were located. Regina paid the bill and wandered into the lobby. When she was certain she was not being observed, she walked over to the bank of elevators, reached for the up button, and froze. She couldn't remember the floor or the room she wanted.

Regina dropped her hand to her side. Her stomach knotted and she started to perspire. Then she remembered her purse. She snapped it open and jabbed her fingers inside, her anxiety rising until she found the paper on which she had written the information she needed. Relief washed over her just as one of the elevators opened and a group of laughing teenagers got out.

Regina entered the car, consulted the paper, and pressed the button for the ninth floor. While the car rose, she took deep breaths, and she was composed by the time the elevator stopped. Moments later, she was knocking on a door at the end of the ninth-floor corridor. Shortly after she knocked, Stanley Cloud let her into his suite.

"What took you so long, Reggie?" he asked.

Regina raised an eyebrow. "What made you so sure I'd come?"

"I always make you come," the chief justice replied with a sly grin.

Regina threw her head back and laughed.

CHAPTER THREE

Three days after Caleb White rescued Meredith Fenner, Carrie Anders fielded a call from Harry White. Carrie, who had been a detective with the Hammond County Sheriff's Office before moving to Portland several years ago, was a large woman who was a little taller than Harry's six one and as strong as some of the men in both police departments. Harry had seen her wade into a bar fight and beat the crap out of belligerent drunks who thought they could take her because she was a woman.

Carrie had sad brown eyes, a large, lumpish nose, and short, shaggy black hair. Her lumbering appearance and slow drawl often fooled people into thinking that she was slow-witted, but Harry knew that she was wicked smart.

"Hey, Harry, what can I do for you?" Carrie asked as soon as Harry identified himself.

"It's what I might be able to do for you. Is anyone in your office working a serial case where women have been tortured with cigarettes and bound with duct tape?"

Carrie sat up. The information about the cigarette burns and duct tape had not been released to the public.

"Why do you ask?"

"Two days ago, a young woman staggered out of the forest and collapsed on County Road Twenty-four. She was in terrible shape, in shock, and reluctant to talk about what had happened . . . until this afternoon. As soon as I heard her story, I remembered an email from your department and an article in the Portland newspaper. I could be way off base, but I think it would be worth your while to talk to her."

Carrie Anders, dressed in navy blue slacks, a blue blazer, and a white tailored man's shirt, entered Meredith Fenner's hospital room the afternoon after Harry White's call. Fenner turned toward the detective as soon as the door opened, and Anders could see she was scared.

"Hi, Meredith," Harry said as he walked in. Meredith relaxed a little when she saw him.

"This is Carrie Anders. She's a detective from Portland, but she used to work with me here. I asked her to talk to you because she's been investigating the deaths of two women who may have been murdered by the man who kidnapped you."

"Do you mind if I sit?" Carrie asked.

When Meredith shook her head, the detective pulled a chair up next to Meredith's bed. Harry had shown Anders photographs of Meredith that had been taken when she arrived at the hospital. She'd looked hideous in them. Now that a lot of the damage to her face was fading and her hair had been washed, cut, and combed, Carrie could see she was an attractive young woman.

"I know you've been through a lot," Carrie said. "I'm glad you're safe now. How are you feeling?"

"Better," she said quietly.

"Would it be okay if I asked you some questions?"

"I already told Detective White what happened. I really don't want to have to think about it again."

"You're not the first woman I've talked to who's been through a horrible experience, so I know it's painful to relive it. But I'm afraid that you might be the third victim of a very sick and dangerous man and I want to stop him before a fourth woman has to go through what you did— or worse."

Carrie paused and looked into Meredith's eyes. "Will you help me stop him?"

Meredith hesitated. Then she nodded.

"Would you mind if I record our conversation? This way, I'll have an accurate account of what you tell me and I can save you from having to repeat it again."

Meredith nodded.

"Thank you," Carrie said as she took out a recorder and dictated an introduction that established the time, date, and location of the interview and who was present.

"Can you tell me everything that happened from the beginning? And if it gets too intense, we'll take a break. Okay?"

"Okay."

"Why don't we start by talking a little about you? How old are you?"

"Twenty-three."

"Are you in school, working?"

"I'm a barista at People's Coffee House in Portland. I'm trying to make enough money to go to Portland Community College."

"What are you planning to study?"

"I . . . I'd like to be a nurse."

"That's good. There's a shortage of nurses. Do you have any credits toward a degree?"

"Some from a community college in Florida."

"So you're not from Oregon?"

"No. I moved here a few months ago."

"Detective White says you told him you were attacked after work," Carrie said after a few more preliminary questions. "What happened?"

"I work until ten. Then I help clean up after we close. There's an employee parking lot in back of the store. That's . . . that's where he was waiting."

"It was a man? You're sure."

Meredith nodded.

"Was he alone?"

"I think so. I never saw anyone but him."

"Okay, tell me what happened. You're going to your car . . ."

"He grabbed me from behind and pressed a cloth over my nose."

She paused and turned her head away. Carrie thought that Meredith was fighting back tears, and she waited patiently for her to regain her composure.

"Do you want some water?" Carrie asked.

"Yes, please. This is very hard."

Harry poured a glass of water and handed it to Meredith.

"Thank you," she said when she had sipped a little.

"What do you remember after the man pressed the cloth to your nose?"

"I blacked out. When I came to, I was in a car trunk and the car was bouncing. I was woozy when the car stopped. Before I could see anything, he put the cloth over my nose and knocked me out again. But I saw a dirt driveway that leads up to the cabin where he held me when I escaped."

"We'll get to your escape in a bit. Let's get back to your abduction. You're in the trunk. It opens?"

Meredith nodded.

"What do you see?"

"Him. He . . . he was leaning in and he pressed the cloth on my nose and mouth again."

"Could you see his face?"

"No. He was wearing a ski mask."

"Okay. What's the next thing you remember?"

28

"I was in a room, spread-eagled on a bed, and my hands were secured to the bedposts with duct tape."

"Did you still have your clothes on?"

"He'd taken off my pants and bra, but I had on my underpants and blouse."

"What did the room look like?"

"There was just the bed. The walls were wood. It was a log cabin. There was nothing on the walls, no photographs or paintings. My room was small. There was a window, but it was covered by blackout shades. There were sheets on the floor around the bed." Meredith shuddered. "There were stains on the sheets, and I think it was blood."

"Do you want some more water?" Carrie asked.

"No, I just want to get this over."

"How long were you alone?" Carrie asked.

"I don't know. I'd lost track of time. It seemed like hours, but I don't know. I . . . I started feeling very hungry and thirsty. I called out, but no one answered. I was groggy when I came to, but whatever he used to dope me wore off. Then I was really scared. I did get light-headed from hunger, so I could have been there a day. I don't know. I had to pee. I tried to hold it in, but I . . . I couldn't."

Meredith started to cry. Carrie heard her gulping in air. She laid a hand gently on Meredith's shoulder.

"It's okay. You don't have to be embarrassed."

29

Carrie waited for Meredith to calm down. Then she asked her what happened next.

"He came in."

"Describe him."

"He had black clothes on, a bulky black sweater and dark jeans and gloves. And he was still wearing the mask."

Carrie stood up. "You're on a bed, so you have a different perspective from someone standing. Was he as tall as I am? I'm six two."

"He was shorter, average height, not short, but not tall, either."

"What happened after he came in?"

"He stood at the foot of the bed and just stared at me. I asked him what he wanted. I begged him to let me go. He just stood there. When I realized I was just turning him on, I stopped talking. That's when he walked around the bed and punched me in the face. I screamed, and he put his hand over my mouth and squeezed my nostrils shut. I panicked. I couldn't breathe. When I was about to pass out, he took his hands away and leaned close to me and said that I must never talk unless he gave me permission. He said I would be punished if I disobeyed.

"I think my nose was broken, because the pain was intense when he squeezed my nostrils. When I was quiet, he said I was a bad girl and bad girls must be punished. That's when he ripped my blouse open and took out a pack of cigarettes."

Meredith started to shake.

"It's okay. Relax. He's not here and he can't hurt you. Detective White and I won't let him," Carrie said.

Meredith took a deep breath. "He burned me. When I screamed, he reached down between his legs. He . . . he was touching himself. When he burned me again, I begged him to stop. He said that I had spoken and had disobeyed him. He said I was a bad girl. He hit me in the stomach and I couldn't breathe. Then he punched me in my eye. I had no air. I couldn't scream. I thought I would die. While I was gasping for air, he burned me on the waist. I had enough air to scream. When I stopped, I could hear his breathing. It was heavy and he was stroking himself some more. He shivered and I think he . . ." She gulped in some air. "I think he ejaculated. After that, he put a strip of duct tape across my mouth and left."

"Thank you," Carrie said. "I know this is rough, but you're coming through like a trouper. Now I want you to think. You said he spoke to you. Was there anything distinctive about his voice?"

"I . . . He didn't speak much, but . . ."

Suddenly, Meredith's eyes opened wide.

"He did have an accent. There were a lot of New Yorkers where I lived in Florida, snowbirds and retirees. He sounded a little like them."

"That's terrific!" Carrie said. "Anything else, any scars, distinguishing marks?"

31

"I'm not certain. The only time I saw any of his flesh was when he took off the glove on his right hand to . . . to stroke himself. When he started . . . when he was masturbating, I was disgusted and really scared, but I did see his hand."

"When you saw his skin, could you tell his race?"

"He was white."

"Okay. What happened after that first time?"

"He left me. There was no food or water. I was in a lot of pain. I can't say how long it was before he came back. I was tied to the bed. I tried to get my wrists and ankles free, but I couldn't. The second time, it was more of the same. I didn't talk, but he still beat me. This time, he cut me with a knife. Not bad cuts, but they were painful. Then he would burn the cuts with a cigarette. He knocked me out again and I woke up in a closet.

"My wrists and legs were both taped together. I still had my underpants and shirt on, but I had soiled myself. I was gagging from the smell and starving. Thirst was the worst. I knew I had to escape or I would be tortured again and again until he finally killed me. That's when I got lucky. I felt around the closet for anything I could use. There was a nail sticking out of the floorboard. It was dark in the closet and he probably never saw it. I sawed through the tape on my wrists, freed my legs, and used what was left of my strength to break open the door. It wasn't very strong and I was desperate.

"It was night and he wasn't there. I was afraid to go down the driveway because I thought he could come back at any moment, so I went through the woods, and Mr. White saved me."

"Okay, you did great. I only have one last question. The area where Caleb White found you, there are a lot of summer cabins around there. Do you think you'd recognize the place where you were held if you saw it?"

"I might. I only saw it at night when I ran away, but I remember a toolshed, and the cabin was big. It didn't look like an old cabin. It looked new, like something rich people would build."

"When you're stronger, would you be willing to look at cabins near the place where you came out of the forest? You'll have police all around you, so you'll be safe, and if you can identify the cabin, we can get him."

"I'll do it." Suddenly, Meredith's voice sounded stronger. "I want him caught. I want him dead."

CHAPTER FOUR

Robin had driven home from the CLE at the Hilton sky-high with excitement. She'd wanted to be a lawyer from the moment her attorney defeated the school board's attempt to keep her off the wrestling team, and criminal law had the greatest appeal for her. Placing in Districts, being the first person in her family to graduate from college, getting into Yale Law School, and clerking for Justice Cloud were among the most amazing moments in her life, but working with Regina Barrister would be way up there.

Robin had started to hear about Regina while she was in law school. One of the cases Regina had argued in the United States Supreme Court had been required reading in Constitutional Law, and even the East Coast newspapers occasionally carried accounts of her cases. Robin had graduated near the top of her class and could have gotten almost any federal or state clerkship she wanted, but clerking in Oregon, where Regina Barrister practiced law, had been a big selling point when she was weighing where to go. During her year at the Oregon Supreme Court, Robin had even played hooky a few times so she could drive to Portland and watch Regina in action.

Justice Cloud had never mentioned that he knew Regina, but Robin remembered a conversation a few months ago in the judge's chambers. After they had finished discussing a memo she had written, Justice Cloud had asked her what she wanted to do when her clerkship ended. She'd told the judge that Regina's firm was high on her list of places where she'd like to work. Justice Cloud hadn't said anything about Regina during the conversation or afterward, but he'd been instrumental in helping her get her dream job.

Robin parked in front of her garden apartment at ten. The apartment was small, furnished, and messy. Robin was so busy between work and working out that she felt cleaning was an imposition on her precious free time. There would usually come a point where the mess was too awful to ignore and Robin would go into a frenzy of garbage collection, washing, and vacuuming, but she hadn't reached that point in a while. She walked to her bedroom, passing take-out boxes, stacks of old newspapers, and general clutter.

Robin fell into bed but was too excited to sleep. She conked out a little after midnight and was up at five on Thursday. A half hour of calisthenics and a five-mile run cleared the cobwebs. Then she showered, scarfed down a bagel, and walked to the supreme court building. As soon as she arrived, Robin went to Stanley Cloud's chambers, but the chief justice wasn't in yet.

Robin tried to distract herself by working on a draft of an opinion, but she couldn't concentrate. She wanted to tell someone about her new job, but she didn't want to bother the other clerks or give the impression that she was bragging. The natural thing would be to call her mother, but her mother disapproved of almost everything she wanted to do.

Robin's high school wrestling career had thrilled her father and embarrassed her mother, who wanted a "normal" girl who would stay in her hometown, marry a local boy, and have children. Robin's mother had not been in favor of Robin's going to college. None of her brothers had gone. But she had tolerated Robin's attending the state university because it was a short drive from home. She had never understood why Robin would want to go to law school, especially one that was clear across the country. Still, Robin knew that deep down her mother loved her and had her best interests at heart, so, after a moment's hesitation, she called home.

"Hi, Mom," she said when her mother answered.

"Hello, Robin. It's nice of you to call," her mother said, her tone frosty. "I haven't heard from you in a while."

"I've been super busy, but I have some great news to tell you."

"Yes?"

"You know my clerkship is almost over. Well,

36

I've just been hired by Regina Barrister, the best criminal lawyer in the state, and I'm starting as her associate on Friday."

"You're staying in Oregon?"

"Yeah."

"I thought you'd try to get a job nearer to home."

"I was thinking about that," Robin lied, "but this is an amazing opportunity."

Robin's mother went quiet and Robin could almost feel her disapproval flowing across the ether.

"It's a really great job and I'd be learning from one of the best."

"I guess you have to do what you think is best for your career."

"This is definitely what's best."

"Then I'm happy for you," she said grudgingly.

"Thanks, Mom. I love you."

"I love you, too."

"Well, I've got to get back to work. I just wanted you to know about the job."

Robin hung up. Calling her mother had been a mistake. The call had killed the joy she'd felt since Regina Barrister had offered her the job. But she'd known it probably would and she'd called anyway.

Justice Cloud had still not shown up by the time Robin went to lunch, which was unusual, but he was in his chambers when she got back. Robin knocked on Cloud's doorjamb and he looked up from a brief he was reading. When he saw who was knocking, he broke into a grin.

"I'm guessing that I've lost you to free agency," Cloud quipped.

Robin returned the grin. "Miss Barrister said you set this up, and I can not thank you enough."

"I thought you'd like working with Regina, and I told her she was lucky to get you. I was certain you two would hit it off."

"We did. I really felt comfortable with her."

Robin stopped smiling. "One thing, though. She wants me to start next week. She said she cleared it with you, but is that okay?"

"Oh, yeah. The associate you're replacing is leaving today and she's got tons of work for you. I've already lined up your replacement. He's coming in Monday. He's a good kid, second in his class at Lewis and Clark. Get him oriented, then take off."

"You're the best, Judge."

Cloud grinned. Then his expression became stern. "Enough chitchat, Lockwood. I need that draft of the Sierra Club opinion on my desk pronto."

"Yes, sir," Robin said as she saluted and did an about-face. As soon as her back was turned, she couldn't help breaking into another grin.

CHAPTER FIVE

"What do you think?" Carrie Anders asked Dr. Sally Grace.

Everyone in the room was watching the assistant medical examiner, a slender woman with frizzy black hair and sharp blue eyes. Dr. Grace was known for her sense of humor, but she wasn't smiling as she looked at the pictures of Meredith Fenner that Carrie had laid on the conference table after playing the recording of her interview with the young victim.

Dr. Grace had examined the corpses of Portland prostitutes Patricia Rawls and Tonya Benson. Benson's body had been found in a Dumpster behind a restaurant forty miles west of where Caleb White had found Meredith Fenner. Rawls's body had been discovered a month later in the woods at a rest stop by a couple who were walking their dog. The rest stop was thirty-seven miles east of the spot where Fenner had stumbled out of the forest a week after Rawls was killed.

"I think there's a good chance that the person who murdered Rawls and Benson is also the person who kidnapped and tortured Meredith Fenner," Dr. Grace said.

Deputy District Attorney Kyle Bergland and the detectives grouped around the conference table let out a collective breath. They had been hoping for a break and it looked like they might finally have one.

Dr. Grace put photographs of the battered faces of Benson, a black woman, and Rawls, a white woman, next to a picture of Meredith Fenner's face.

"The damage to the faces of all three women is similar and Fenner said her kidnapper sealed her mouth with duct tape. Traces of duct tape were found around the mouths of Rawls and Benson. All of the victims were found wearing only underpants and a top.

"By the way, has the lab come back with any results?"

Bergland nodded. "We have partial prints on the duct tape removed from Meredith Fenner's wrists and ankles. They're not good enough to run, but there are several points that could be used for comparison. The really good news is that Fenner's kidnapper used his teeth to rip the duct tape on Fenner's ankle and he left some saliva on it, so we have a sample of his DNA."

Dr. Grace placed photographs of the torsos of Rawls, Benson, and Fenner on the table.

"Look at these burn marks and the cut marks on the victims' waists and breasts. They're almost identical, as if the perpetrator was following a ritual. And there is no indication that any of the women were raped, which makes sense if the perp masturbated while he was torturing the victims instead of seeking to penetrate them."

"Does anything else connect the crimes?" Anders asked.

"Yes," Dr. Grace replied. "Rawls and Benson also had dried urine and feces in their underwear. My guess is that the killer wanted to humiliate and infantilize his victims by making them soil themselves, like he did with Fenner."

"This has been tremendously helpful, Sally," Bergland said.

"I'm glad. You guys are dealing with one sick fuck and I hope you stop him fast. I'm guessing that as soon as he finds his captive is gone, he's going to go after someone else."

"There's a rush on the DNA," Anders said, "but our best bet for identifying Fenner's kidnapper is Fenner. We have property records for cabins in the area where she was held. Her doctor says she'll be healthy enough in a day or so to go house hunting. If she ID's the cabin, we may have our killer."

CHAPTER SIX

After spending Tuesday and Wednesday breaking in Justice Cloud's new law clerk, Robin drove to Portland, where she got lucky. By Thursday afternoon, she'd found a furnished apartment over a Thai restaurant on the east side of the river. Several other ethnic restaurants, an old-time movie theater that showed indie films, and blocks of funky locally owned stores gave her new hood character. Finding a furnished apartment made the move from Salem easy, and living in a neighborhood where there were a lot of restaurants that had takeout was great, since she wasn't much of a cook.

Once she was settled in her apartment, Robin joined a gym on the west side of the river that was within easy walking distance of her office. Most mornings, she got up at five, donned sweats, and ran several miles to the gym, a duffel bag filled with her work clothes slung across her back. After working out for an hour and then showering, she would walk to work, stopping to pick up the large latte and scone or bagel that made up her breakfast.

Regina Barrister had a corner office in a glass-and-steel high rise in downtown Portland. Glancing out her floor-to-ceiling windows, she could see the snowcapped majesty of Mounts Hood and St. Helens and sailboats and rowing crews cutting through the current in the Willamette River.

Robin Lockwood had no window in a narrow office that barely accommodated her desk, a bookcase, and a small filing cabinet, but she didn't mind because she was enjoying her job so much. Mark Berman, Regina's other associate, had gone out of his way to make Robin feel at home. Mark was tall and handsome, with long brown hair and a pleasant smile. He was married, had a three-year-old daughter, and seemed to be immune to stress.

Robin was dying to get into court, but Regina had her handling some very interesting research projects because of her appellate background. At Regina's suggestion, she had put her name on the list for court appointments, and Mark had invited Robin to sit at counsel table with him for motions and a few misdemeanor trials.

On her second day, someone walked into Robin's office and said, "So you're Regina's new victim."

Robin looked up from the memo she was writing. She saw a man about six two with shaggy reddish blond hair that almost touched his broad shoulders, green eyes, and pale, freckled skin. But what drew Robin's attention were the faint tracery of scars that crisscrossed his face.

"Jeff Hodges," the man said as he extended his hand. "I'm Regina's investigator, which means that I'm also your investigator."

Robin realized that she was staring at Hodges's scarred face and felt a burn in her cheeks. She stood up and walked around her desk, grateful for the chance to avert her eyes.

"Robin Lockwood," she said as they exchanged firm handshakes.

Robin guessed that Hodges was used to people staring, because he ignored her reaction to his face. Instead, he gestured at the stack of briefs and memos piled on her desk.

"I see the boss has you toiling in the coal mine already."

Robin smiled. "I love research, and the issues are really interesting."

"Different strokes for different folks," Hodges said. "I'd go nuts if I had to be cooped up all day. Well, I'll let you get back to work. I just wanted to introduce myself. If you need help on any of your cases, I'm just down the hall."

"Thanks," Robin said.

When Hodges walked out, Robin noticed that he limped, and she wondered what had caused the damage to his face and leg.

CHAPTER SEVEN

Harry White, Meredith Fenner, Carrie Anders, and Roger Dillon, Carrie's partner, drove in one car to the spot in the road where Meredith had come out of the woods. Two Hammond County deputies followed in another car with Kyle Bergland. Harry pulled to the shoulder and Bergland's car parked behind him. Everyone but Meredith got out. She looked pale, drawn, and frightened.

Harry spread a map of the area on his hood. "We're here," he said. Then he pointed at two lines on the map. "Roads lead to Whisper Lake here and here. There are summer cabins all around the lake." Harry pointed at one of the roads that led away from Country Road 24. "Let's concentrate on the cabins in this area."

Everyone got back in their cars and Bergland's car followed Harry's car down a poorly paved, narrow road that led toward Whisper Lake. Carrie noticed that the car was bouncing.

"Close your eyes, Meredith. Is this how you remember the ride when you came to in the trunk?"

Meredith closed her eyes for a few moments. Then she opened them.

"I can't be certain because I was still woozy, but I think it was like this."

"Great." Carrie reached over from the backseat and laid her hand on Meredith's shoulder. "We're going to get him. You're going to get justice."

After a short drive, the road turned and they drove past an unpaved driveway. Harry turned in and a cabin appeared. They could see the lake through the trees. Harry stopped the car and looked at Meredith.

"No. This isn't it."

Harry turned the car around and drove back to the road.

"What if I don't remember?" Meredith asked after they had driven down three driveways without success.

"That won't be on you," Harry assured her. "Just try your best. Don't make up anything. You'll either recognize the place or you won't."

Harry turned into the next driveway and Meredith gasped when a large modern cabin with a blue metal roof came into view.

"That's it! I remember the roof. And there's the shed."

Harry stopped the car and Bergland pulled in behind him.

"Stay in the car," Carrie said as the detectives and the deputy DA got out. "Harry, you stay with Meredith, just in case our guy is here."

Harry stood beside the car and Bergland leaned in the window on the passenger side.

"I've got a judge waiting," Bergland told Meredith. "We're going to get a telephonic warrant. Are you certain this is where you were held?"

"Yes, definitely." Meredith pointed toward an area where the lawn met the woods. "That's where I ran into the forest. And I told you the cabin was big and new, like something a rich person would have built."

Dillon, Anders, and the deputies approached the house with guns drawn. Harry, Bergland, and Meredith waited. Ten minutes later, the detectives returned to the car.

"The back door was open, just like Meredith said," she told the DA.

Bergland dialed a number and spoke to the judge. "We can go in," Bergland said as soon as he hung up. He turned to Meredith. "I know this is going to be hard on you, but I need you to come with us and show us where you were held."

Meredith turned pale. "I really don't want to go back in there."

"I know you don't, Meredith, but we have to be certain this is the right cabin."

"I'll be with you all the way," Harry said.

Meredith swallowed. Then she nodded. The detectives and sheriff's deputies surrounded her and they led the way around the back. When they got to the rear door, they stopped.

"Is this what you remember?" Carrie asked.

"I wasn't paying attention. I just found a door, opened it, and ran."

"But you were in the back, not the front?"

"Yes."

Carrie opened the door and switched on a light. They were in a large kitchen with an island covered in gray slate.

"Show us where you were held," Carrie said.

"I never turned on a light. I just felt my way along."

Meredith looked in the direction of a hall that led off to one side of the house.

"There, I think."

Carrie took the lead and turned on a light as she started down the hall. Every time they came to a closed door, the detectives stood on each side and opened it cautiously, even though they were convinced no one was in the house. The rooms looked ordinary until they opened a door in the middle of the hall. An odor swam out, and Carrie held her breath. When she flicked the wall switch, bleak light from a low-watt bulb showed them a bed surrounded by bloodstained sheets. Meredith peeked in, then blanched. She wobbled on unsteady legs and Harry braced her.

"Is this it?" he asked, even though they all knew it was.

Meredith nodded.

"Who owns the house?" Bergland asked.

Carrie pulled a sheaf of papers out of her jacket

pocket and ran a finger down a list. When she got halfway down the list, she stopped.

"Hey, I know this guy," Carrie said. "He's a lawyer; a real asshole."

"Who is he?" Bergland asked impatiently.

"Alex Mason."

CHAPTER EIGHT

Tremaine, Mason, Ozaki and Holt, the leading plaintiff's firm in Oregon, occupied the top three floors of a twenty-five-story office building in downtown Portland. The senior partners had made millions suing corporations for manufacturing faulty automobiles, using asbestos in buildings, and selling pharmaceutical products with drastic side effects. Alex Mason was the leading rainmaker in the firm and rated the largest corner office. When his intercom buzzed, Mason looked up from a complaint he was drafting.

"Yes."

"Two police detectives are here," Mason's secretary said. "They want to talk to you."

Mason frowned. "Detectives?"

"Yes."

"Did they say what they want?"

"No, sir. Just that they wanted to talk to you."

"Show them back," Mason said after a brief pause.

A few minutes later, the secretary held open Mason's door and Carrie Anders and Roger Dillon, walked into his office. Dillon, a lanky African-American with close-cropped salt-and-pepper hair, was four years away from retirement. He had been around the block so many times that he was considered a reference tool by the other detectives, thus his nickname, "OED," which stood for the *Oxford English Dictionary.*

"What can I do for you?" the lawyer asked.

Carrie noticed the New York accent that Meredith had described.

"I'm Carrie Anders and this is Roger Dillon," she said as they showed Mason their IDs. "We're detectives with the Portland Police Bureau and we were hoping you could help us with an investigation we're working on."

Mason frowned as he pointed to a pair of client chairs in front of his desk.

"Please sit down. What kind of investigation?"

"It's a homicide, sir," Dillon replied.

Mason looked confused. "Why do you think I can help you?"

"Do you own a cabin on Whisper Lake?" Carrie asked.

"Yes."

"How long have you owned it?"

"Fifteen years. There was an old cabin there originally, but it was small and in very bad shape. I had it torn down and we built a modern cabin."

" 'We'?"

"Christine, my first wife." Mason paused. "She passed away just after the cabin was completed and she never got to use it."

"I'm sorry for your loss," Carrie said.

"What does my cabin have to do with a murder

investigation? And why are Portland detectives investigating something in Hammond County?"

"Bear with me for a moment more and we'll explain why we're here," Carrie said as she flashed a reassuring smile.

Mason looked like he was going to protest. Then he said, "Go on."

"Can you tell us how often you use the cabin?"

"We go out several times in the summer. Less when the weather gets bad."

" 'We'?"

"I remarried."

"Who other than you and your wife uses the cabin?"

"I've taken clients and friends out there."

"Have you or any one else been at the cabin recently?"

Mason looked annoyed. "Look, I want to help, but I'm not going to answer any more questions until you explain why you're here."

"Yeah, Mr. Mason, about that," Dillon said. "We have evidence that three women were kidnapped in Portland and tortured in your cabin."

"What?"

"The first two were murdered, but the third victim escaped and identified your cabin as the place where she was imprisoned," Carrie said.

"That's . . . that's ridiculous."

"Actually," Carrie said, "it's not. We found

52

bloody sheets in the room where the surviving victim was tortured. DNA tests prove that some of the blood is hers and the rest matches the blood of the two dead women. What troubles us is the DNA we found on the duct tape that was used to bind the last victim."

Mason blanched when Carrie mentioned the duct tape.

"Want to guess whose DNA we found on the tape?" Dillon asked.

Mason just stared at the detectives. Carrie and Dillon stared back. Then Carrie produced an arrest warrant.

"Alexander Mason, I am placing you under arrest for the murders of Tonya Benson and Patricia Rawls and the kidnapping of Meredith Fenner."

"That's absurd. I didn't murder anyone."

"If that's true, you'll be exonerated," Carrie said. "For now, you're going to have to come with us."

Mason tensed and the detectives stood up. Dillon pulled back his jacket so Mason could see his firearm. Mason stared at the gun, then raised his eyes.

"I want to call an attorney."

"That's your right, sir," Carrie said. "And you can make your call after you're booked. Now please stand up so we can handcuff you."

"Handcuff? That's not necessary."

"I'm afraid it's procedure."

"All right, but let me tell my secretary where I'm going."

Carrie hesitated. Then she nodded.

"Maria," Mason said into his intercom, "call Regina Barrister and have her meet me at the jail. Tell her I've been arrested."

CHAPTER NINE

"You have a call on two from Alex Mason's secretary. She sounds upset. Do you want to take it?" Regina Barrister's receptionist asked.

Regina's brow furrowed. Why would Alex Mason's secretary be calling her? She didn't have any cases with Mason, which made her very happy. They had squared off against each other on two occasions and Mason had been thoroughly obnoxious. If Mason were a Buddhist, Regina imagined that he would be reincarnated as a weasel. He even looked like a weasel with his thinning black hair, narrow face, close-set brown eyes, slight overbite, and sallow skin that still bore signs of teenage acne.

"This is Regina Barrister. How can I help you?" Regina said when her receptionist put the call through.

"Mr. Mason told me to call you. He's been arrested. Two detectives took him away in handcuffs. He wants you to go to the jail."

This was unexpected and interesting. "Do you know why he was arrested?" Regina asked.

"No. They just took him away."

"Do you know the names of the detectives?"

"I can't remember."

"Can you describe them?"

As soon as she heard the description, Regina was certain that Carrie Anders and Roger Dillon had made the arrest. She hung up and called the Portland Police Bureau.

"Anders," the detective said as soon as Regina was connected.

"I know you don't like lawyers, but isn't arresting them going a little too far?"

"This isn't funny, Regina."

"Oh. What's Alex Mason supposed to have done?"

"We think he kidnapped three women, tortured them, and killed two of them."

There was dead air for a moment. Then Regina said, "You're serious?"

"Dead serious."

"Okay. No more jokes. Is he with you or at the jail?"

"He's been processed in. Are you going to represent him?"

"He's asked me to. I assume he told you he wanted a lawyer."

"First thing."

"Did you talk to him before you made the arrest?"

"You'll get discovery when you're entitled to it."

"So that's how you're going to play this."

"Your client is very dangerous, Regina. He's behind bars and he's going to stay there."

"We'll see. In the meantime, I don't want

anyone talking to Alex without my being present."

"Don't worry. This case will be handled strictly by the rules. When Mr. Mason is convicted, there will be no reversible error in the record."

As soon as Regina hung up, she headed across town to the Justice Center, a sixteen-story concrete-and-glass building whose fourth to tenth floors housed the Multnomah County jail.

Regina showed her Oregon State Bar card to the duty officer. After she went through the metal detector, he sent her up to the floor where Mason was being housed. The elevator doors opened onto a narrow concrete hall with a thick metal door at one end. Regina called to a guard through an intercom mounted on the wall next to the door. A few minutes later, the door swung open and the guard led her along another narrow hall, this one with a solid concrete wall on one side and bulletproof windows that gave a view into three contact visiting rooms on the other. The guard opened a steel door and let Regina into the middle room. Alex Mason, wearing an orange jumpsuit that was a size too large, was sitting on one side of a metal table that was bolted to the floor. The lawyer jumped up as soon as Regina entered.

"What took you so long?" Mason demanded.

Regina was used to dealing with newly arrested clients, so she didn't react to Mason's angry outburst.

"I got here as fast as I could, Alex. How have you been treated?"

"Like a common criminal. As soon as you get me out of here, I am going to sue everybody in the county for false arrest."

"Did the detectives who arrested you mistreat you?"

"They put me in fucking handcuffs and perp-walked me out of my office in front of everyone! I'm going to own their pensions when I'm through."

"Did you talk to them?"

"Do I look stupid? As soon as I realized what was happening, I demanded a lawyer."

"Did they say why they were arresting you?"

"It's nuts. They claim I kidnapped and tortured women at my cabin at Whisper Lake. I haven't been out there in months and I certainly didn't kill anyone."

"Did they ask you about the cabin?"

"Yeah, before they told me what allegedly happened there."

"What did you say?"

"I can't remember exactly. Just that I bought the property with an older home on it and tore that cabin down and built a new one."

"Did you say anything else about the cabin?"

Mason thought for a moment. "Yeah, I said my wife and I used it and I entertained friends and clients there."

Mason hesitated.

"Is there something else?" Regina asked.

Mason broke eye contact for a moment. "They said something about my DNA being found on some duct tape that was on a victim," he said reluctantly.

Regina frowned. She wanted to ask Mason about the DNA, but this wasn't the right time to do it.

"I'll hire an expert to look into that, but we have to get a few things cleared up first. I talked to Carrie Anders. The authorities are going to go after you with everything they have and I assume they'll be seeking the death penalty. That means that this case is going to get very expensive. You have some idea what the defense of a capital case costs. Can you afford to hire me?"

Mason nodded.

"Okay. I'll prepare for a bail hearing and get discovery. Once I know what we're dealing with, I can start lining up experts and we can concentrate on clearing your name."

CHAPTER TEN

Robin was sipping a latte and reading a case when her intercom buzzed. Mary Stendahl, Regina's secretary, told her that the boss wanted to see her. Robin finished a paragraph, took one more sip of her latte, then walked down the hall.

"Have a seat," Regina said, gesturing to one of her client chairs while she squared up some files on her blotter.

"What's up?"

"You remember arguing with Alex Mason about capital punishment at the cocktail party at the Hilton?"

"Yeah. He's definitely not someone I'd want on a jury in a criminal case."

"He may be changing his tune, since he's been arrested on charges of kidnapping and murder."

"You're kidding?"

"The police think he's a serial killer, the district attorney is going to seek the death penalty, and Mr. Mason has asked me to represent him."

Robin cocked her head to one side and watched Regina carefully, hoping she knew where the conversation was going.

"A lawyer defending a death case needs a second chair," Robin's boss said. "I want you to be second chair on Mason's case. We would divide up the work. With your appellate experience, you're a natural to handle pretrial motions, evidence issues, jury instructions, and anything else that requires research. This will allow me to concentrate on both direct and cross-examination of the witnesses and directing the investigation into the facts of the case."

Regina paused and smiled at Robin. "Well, what do you think?"

Robin's first instinct was to leap across the desk and hug Regina, but she restrained himself.

"Count me in. What can you tell me about the case?"

"Not much right now. I just received discovery. Jeff will give you a copy. I don't want to discuss the case until you've read through the police reports, because I don't want to prejudice you."

Robin went to Jeff's office as soon as she left Regina's.

"Did you hear that Miss Barrister is going to represent Alex Mason in a death case?" Robin asked.

Jeff looked very serious and stroked his chin. "From the way you're grinning, I deduce that the Sorceress asked you to be second chair."

"Correct, Mr. Holmes." Robin laughed. "And you're supposed to give me a copy of the discovery."

Hodges pointed to a stack of reports that was sitting on a corner of his desk.

"Thanks," Robin said. Then her brow knit. "Why did you call Regina 'the Sorceress'?"

"That's right. You've only been in Oregon a short time, so you probably haven't heard the story about the case that made Regina's reputation."

"No."

"Six months after Art McCallum reported her missing, his wife, Karen, was found in a freezer in their garage, wrapped in her favorite mink coat. Instead of breaking into tears when he was shown the body, Art started laughing and said, 'So that's where she went.'

"Somehow, Regina convinced the jury that Karen had committed suicide, and Art was acquitted. That's when the newspapers started calling her 'the Sorceress.' I don't think she liked that nickname, but she never disavowed it, because it brought her a raft of clients." Jeff shrugged. "Who wouldn't want to be represented by a sorceress if you were charged with a crime and there was overwhelming evidence of guilt?"

CHAPTER ELEVEN

Carrie Anders got out of the passenger seat as soon as Kyle Bergland parked in front of Alex Mason's McMansion, a gaudy bright yellow attempt to copy an Italian villa. Bergland was short and bald, with a narrow mustache and goatee. Wire-rimmed glasses magnified watery blue eyes and perched on a thick nose. The deputy DA had asked Carrie to accompany him because he thought that Allison Mason might feel more comfortable being interviewed by a female detective.

Allison opened the front door moments after Bergland rang the bell. She wasn't wearing makeup and her only jewelry was her wedding ring. Her flame red hair was tied in a ponytail and she was dressed in tan slacks and a sky blue blouse.

"I don't know if you remember me, Mrs. Mason," Bergland said, "but we met at a cocktail party at the Hilton a week or so ago."

Allison stared at Bergland. Then she shook her head. "I'm sorry."

"That's okay." Bergland smiled. "I'm not that memorable. Anyway, I want to thank you for taking the time to talk to me and Detective Anders. Under the circumstances, I would have understood if you didn't want us here."

Allison hesitated for a moment, then said, "Come in."

A crystal chandelier illuminated alternating squares of black and white marble in a spacious foyer and a curved stairway with polished wooden banisters that wound up to the second floor. Carrie took in the posh surroundings as she followed Allison into the living room. Their hostess sat in a high-backed armchair and indicated a comfortable sofa for her guests.

"Why have you arrested Alex?" Allison asked.

"Hasn't he told you?" Carrie asked.

"When he called from the jail, he said he was suspected of murder and that he was innocent. He didn't go into details."

"Have you read the papers or seen the news on TV?" Carrie asked.

"Well, yes. They say he killed two prostitutes and kidnapped a girl, that he tortured them. But they didn't say why you think my husband is . . . why he did this."

Carrie and the DA noticed that Allison didn't appear shocked by the allegations and didn't protest her husband's innocence.

"The women were held at your cabin at Whisper Lake," Bergland said.

"Oh God," Allison said. Her hand flew to her mouth. She looked as if she might be sick.

"There's other evidence connecting your husband to the crimes," Bergland added.

Allison looked panicky. "Why do you want to talk to me?"

"We were hoping you could clear up some things for us," Carrie said.

"I don't know anything about those women."

"We have no indication that you do, but you can still help us."

Allison sat up straight. She folded her hands in her lap. "Go ahead," she told Carrie, who decided to start the interview by throwing Allison a few softballs.

"How long have you and Alex been married?"

"Just a few years."

"How did you meet?"

"I moved to New York four years ago and I met him three years ago, when I was working as a temp at a law firm in Manhattan. Alex was suing a corporation that the firm represented and he was in New York for depositions. I was helping in the conference room, getting coffee, taking notes.

"Alex was staying at a hotel down the street from the firm. Some of the other girls and I went to the hotel bar after work. When the girls left, I stayed to finish my drink. That's when Alex came into the bar. He hadn't seemed to notice me during the deposition, but he must have, because he came over and introduced himself and asked if he could join me."

Allison blushed. "I was sort of honored, you

know." She looked down at her lap. "I'm not that smart. I dropped out of high school." She looked up at Carrie. "I did get my GED, but I'd heard the lawyers talking about Alex before he arrived, so I knew he'd gone to Harvard. I was surprised that he wanted to spend time with me."

One look at Allison's perfect figure and stunning good looks solved that mystery for Carrie, but she didn't reveal this to Allison. Instead, she asked, "What did you talk about?"

"New York. He said he grew up there and moved to Oregon after law school. I told him I felt pretty lonely and that I found the city a cold place to live. He said he was all alone in the city, too, and he asked me if I would have dinner with him. I said sure."

For the first time since they had entered the house, Allison smiled.

"To be honest, Alex did make a good first impression, but that's not why I accepted the invitation. I didn't make much as a temp and I was living on cheap food, mostly takeout, and I'd heard the attorneys at the firm say that the restaurant at the hotel was terrific."

Carrie returned the smile. "How did the dinner go?"

"Real good. He treated me very nice. He didn't talk about himself a lot and he really seemed interested in me. I told him I wanted to be a paralegal and was saving up for school. He said he admired me because I didn't have his advantages but was trying to make something of myself.

"Later on, I got him to open up and I found out that he was recovering from a vicious divorce. He told me he had this great job and great house and people thought he had it made, but that he was really lonely." She looked at Carrie. "I sort of felt sorry for him."

"What happened after dinner?" Carrie asked, although she was sure she already knew.

Allison blushed. "He asked me up to his room for a nightcap and, well, we ended up in bed."

Allison stared at Carrie, defying the detective to say anything. When she didn't, Allison looked away, and Carrie thought Mason's wife looked very sad.

"You know, the lawyers at the firm said Alex was vicious and unprincipled, but he was very nice to me and he was very considerate."

"It sounds like you cared for him."

"Yeah. It was what he said about being lonely. I think he really was."

"What happened between you two after that first night?" the detective asked.

"Alex was in New York for three days and we spent every evening together. Then he had to go back to Oregon, but he asked me to follow him. He promised to get me a job and . . . Well . . ." She looked down again. "He said he loved me."

"What did you do?"

"I thought real hard about what he'd said for a month and a half." She shrugged. "I mean, we'd only had those three evenings together and that wasn't really enough time to fall in love or get to know someone, but I didn't have anything going for me in New York. I figured I could go somewhere else if things didn't work out, so I called Alex and asked if he still wanted me to come out. He bought me a plane ticket and that was that."

"Can I ask you something?" Kyle Bergland said.

Allison looked at the DA.

"I noticed that you didn't seem shocked when we asked you about the charges against your husband. Is there a reason for that?"

Allison looked down at her lap. Carrie thought that she looked upset and confused.

"I . . . I read about the girl who escaped and what happened to her and those other women."

Allison bit her lip. Then she took a deep breath and looked at her visitors.

Allison blushed. "I . . . This is embarrassing. If this whole thing wasn't so serious . . ." She paused and took a deep breath. "It's about our sex life."

She looked back and forth between her interrogators.

"Is there any way you can keep this off the record?"

The DA looked directly at Allison. "Mrs. Mason, what happened to these women was horrible. I can show you photographs of what was done to them, but I don't really think you want to see them. If you have any information that will help us prosecute the man who tortured these women, you should tell us. We don't want to charge an innocent man. In fact, if your husband is innocent, we want to find that out very quickly so we can catch the real killer. But—if he did this—he is a very sick man and a danger to you as well as to other potential victims."

"Yes, I see that. It's why I was willing to talk to you. It's just . . . I feel very uncomfortable talking about what . . . what we do in our bedroom."

"Talking about sex is always uncomfortable," Carrie said sympathetically. "But these women are the victims of sex crimes, so your sex life could be relevant."

Mason's wife looked down for a few moments. When she looked up, she seemed nervous.

"Those first few months, sex with Alex was normal; it was good. Then, at some point—I don't remember when exactly—he started suggesting that we try . . . different things."

"Different how?" Carrie asked.

"Alex said that one reason for his divorce was that his ex-wife didn't like sex. He said she never wanted to experiment and that soon after the marriage she started refusing to have sex

69

altogether. I didn't want to disappoint Alex like his other wife had, so I said I would try some things."

"What did Alex want you to do?" Carrie asked.

Allison looked at her lap and her voice dropped. "S and M."

"What kind of S and M?"

"First it was just me tying him up and teasing him. He told me I was in control and I should excite him and . . . and not let him cum until he begged. I could see he liked what I did, so I didn't mind. But then . . ."

"Yes?"

"He wanted to tie me up." Allison looked at Carrie, her eyes pleading for understanding. "Since I had done it to him, I had to say yes."

"How did he bind you?" Carrie asked, fighting hard to suppress her excitement.

"He used duct tape. I had to put my wrists at the ends of the bed and my ankles at the other ends. I would be—what do you call it?—spread-eagled. And he would make it so I couldn't move."

Carrie didn't want to chance a look at Kyle, but she bet his heart rate had gone up as fast as hers had.

"Okay. Go on. What happened?"

"At first it was exciting. It made the sex so much more intense. But then Alex wanted to take it to another level."

"How?"

"Pain. He wanted the sex to be more violent."

"Violent in what way?"

"He would burn me with cigarettes. It hurt. I begged him to stop, but he said I would come to enjoy the pain." Allison dropped her gaze. "Only I didn't."

"How far did he go with this? Did he ever cut you?"

"No. I wouldn't let him. One time, he stood over the bed with a knife. I said I wouldn't do it. That I'd stop having sex if he cut me. He apologized and swore he would never do anything I didn't want to do."

"So that's as far as it went?" Carrie asked.

"No, not really. He never did anything more than burn me a few times, but he did start . . . I don't know how to say this."

"Take your time."

"He would get real mean and humiliate me. He started berating mc at home and sometimes even in public. He would say I was stupid and a bad wife, but he wouldn't tell me what I'd done wrong. He would say I had to be punished."

"How would he punish you?"

"There were three times that Alex tied me up and left me and wouldn't say how long he would be gone. I begged him not to leave me, but he said it would heighten my sexual tension because I couldn't be sure when he would come back. He even hinted it might be several days or a week."

Allison started to cry. "I begged him not to do it, but he just left. After a while I . . . I had to go and . . . and I couldn't hold it in and I wet myself."

Allison took several deep breaths. Anders waited while she regained her composure to ask her next question.

"You said you read about the women who were kidnapped," Carrie said when Allison was ready. "Were the times your husband tied you up and left you around the times the women disappeared?"

"I can't be sure."

"Why did you put up with what he did to you?" Carrie asked.

Allison looked ashamed. "He wasn't mean all the time. Most of the time he was good to me. I love him. I wanted to make the marriage work." She looked at Carrie with beseeching eyes in which tears had begun to appear. "And he did treat me like a queen. He bought me jewelry and took me places I'd only dreamed of going— Venice, Paris. But now . . ." She shivered. "If he did these things . . ."

"Mrs. Mason," Carrie said, "do you still have marks or scars from Mr. Mason's abuse?"

"Yes."

"Could I take a photograph of the marks? We'd do it in a private place. Kyle wouldn't be there."

"I'd rather not."

"I can understand that, but the photographs

72

might be very important. I can't tell you why, but I can assure you they might have significant evidentiary value."

Allison spaced out for a moment and stared at the wall across from her. Then she looked down and nodded.

"Thank you," Carrie said.

"We've got him, Carrie," Bergland said. He'd kept his emotions bottled up during the rest of the interview, but he exploded as soon as they were in the car and headed back to town.

"It sure looks like it. The burn marks on her body are similar to the burn marks on our victims, and there was even some chafing on her ankles from the duct tape that resembles the marks on Meredith Fenner's ankles."

Bergland smiled. "It always feels great when a case comes together."

CHAPTER TWELVE

Miles Poe paced back and forth outside room 220 of the Weary Traveler Motel, muttering, "This is bad; this is bad," and holding his pistol so tight that it cut into his palm. Mordessa screamed again. Poe squeezed his eyes shut and pounded his fist into his temple. "Fuck, fuck, fuck," he screamed, every muscle in his body tight as piano wire, his gut in a knot. Then another scream cut through the door and raced down the hall and Poe knew he had to move or Mordessa would become damaged goods.

Poe had bought a skeleton key from the night clerk when his whores started using the motel. He jammed it home and wrenched open the door. Arnold Prater's head snapped around and he paused with his fist in the air.

"What the fuck!" Prater exclaimed.

Poe looked past Prater to Mordessa, who was naked and had her wrists secured to the headboard of the bed with a pair of handcuffs. Her right eye was swelling and her bloody nose was bent to one side. But what shocked Poe the most were the tears in her eyes. Mordessa was one tough bitch. Mordessa did not cry.

"This has got to stop, Arnold," Poe said, trying to keep his voice from trembling so that he would sound tough.

"Get the fuck out, asshole," Prater yelled.

Poe was shaking, but he sucked it up. "This is no good. I told you the last time, a little rough stuff is okay, but this shit is out-of-bounds."

"I'll tell you what's out-of-bounds, dickhead, peddling dope and selling whores, and that's something you won't be doing if I throw your ass in jail."

"Throwing my ass in jail would put a serious dent in your income, and beating Mordessa so bad that she can't work will put a dent in mine, so this session is over, right now."

Prater took a menacing step toward the pimp, and Poe pointed his gun at Prater's groin.

Prater laughed. "You gonna shoot a cop, Miles?"

"It's a gamble, but I figure if they find you dead with your dick hanging out and Mordessa all beat to shit, a good lawyer will have me on the street pretty quick. So let's negotiate instead of getting angry. Say I slip you two hundred bucks to compensate you for the time you've lost fighting crime. That way, you leave richer, Mordessa goes back to work, and we avoid violence."

Prater stared hard at Poe. Then he walked to the side of the bed and grabbed his clothes. When he bent down for his pants, his lips were close to Mordessa's ear and he whispered something to her that Poe didn't catch. Mordessa turned her head away and squeezed her eyes shut. Prater laughed and pulled on his pants before unfastening the handcuffs.

While Prater was dressing, Miles had pulled a wad from his sock and peeled off two one-hundred-dollar bills. Prater snatched them from the pimp's hand.

"You just made a big mistake, Miles, one you are going to regret."

Prater walked out and slammed the door. Poe collapsed on the bed. He hadn't been this scared since he was a kid and his father came home drunk. Prater was not just a crooked cop; he was sick in the head and capable of doing just about anything.

"Thank you, Miles," Mordessa croaked.

Poe turned toward her. This close, he could see how much damage Prater had done. There were the blood and broken bones, but there was also a lit cigarette on the end table next to the bed and several festering burns on Mordessa's torso. Miles shook his head. This bitch wouldn't be working for a while, that was for sure.

Mordessa was weeping, and that tugged at Poe's heartstrings. He reached out and stroked Mordessa's forehead.

"It's okay, baby. Nobody hurts my women; you know that. You work hard and I'll always be there to protect you. Miles gonna give you something good for the pain soon as we get back to our crib, something that will make you forget all about this shit."

But Poe knew she wouldn't forget. He wouldn't, either, because Arnold Prater was an evil bastard and Poe had no idea what kind of revenge he was planning.

CHAPTER THIRTEEN

Harry White had a big smile on his face when he walked into Meredith Fenner's hospital room. Fenner smiled back when she saw who was visiting. Harry studied Meredith's face. There was still evidence of the abuse she had suffered, but the signs were mere shadows of the way she had looked when she'd been admitted to the hospital. When Harry had seen her that first night, he had suspected that Meredith was beautiful. Now he was certain.

"You know, you look great," he said with a grin.

Meredith blushed and looked away. "No I don't."

"Well, that's just my opinion." He shrugged. "Someone else might think you're really ugly."

Meredith's mouth opened for a second. Then she laughed.

"You sure know how to build up a girl's self-esteem," she said.

"I learned my people skills at the police academy. And I learned a few more things today. I've got good news for you. Actually, I've got more than one piece of good news."

Meredith stopped smiling and looked wary.

Harry smiled to reassure her. "Sometimes good

things really do happen to good people. First piece of good news: Nick thinks you're well enough to be discharged."

Harry saw fear in Meredith's eyes.

"That's the second piece of my gool news. You don't have to worry. Alex Mason is in jail. You're safe now."

"He . . . he can't get out?"

"There's no automatic bail in a murder case and you can bet no judge will let Mason out when they see what he did to you and those other poor women."

Meredith didn't smile, but she did take a deep breath.

"So," Harry asked, "what will you do now?"

"I . . . I guess I'll go back to my apartment in Portland and see if I still have a job."

"Do you have someone who can drive you?"

Meredith shook her head. "I haven't made any real friends since I moved to Oregon."

"How about I drive you?" Harry asked.

Meredith looked at the detective, wide-eyed. "Would you? That would be so great."

"It's all part of the service," Harry replied.

Meredith smiled. "Thank you."

"It's nice to see you smiling," Harry said. "I haven't seen too many smiles since Caleb rescued you."

Meredith looked down. "I haven't had much to smile about."

"Well, you do now."

"I . . . I still have nightmares, Harry."

"I know, but they'll stop and you'll get better. No one should ever have to go through what you did, but look at how you dealt with it. You didn't cave; you didn't fold like some people would. You were strong and *you* escaped all by yourself. No one helped you.

"You're one tough cookie, Ms. Fenner, and because you're tough, Mason is behind bars. You're responsible for saving all the other women who could have been his victims. They don't know it, but there are young women walking the street without fear because of what you did."

Meredith's breast swelled. "Thank you, Harry. I am still scared, and I won't feel completely safe until they execute that bastard, but I always feel safe when you're around."

Harry blushed. "Go get dressed," he said. "Then I'll get you back to Portland."

CHAPTER FOURTEEN

Regina Barrister had been working nonstop for the past four days on Alex Mason's case when it dawned on her that she was ignoring the rest of her caseload. When she arrived at the office at seven in the morning, she vowed to finish writing a motion to suppress in a federal drug conspiracy case. She'd had the best of intentions, but she had trouble concentrating because she kept thinking about the way Stanley Cloud had made love to her the night before. No one had made Regina feel that way in a long while and she could not get enough of the time they spent together. Unfortunately, that time was limited to clandestine getaways or stolen moments because the chief justice of the Oregon Supreme Court had to be free from scandal.

Regina's first and second marriages had been brief and painful. She had married husband number one while still in college. He was a mediocre student with a gigantic ego and had informed Regina that she would work to support him while he was getting his MBA, then spend her days at home hosting dinner parties that would help him build his career in finance.

Regina, an academic all-star, received a full ride to a top-tier law school. When she made it clear that was where she was bound, hubby number one opted out of the marriage. Regina heard through the grapevine that her ex had married a secretary, whom he had dumped as soon as she'd paid his way through the graduate program at a middling state university.

Hubby number two, another disaster, was a suave and apparently successful partner in a big firm. He was a whiz at cocktail-party conversation and really good in bed. Unfortunately, he was totally lacking in substance. Regina had ignored the rumors that her fiancé's firm was looking for a way to dump him and the warnings given her by his former girlfriends. By the time Regina figured out that number two had married her to shore up his shaky finances, she was out a considerable sum and ready to give up on men forever.

Then Stanley came along. He was everything she'd ever wanted in a man, but he was also trapped in marriage to a mentally ill, drug-addicted wife who was frequently in rehab and was an expert at making his life hell when she was out. Stanley had made it clear to Regina that he was very much in love with her but that he could not divorce his wife. The chief justice was a devout Catholic. His religion played a part in his decision, but guilt created by his belief that he was partially responsible for his wife's condition kept him from abandoning her. Cloud was convinced that he had been so driven in his early quest for success that he had ignored the signs of his wife's disease when he could have helped her.

Regina was slipping past middle age and had given up on love when she and Stanley began their affair. She was certain that he loved her and she knew she loved him, so she had resigned herself to moments of wonder and stretches of loneliness. Regina's memories of her evening at the Hilton were interrupted when Robin Lockwood rapped on her door and entered.

"A man named Arnold Prater is in the waiting room. Do you have time to speak to him?" Robin asked.

Regina pulled herself out of her reverie and looked at her watch.

"Send him in and sit through the interview. It will give you some ideas about how to handle a meeting with a client."

Robin grinned. "Thanks."

"Oh, and bring me Mr. Prater's . . ." Regina's features clouded. Then she forced a smile. "The thing with all the police reports and witness statements."

"His file?" Robin asked with a laugh.

"Yes," Regina said, trying not to sound flustered.

"This is Mr. Prater's first appointment. We don't have a file yet."

Regina reddened. "I know that," she snapped. "Send him in."

Robin flushed, startled by her boss's rebuke, and left Regina's office.

A few moments later, Arnold Prater strutted into Regina's office and made a bad first impression. But most of Regina's clients were criminals and few made a good first impression.

Prater was of medium height, with a stocky build and a slight paunch. Tufts of hair grew on his ears, and thick eyebrows arced over close-set muddy brown eyes. His face was puffy, and Regina spotted early signs of alcoholism.

"How can I help you?" she asked when Prater was seated.

Prater looked at Robin, who had taken a seat on a couch set against the wall.

"Who's she?"

"Miss Lockwood is one of my associates. She'll take notes so that I can concentrate on what you have to say. And don't worry. She's covered by the attorney-client privilege, so anything she or I hear is confidential. Now, what can I do for you?"

Her visitor slapped a stack of legal papers on Regina's desk. "A scumbag named Miles Poe had me served this morning. He's suing me, and I want you to crush this asshole."

Regina didn't react to Prater's outburst. Instead, she picked up the complaint and read it over while Prater seethed in silence.

"You're a policeman?" Regina asked.

"And Poe is a nigger pimp and drug dealer."

Regina smiled tolerantly. "If I'm going to represent you, you'll have to banish the *n* word from your vocabulary. If it slips out while you're in a deposition or on the witness stand, you can kiss your case good-bye."

Prater didn't look chastened, but he nodded conspiratorially. "Yeah, I get it. From now on, Mr. Poe is a 'person of color.' "

"I'm very serious, Mr. Prater. Do you remember what happened in OJ's case when Mark Fuhrman was tagged as someone who called African-Americans 'niggers'?"

"Okay, okay."

"Now, why don't you tell me what this is all about?"

"Poe is a drug-dealing pimp and he's pissed at me because I interfere with his illegal businesses."

"It says here that you and other Portland police officers stopped him almost every other day last month—thirteen times in all—to give him traffic tickets and that you arrested some of the female employees from his pool hall for littering, public intoxication, and other minor crimes when there were no legal bases for the arrests."

"Poe is paranoid. I did give him two traffic tickets, but different officers gave him the other tickets."

"Mr. Poe alleges a conspiracy that started

when he prevented you from beating up a female friend."

Prater laughed. "Good luck proving a conspiracy."

"What about the woman?"

"She was one of his whores and she resisted arrest. And about that pool hall, it's a front for prostitution. Some of his girls hang out there. There are rooms in the back. You can use your imagination to figure out what goes on in those rooms."

"So you're saying that there is no basis for Mr. Poe's claims?" Regina asked.

"Absolutely none. Talk to the officers who issued the tickets and arrested the girls. They'll tell you that I had nothing to do with them."

Regina decided to switch gears. "I notice that you have a New York accent. Is that where you're from originally?"

"Yeah," Prater replied after a moment's hesitation.

"When did you move to Oregon?"

"About four years ago."

"Were you a policeman in New York?"

Prater nodded but did not elaborate. Regina suspected that the move and the reasons for it were not something Prater wanted to discuss, but they were something she had to know if she was going to represent him.

"Why did you decide to come west?" she asked.

Prater shrugged. "I felt like a change of scenery."

Regina was an expert at reading body language and she could tell that her potential client was very tense.

"Is that what the investigators for Poe's attorney are going to find when they contact your old precinct? And remember, anything you tell me is confidential. So honesty is the best policy. Believe me, nothing blows a case to pieces like surprises in the middle of a trial."

"Okay," Prater said as he shifted uncomfortably in his chair. "Some gangbangers made a complaint about excessive force. It was bullshit, but there were some police shootings around the country and you couldn't lay a finger on a *person of color* without a hundred unemployed *African-Americans* protesting outside city hall."

"And you didn't use excessive force?"

"Every ounce of force I employed was reasonable, but the chief was covering his ass and he wanted me gone. You look at my file and you'll see I left of my own free will. So, will you take the case?"

"I will, but we need to talk business. I'm going to need a retainer. . . ."

"I thought lawyers handled cases like this on a contingency fee."

"The lawyers who sue on behalf of the plaintiff receive money only if they win, but the lawyer defending the case doesn't receive any money if she wins. She just defeats the claim."

"Can't you countersue?"

"We could, but I'll need a fifty-thousand-dollar retainer if you want me to represent you. There may be more down the line."

"Fifty thousand! I don't have that kind of dough."

"Mr. Poe is also suing the city. Have you talked to the city attorney? Maybe they'll provide you with a lawyer."

"I don't want a free lawyer. I want someone good."

"Why don't you think about my fee and get back to me."

"Yeah. I'll do that," Prater said. Then he stood up and left. When he was out of sight, Regina breathed a sigh of relief.

"Good riddance," she said. Regina shook her head. "Everything about Mr. Prater screams 'dirty cop.'"

"Is that why you asked for a high retainer?"

Regina smiled. "That is my retainer for a case like this, but I was hoping Prater didn't have the money. He made my skin crawl and I'm glad we won't have to see him again."

Regina's cell phone rang and she put down the police reports in Alex Mason's case she'd been reading since she'd gotten rid of Arnold Prater.

It was dark outside and she noticed that it was almost eight o'clock.

"Stanley?" she asked when she saw the caller ID.

"Where are you?" he said.

"At the office. I just got a new case and I'm going over the discovery."

"Did you forget about dinner? We had a seven-fifteen reservation."

Regina panicked. She had no memory of a dinner reservation.

"I'm sorry. I just got wrapped up in my work and lost track of time," she said, lying.

"That's okay. Just come over."

"Where are you?" she asked.

Cloud laughed. "Our favorite restaurant. Where we had our first date."

There was dead air and no response.

"The Seville. It's going to take you at least twenty minutes, so hurry. I'm starving."

"Yes, of course," Regina said. "I've been reading police reports nonstop and my brain is mush."

"See you soon. I'm at our table in the back."

Stanley disconnected and Regina realized that her hand was shaking.

CHAPTER FIFTEEN

When Regina woke up, her room looked strange. She sat up slowly and glanced around. It was her room, but she didn't remember some of the furniture being where she saw it. Her heartbeat accelerated and she took deep breaths.

"I'm just groggy," she told herself. And, in truth, she was after spending most of the night in a motel room halfway between Portland and Salem, where Stanley lived and worked.

Regina closed her eyes. She tried to convince herself that everything was okay and she distracted herself by reminiscing about sex with the chief justice. After several erotic moments, she got out of bed and walked to her bathroom with her eyes on the floor so she wouldn't have to look at her bedroom.

Regina lived in a classic Tudor house on an acre of land in Dunthorpe, Portland's most exclusive neighborhood. The house was too big for a single person, but Regina entertained a lot and she needed the space. Her breakfast nook looked across a flower bed and a rolling lawn to the river and she watched the boats floating by as she ate a quick breakfast of coffee, yogurt, and toast. While she ate, Regina looked at her schedule for the day. This morning, she was going to visit Alex Mason at the jail. She didn't remember making the arrangement, but it was in her phone, so she must have. Regina looked in her attaché case. Mason's file was in it, but she didn't remember putting it in when she left the office. She told herself that she had the file and plenty of time to get to the jail, so there was nothing to worry about.

Regina put her plate and cups in the dishwasher and walked into her foyer, where the door to her garage was located. As she walked, she searched in her purse for her car keys. She couldn't find them. A sick feeling formed in her stomach. She emptied her purse on a table and raked through the contents. She grew more agitated when it became clear that the keys weren't in her purse.

Regina took deep breaths to calm down. She'd driven home from the motel. She'd parked in the garage. So she'd had the keys when she parked. And then . . . Nothing.

The steps to the second floor were in the entryway. Regina sank down on them and held her head in her hands. Where were the keys? She couldn't get to the jail to see Alex Mason if she couldn't find her keys.

Suddenly, Regina saw something out of the corner of her eye. A Post-it note was stuck to the inside of the door to the garage. She walked to the door and read the note. It was in her handwriting, but she didn't remember writing it.

KEYS IN DRAWER OF TABLE
NEXT TO GARAGE DOOR.

Regina pulled out the drawer. They were there! Her keys were in the drawer! She gulped in air and steadied herself. She'd found them. She could go to the jail now. Everything was okay.

Only it wasn't. This wasn't the first time she'd misplaced her keys, and two days ago she'd come home and found the stove on. But everyone had memory lapses, and she was almost sixty. Many of her friends complained about forgetting names and movie titles. Slow memory retrieval was a side effect of aging. It was normal. Only what if her problem wasn't?

Regina felt panicky. She shut her eyes and took slow, deep breaths. She didn't want to think about *that*.

Regina grew angry. There was nothing wrong with her. She was perfectly normal. Everyone forgot things from time to time. Regina took a deep breath and calmed down. This wasn't a big deal. Certainly nothing to get upset about, she thought, trying to convince herself as she walked into the garage.

Alex Mason was waiting in one of the contact visiting rooms at the jail when the guard opened the thick metal door and ushered Regina inside. Her client looked scared and exhausted. Copies of the discovery in his case were piled high in front of him on a metal table.

"How are you holding up?" Regina asked.

"I'm not. This place is a zoo. I haven't slept more than an hour or so since they locked me up. You've got to get me out of here."

"I've scheduled a bail hearing for next week and I'm lining up witnesses. I didn't want to go to court until I had a good grasp of the evidence against you and strong testimony about your character."

"How does it look?" Mason asked anxiously.

"I'm not going to sugarcoat this, Alex. It doesn't look good. Meredith Fenner is definite that she was held at your cabin, and DNA evidence puts her and the other victims there. Then there's your DNA on the duct tape."

"I had absolutely nothing to do with these women. Do you think I'd be stupid enough to leave evidence at my cabin, like those blood-stained sheets, once I learned that Fenner girl had escaped?"

"The DA will argue that you would have thought the cabin was being watched."

Mason put his head in his hands. "This is insane."

"We have another problem. Your wife's statements really hurt your case."

Alex looked desperate. "A lot of what Allison said isn't true."

"Let's talk about that. Why don't you walk me through her statements and tell me where she got it wrong."

"We did meet in New York, but her account of what happened isn't completely accurate."

"Okay."

"I was in Manhattan for depositions. I saw her for the first time in the conference room at the law firm that was representing the defendants. She was getting everyone coffee, taking notes. I learned later that she was a temp and she'd only been working at the firm for about a month."

"Did you talk during the deposition?"

"Maybe to thank her for the coffee. I don't remember anything else."

"What was your next contact with Mrs. Mason?"

"I was staying at a hotel a block from the law office and I went to my room after the meeting broke up. I changed out of my suit and went into the bar to unwind before getting dinner. Allison was with some other women when I came in. I remembered her, but I didn't pay much attention until she sat down next to me and said hello."

"Mrs. Mason says that you initiated the conversation."

Mason shook his head. "That's not how it happened. I read what she told the detectives, but it was the other way around. Right before I flew to New York, I'd wound up the proceedings in

94

my divorce from my second wife and I was gun-shy about getting involved with any woman."

Mason paused and looked down at the table. Then he looked back at Regina.

"I know what everyone will think. Allison is beautiful—stunning—and I definitely noticed her, but Carol had put me through hell and I didn't know Allison, and I was only going to be in New York a few days."

"So what did happen?"

"It was Allison who took the initiative. She sat on the bar stool next to me and asked me how the deposition was going. I laughed and said I wouldn't tell her, since she was working for the enemy. She blushed and apologized for asking. She told me she was a temp and had never worked in a law firm before, so she didn't realize she was out of line. I told her not to worry.

"I don't remember everything about the conversation in the bar. I know I asked her if she was from New York and she said she'd just moved about a year ago. I don't remember where she'd been living. She said she was taking temp work until she could find a full-time job. She asked me where I lived and I told her Portland but said I'd grown up in New York. To make a long story short, she was easy to talk to and I was hungry, so I asked her if she'd like to have dinner with me."

"And she acccpted?"

Mason nodded.

"What did you talk about at dinner?" Regina asked.

"Lightweight stuff for the most part. You know, how she liked New York. But the subject matter got a little heavy by the end of the meal."

"Oh?"

"I don't know how it came up, but I told her about how draining my divorce had been and she said she'd been through a bad relationship, too. Only hers had involved bad physical abuse. Then she told me that her stepfather had tried to rape her. When her mother refused to believe her, she ran away from home and had been supporting herself ever since by waitressing and working as a model and a salesclerk. Basically, any work she could find."

"That's pretty heavy for a first date," Regina said.

"Yeah, it was. And I felt . . . When she opened up like that . . . I can't explain it, but what she told me was so intimate. And it made me feel . . ."

"Sorry for her?"

"Yeah. And close to her because we'd both gone through hard times. I mean, not that getting raped and having to run away from home was the equivalent of a bad marriage, but we were both emotionally beat-up."

"You don't think she was playing you?"

Mason thought before answering. Then he shook his head.

"I don't want to believe that. The conversation seemed very natural at the time. But with what she's saying now . . . She might have."

Regina didn't press her client, but she did make a note on her legal pad.

"What happened after dinner?"

"We went to my room. I'd been drinking and I felt sorry for Allison and what she'd been through, and I was smitten. I know that sounds ridiculous, but it was like one of those romances at summer camp or something that would happen on a vacation in a foreign country. You never expect to see the person again and you don't see any of her flaws, just the good parts. And she was—she is stunningly beautiful."

"You slept together?"

Mason nodded.

"Just the one time?" Regina asked.

"No. We were together every night I was in New York and the sex was incredible. Allison made me feel alive again, and after what I'd gone through with Carol . . . I don't know how to explain it other than to say it was the best three days of my life."

"Allison says that you asked her to move to Portland."

"No, that's absolutely false. The wounds from my divorce were still too raw for me to think about commitment. And I thought Allison understood that we were just two adults having fun. That last morning, she left around four to go to her apartment, and I went to the airport and flew home."

"So how did Allison end up in Portland?" Regina asked.

"I had nothing to do with that. She just showed up about a month and a half after I got back. She came to my office. I had no warning."

"What did she want?"

"She said that she couldn't stop thinking about me. She told me she knew flying to Portland was crazy but that she felt she had to take a chance that our time in New York wasn't just a fling, that we'd really made an emotional connection. She told me that she'd fly back if I didn't want her to stay, no hard feelings.

"I pointed out the difference in our ages and she said she'd thought about that, too. Then she said that she'd given up on love until she met me and she didn't want to go through the rest of her life wondering if she'd lost her only chance at happiness because she didn't have the courage to take a risk."

Mason paused and took a deep breath. He looked at Regina, his eyes pleading for understanding.

"I was blown away. I had replayed our nights together many times in the month after I returned to Portland and what she'd said. . . . It seemed straight from the heart. I was really moved."

"What did you tell Allison?" Regina asked.

"I told her that I'd been thinking about her, too, and I'd felt a loss when we parted. I told her that I didn't want to act impulsively, no matter how strongly I felt. I suggested that I find her a job at another firm—not mine, because that would be awkward. I told her I'd pay for an apartment where she could live while we decided if we really wanted to be with each other.

"She agreed. She said she'd had too many disappointments in her life to make a rash decision. So that's where we left it. We agreed that we would date for a while before we slept together again, because we had to see if there was more to the relationship than sex. It was all very civilized, very adult."

"So what happened?"

Mason sighed. "We were in bed before the week was up and we were married two months later."

"Was it true love?" Regina asked without sarcasm.

"I thought so. I couldn't keep my hands off Allison. I thought about her every minute we were apart. And she was good for me. She cooked, she built me up, and she helped me forget my failed marriage."

"Did you have Allison sign a prenup?"

Mason reddened. "No."

Regina looked surprised. "You're a very smart lawyer, and you'd just been through a terrible divorce. Why no prenup?"

Mason looked down. "I . . . It was stupid, I know. But no one had ever made me feel like Allison did. I didn't want to upset her by making her think our marriage was just a business deal."

"How long did the good feelings last?"

"Until she started to disappear."

Regina had been writing a note, but she stopped and looked up.

"When did that start?"

"We'd been married maybe six, eight months."

"What do you mean when you say that she disappeared?"

"It was never more than a night and it wasn't often. The first time she stayed away, I was really worried, and I was very upset when she showed up the next morning. She laughed it off. She told me she was sorry she'd worried me but said she'd been out with friends from work and had had too much to drink and didn't want to drive. I asked her why she hadn't called. She said she'd passed out at her friend's house and woke up at four in the morning. She claimed that she didn't want to wake me up."

"And you believed her?"

"Yes. I had no reason not to. Everything was going so well."

"Did you suspect she was lying at some later time?" Regina asked.

"Yes. The third time she was away all night, we

had our first argument. She accused me of being jealous and suspicious for no reason. I asked her to tell me her friend's name. I said I'd call the friend. She blew up and said that I either trusted her or I didn't. Then she left. I'd gotten her a job as a secretary at another law firm and I called her at work. She was very contrite and she said she was sorry and that she loved me and would never hurt me. She even told me the name of another secretary at her job. She told me to call the friend if I doubted her."

"Did you?"

"I couldn't. It would have been an act of betrayal. I wanted to call, but I decided that I had to trust Allison if I loved her. I let the matter drop and everything returned to normal."

Regina consulted a list she'd drawn up. Then she looked at her client.

"I'm going to read you the dates and times that Tonya Benson, Patricia Rawls, and Meredith Fenner were kidnapped. I need to know if you have an alibi for any of them."

Mason looked embarrassed. Before Regina could read the list, he said, "I might not."

Regina could see that her client was very uncomfortable. "What's going on, Alex?"

"She told the cops about our sex life, so it's not private anymore. I'm not one hundred percent sure, but there's a possibility that I was at home alone on the nights those women were kidnapped.

And I may have an explanation for my DNA on the duct tape, though I hope I'm wrong."

"Go ahead."

"Allison makes me sound like a pervert, but the S and M was all her idea. Sex with my first two wives was very conventional. I met Christine when we were students at Harvard. I was in law school and she was an undergrad. She was from a prominent Oregon family and I moved west after we graduated. The marriage wasn't great. We fell out of love after a few years. I think some of it had to do with my work hours and her inability to have kids. Anyway, we did have sexual relations, but they were few and far between. It was your normal missionary position type of sex. And then she got cancer and was sick for a few years."

Mason paused and took a deep breath. Regina thought his distress was genuine. After a short pause, Mason resumed.

"My relations with Carol weren't much better. I thought of marriage as a partnership where you shared everything. We had a joint bank account and I used money from it for two investments that turned out to be very bad ideas. She went ballistic because I hadn't consulted her when I took the money. Before we argued, she'd transferred all of the money from the joint account into her personal account. Some of that was my money, but she wouldn't acknowledge that and said I had to cover the loss from the investments. The marriage went downhill from there and so did our sexual relations."

"Let's get back to your relationship with Allison."

"At first, Allison was a passionate lover, but she wasn't kinky. That changed about six months into the marriage. We had this conversation about sexual fantasies and she suggested that we could spice up our sex life by acting out some of them."

Mason looked at his lawyer. "This was all role playing, a game."

"Explain that."

"Do you remember the cocktail party at the Hilton? You walked up when I was arguing with your associate about the death penalty. One of our scripts involved a stern husband and a disobedient wife. Allison triggered the game by interrupting me. I pretended to be angry with her and she pretended to be contrite. When we got home, I told her she was a bad wife who had to be punished. Then we went through this ritual where I made her strip and I bound her to the bed and . . . Look, I'm not proud of this, and I didn't want to do it, but Allison said that pain heightened the sexual experience for her. I didn't want to hurt her, but she insisted. I think she might have been punishing herself for things that happened when she was a child. I'm no psychiatrist. I tried to talk her out of it, but she insisted, and the sex was intense when I burned her or spanked her."

"Wasn't this dangerous?" Regina asked.

"Yes, but Allison said the danger made it better for her. And we did have a safety word that Allison suggested. It was *pumpkin* and either one of us could use it if our game got out of hand and we got scared."

Regina made another note.

"Did Mrs. Mason bind and torture you, too?"

Mason nodded. "After I'd bound her a few times, she said I should try it. I couldn't say no after binding and tormenting her, so I let her do it."

"Did you buy into it?" Regina asked.

Mason flushed. "Yes," he replied softly. "I can't explain how I felt. I was powerless and she could do anything to me. It made the sex unbelievably intense. Sometimes she'd duct-tape me to the bed, get me aroused, then leave without a word. The first time, I got frantic. I was really scared. But the sex was incredible when she came back an hour later. Then things got out of hand."

"What happened?"

Mason flushed again. "She started tying me up and staying away all night. She did it three times. The last time was right before that Fenner woman was kidnapped."

"Did the other times coincide with the dates the other victims disappeared?"

"I can't say for sure, but it was close to the times the bodies were discovered. I remember reading about that in the newspaper."

"Let's change the subject," Regina said.

"Meredith Fenner. She swears that a man with a New York accent kidnapped her and took her to your cabin. And there is a lot of evidence that she was tortured there. How do you explain that?"

Mason started to speak. Then he just looked down and shook his head.

"I can't."

"You said you might be able to explain how your DNA got on the duct tape that was used to bind Fenner."

Mason looked sick. "I used duct tape to bind Allison and I ripped the tape off of the roll with my teeth a few times instead of tearing it with my hands."

"You're saying Allison may be responsible for the duct tape winding up on Meredith Fenner's body?"

"That's what I mean."

"You realize the implication if that's true?"

Mason nodded and his face darkened. "I definitely do. It means the bitch is setting me up. If Allison is trying to frame me, it would explain a lot of things she told the police."

"It would also mean that she was involved in three kidnappings and two murders," Regina said. "What would motivate her to do that?"

"My money. About a year after we were married, my firm settled the case with the company represented by the New York firm where Allison had temped. The settlement was huge and our attorney's fees were in the millions. My cut was fifteen million. We got a lot of business after that and the firm's income exploded. If Allison divorces me, she'll be a very rich woman."

CHAPTER SIXTEEN

Carrie Anders found Alex Mason's second wife on the terrace of the Westmont Country Club. She was sipping iced tea while two middle-aged women volleyed on a court just below her. The sweat from a recent match was drying on her tanned skin and a racket leaned against her chair. Carol Richardson had wide blue eyes set in a broad face and looked tough and self-assured. From her Web search, Carrie knew that the athletic blonde in the tennis outfit was fifty-seven and the recently retired CEO of a software company.

"Mrs. Richardson?" Carrie asked.

"You must be Detective Anders," Richardson said, flashing a welcoming smile.

"Yes, ma'am," Carrie said as she started to reach for her credentials.

Richardson waved them away. "Please, if you flash a badge, there will be more gossip about my ex." She held up her glass. "Can I get you a drink?"

"No thanks. You know, we could have met someplace more private."

"I would have suggested it, but I imagine there's some urgency, given the horrible nature of these crimes."

"You're right."

"So, what do you want to know?" Richardson asked.

"As much as you can tell me about Alex Mason."

Richardson's pleasant smile faded. "Are you convinced that Alex really tortured and murdered those women?"

"Our investigation is ongoing, but there's a lot of evidence pointing in that direction."

Richardson blew out some air. "I have to tell you that I am very surprised. Don't misunderstand. There's no love lost between me and Alex, but . . ." She shook her head. "I would never have thought he would be capable of something this awful."

"How long were you and Mr. Mason married?"

"A little less than three years."

"How did you meet?" Carrie asked.

"I traveled in the same social circles as Alex and Christine, his first wife. They were members of the Westmont and Christine and I played tennis with several other women who had been on college teams. Alex wasn't very athletic, but he's a decent golfer, so we were in foursomes on occasion before I split from my husband."

"Were you friends with Christine?"

"We weren't close. Tennis buddies, really. She didn't work, and my work kept me pretty busy. By the time she discovered she had cancer, she was very sick. I did call and I paid a visit, but she didn't want visitors toward the end."

"How soon after Christine died did you and Alex get together?" Carrie asked.

"About a year. Alex was a very eligible widower and was invited out a lot. We kept running into each other at charity events, social functions at the club. I was into the second year of my divorce and we were thrown together because we were both single. Alex isn't handsome, but he can be charming." She shrugged. "Everybody makes mistakes."

"What led to the breakup of your marriage?"

"A lot of things. Alex spent a lot of money. When I learned that he was draining our joint account, I put a stop to that pretty quickly. Then I learned he was cheating on me. I confronted him and he got very belligerent and denied he was fooling around. He claimed that I was the victim of a vicious rumor. I made the mistake of accepting his word.

"About a year and a half after I suspected he was cheating on me, I found out he was having an affair with a trial assistant at his firm and I confronted him. We had a screaming argument and he slapped me. I will not stand for that. I called the police and locked him out of my house."

"How long had you been married at that point?"

"About two years."

"I hear that the divorce was a knock-down, drag-out affair," Carrie said.

"You got that right, but I hired the best lawyers in town before I filed, and we ended with a draw. I was just happy to be rid of the asshole."

"If you don't like Mr. Mason, why don't you think he murdered those women?" Carrie asked.

Carol thought about the question before answering.

"Alex is not a very nice man. I've heard other lawyers call him ruthless and he can't be trusted, but kidnapping and torturing women is on a whole different level of evil."

"You did say he hit you?"

"Yes, but this was in the middle of a heated argument and he apologized right after he did it."

"So he'd never hit you before?"

"No."

"I'd like to ask you about your sex life because it's very relevant to our investigation. Would you be willing to talk about that?" Carrie asked.

Carol shrugged. "It wasn't that exciting."

"Did Alex ever ask you to do something odd?"

Carol's brow wrinkled. "Like what?"

"Did he ever try to tie you up or burn you with cigarettes?"

Carol laughed. "You're kidding?"

"No, I'm serious."

"You mean S and M stuff?"

Carrie nodded.

"No. When we started going to bed, it was okay, but there was nothing kinky." She shrugged. "I liked it when he went down on me and he liked the occasional blow job, but latex and cat-o'-nine-tails . . ." Carol laughed.

"So he never suggested any kind of bondage or using pain to enhance your sexual experiences?"

"He did bite me one time, but I told him I didn't like that and he stopped. Actually, our sex life got pretty dull to nonexistent pretty soon after we tied the knot. And that wasn't because of me. I like sex, but he seemed to lose interest soon after I closed our joint account and put my foot down about the finances."

"Have you met Allison Mason, Mr. Mason's new wife?"

"A few times. She comes to the club."

"What do you think of her?" the detective asked.

Carol thought for a moment before answering Carrie's question.

"She's gorgeous but a little slow. And she seems out of her depth here. I don't want to sound mean, but she impresses me as trailer trash that's been given a makeover."

Carrie had grown up in a trailer in Hammond, but she masked her emotions.

"What gave you that impression?" she asked.

"The way she acts around men. They all drool over her and she leads them on, though I can't

111

say it's intentional. I mean, if you're not that smart but you're a ten on the sex meter, you learn to use what you've got to get what you want."

"Is there any man in particular she's come on to?"

Richardson pointed at the far court, where a handsome young man was giving a lesson.

"I know this will sound like a cliché, but she seemed pretty friendly with Jake Conroy, our tennis pro, and I've seen her sniffing around one or two of the members of Alex's firm."

"Can you give me a name?"

"Do you mean, is there someone I caught her with in flagrante? The answer is no. She just seems overly friendly at times."

"Can you think of anything else that might help the investigation?"

"Not really."

"Then thanks for talking to me," Carrie said as she handed her a business card. "You've been very helpful. If you do think of anything, please give me a call."

"I will, but I want to tell you that I'm having a hard time believing Alex would do something this cruel."

"That's a common reaction people have when they find out their neighbor or their spouse is a serial killer."

CHAPTER SEVENTEEN

As soon as Miles Poe filed his lawsuit, Arnold Prater vowed to put Poe in a cage or a coffin. Prater hoped that Poe would do something when he came to arrest him that would present him with the opportunity to plead self-defense. Killing Poe would be great, but Prater also imagined a number of ways he could horribly maim the pimp.

Tailing Poe had proved difficult because Poe had become paranoid after Prater started his harassment campaign. But Prater knew that Poe had to move product and he was betting that the pimp would screw up eventually. All that was required was patience, and being patient had just paid off.

Early this evening, Prater had watched Poe trade his fire engine red Porsche for a nondescript brown Toyota Camry. Prater had followed Poe to an industrial district near the river. When night fell, the area was dark and deserted. Poe turned into an area with several warehouses. Prater smiled because he knew exactly where Poe was headed. Jackson Wright, one of Poe's flunkies, worked in a warehouse owned by an export-import firm. The job gave him access to overseas shipments, some of which the DEA had long suspected contained narcotics.

Prater turned off his headlights and parked. He

knew he should call for backup, but he didn't want witnesses. He drew his weapon and moved along the side of a building. When he reached a corner, he peeked around it. What he saw warmed his heart. Poe was standing in front of an open door. A moment later, Jackson Wright handed Poe a package that was just the right size for a kilo of heroin.

Prater hunched over and glided through the shadows. When he was close enough for a good shot, he stepped into the light and leveled his gun at the men.

"Good evening, assholes."

Poe turned, his mouth wide open and a shocked expression on his face.

Prater grinned. He started to say "I'm betting that's not talcum powder," when Poe and Wright dived into the warehouse.

"Fuck!" Prater screamed.

He leaped forward. The door slammed shut. Prater grabbed the knob, yanked, and barreled inside. The door closed behind him, leaving the interior of the warehouse in shadows. Prater froze. Then he heard footsteps running away from him and he ran in their direction.

The first officers to respond to Arnold Prater's call for help found him slumped in his car, ashen-faced and with a deep, bloody gash on the back of his head.

"Are you okay?" one officer asked as his partner went back to their car to radio for an ambulance.

"Do I look like I'm okay?" Prater snapped. "Those two fucks ambushed me."

"Who ambushed you?" the officer asked.

"Miles Poe and Jackson Wright. They're drug dealers. I tailed them to this spot and they took off when they saw me. I followed them into the warehouse, and the next thing I knew, I was coming to on the floor."

"Did you have anyone with you? Is there another officer inside?"

"No. I didn't have time to call for backup."

The policeman straightened up as his partner returned. "Okay, we're going in to check things out."

"They'll be long gone by now," Prater muttered.

"You're probably right, but there may be some evidence we can use."

Prater watched the two policemen go into the warehouse. Moments later, lights shone through the thick glass windows. Fifteen minutes later, one of the policemen came outside and walked over to Prater.

"Find anything?" Prater asked.

"Yeah. Do you have your weapon?"

"No. One of those pricks must have stolen it after they knocked me out."

The cop held up his phone and showed Prater a picture.

"Is this your gun?" he asked.

Prater stared at the photo but didn't answer the question. He could see his weapon lying on the concrete floor between two rows of high metal shelves, but that wasn't why he was speechless. Also in the picture, lying next to his gun with an entry wound in the back of his skull, was Miles Poe.

CHAPTER EIGHTEEN

Jeff Hodges limped into his boss's office and found Regina and Robin sitting on the couch, surrounded by a stack of police reports.

"You rang?" he said.

Regina looked up, then motioned to some items on the edge of her desk.

"Alex Mason's bail hearing is this afternoon. That's the key to Alex's house. The letter is written permission to go inside and take any items that might assist in his defense. There's another piece of paper with his alarm code. Go over there and pick out a suit, dress shirt, and tie for Alex to wear at the bail hearing. Then poke around for anything else you think we can use."

"Haven't the police gone through the house?"

"They seized items like the duct tape and cigarettes Allison says they used in their S and M games. I'm interested in anything that will give me a handle on Allison Mason. I asked Alex about her life before they met. He was surprised when he realized that he didn't know much about her. She told him about running away from home but not where that home was. He knew she moved to New York from Florida, but she was always vague about what she did there and where she lived before Florida."

"Didn't he ask her about that?"

"Yes, but she dodged questions about her past. She'd tell him it was too painful to talk about. So see what you can find. Maybe she has a diary or letters. Look at her emails. Alex gave me the password. It's on the paper with the alarm code."

"What if Allison's home? She's not going to let me rummage around."

"The bail hearing is at one. I asked Allison to meet with me before the hearing. She should be leaving soon."

The Masons' house was located off of an isolated stretch of road in Portland's West Hills. That made it difficult for Jeff Hodges to be inconspicuous while he waited for Allison to leave. After driving back and forth along the narrow two-lane road that bordered the Masons' long driveway, he finally parked on the shoulder of the road, as far away from the driveway as he could while still having a view of it.

An hour later, Allison drove out of the driveway, headed toward downtown Portland. Jeff waited twenty minutes before entering the estate. He rang the doorbell a few times to make certain that no one was home. Then he used Mason's key to get inside and punched in the alarm code.

Jeff looked around the downstairs before going up to the couple's bedroom. He selected a suit, tie, and shirt from Mason's closet and put them

118

in a carrying bag. He laid the bag on the bed and went into the master bathroom. Alex had told Regina that he and Allison had their own sinks, and it took no time at all to identify which sink belonged to Allison. Hodges pulled an evidence bag from his coat pocket and plucked several long red hairs from the hairbrush that sat on the marble counter next to Allison's sink to use for DNA testing. When he spotted a glass that he hoped would have Allison's fingerprints, he ran downstairs and found an identical glass in a kitchen cupboard. Then he returned to the bathroom and substituted the glass he'd just secured for the glass he placed in a second evidence bag.

When Hodges was through in the bathroom, he reentered the bedroom and searched the drawer in the end table on Allison's side of their king-size bed. Nothing in the drawer was helpful.

There was a home office on the ground floor. Jeff booted up the computer and entered Allison's password, but he didn't find anything interesting. As soon as he turned off the computer, Jeff checked his watch. He'd been in the house for an hour. He was tempted to look around some more, but time was growing short, so he left for the jail to deliver Alex's clothes.

CHAPTER NINETEEN

The Honorable Martha Herrera, an elderly jurist who was close to retirement, had been assigned Alex Mason's case. She was slender, with wrinkled brown skin, soft white hair, and a perpetual smile. Herrera refused to wear contacts, and her sharp brown eyes peered at litigants through thick tortoiseshell glasses.

The judge had been in private practice in an insurance defense firm twenty years ago when the governor had tapped her for the Multnomah County Circuit Court. She'd had a few opportunities to fill vacancies on the Oregon Court of Appeals, but she enjoyed trial work and had rejected all of them. Regina felt that Mason was lucky to have Herrera hear his case. She was fair and bright and had the type of judicial temperament attorneys loved.

In all cases except murder, a defendant had a right to bail, but a judge had to deny bail in a murder case when the proof of guilt was evident or the presumption was strong that the defendant was guilty. At trial, the state had to produce witnesses to make its case and the defense had a right to cross-examine them. At a bail hearing, the state was permitted to have the lead detective summarize the state's evidence for the judge.

Alex Mason's bail hearing was the disaster Regina had expected it would be. Kyle Bergland had Carrie Anders give a summary of Meredith Fenner's testimony and a summary of the evidence that would establish that the three victims were held at the Masons' cabin and that Alex's DNA was found on the duct tape that was used to bind Meredith Fenner. Carrie also told the judge that Allison would testify about Alex's sexual preferences, which included using duct tape to bind her and cigarettes to burn her. Allison was sitting in the spectator section, but she would not make eye contact when Alex turned toward her.

Regina presented prominent members of the Oregon Bar, Mason's pastor, and several other character witnesses, but she couldn't counter the state's evidence of guilt. Herrera ruled that the state had met the criteria for a denial of bail.

As soon as the judge issued her finding, Mason's shoulders slumped and his chin dropped to his chest. When the judge left the bench, the guards came over to cuff Mason.

"I'll meet you at the jail in a few minutes," Regina told him.

Mason nodded and the guards led him away.

"Can you take my file back to the office?" Regina asked Robin.

"Sure. Are you going to appeal the bail decision?" Robin asked.

"You're the appellate whiz. Do you see any chance of getting Herrera reversed?"

Robin thought for a moment, then shook her head. "It would be a waste of time."

"I agree. See you in the office."

As she walked toward the door to the corridor, Regina tried to formulate her answers to the questions the reporters were going to ask.

"Miss Barrister?"

Regina looked around and saw a handsome young man in a business suit standing behind her. He was tall and broad-shouldered, with a head of wavy brown hair and soft brown eyes.

"My name is Jacob Heller. I'm representing Allison Mason in her divorce." He held out a legal document. "Please give this to Mr. Mason."

One look at the papers let Regina know that Alex Mason's awful day had gotten worse.

Alex Mason was back in his orange jumpsuit by the time he was escorted into the contact visiting room. He looked furious, and Regina regretted that she was the bearer of more bad news.

"This is total bullshit," Mason raved. "I'm being set up. Why can't Herrera see that?"

"This was just the bail hearing. At trial, I'll get to cross-examine and a lot can change."

"It's that bitch Allison. She couldn't even look me in the eye."

"I'm working on ways to discredit your wife's testimony."

"You'd better, considering what I'm paying you."

Regina sighed. There was no use putting off what she had to tell Mason. "I'm afraid I have more bad news for you," she said as she handed Mason the document she'd been given in the courtroom. "Allison has filed for divorce."

Mason's face grew red. "The bitch! This was her plan all along. First she frames me for murder and then she guts me financially."

"I'm going to start a full-scale investigation into Allison's background. If she planned this, she may have done something similar before."

"If she planned this, she's a lot smarter than we thought and she's probably covered her trail."

CHAPTER TWENTY

Carrie Anders slowed down to maneuver past the pickets outside the Justice Center. Most were African-American, with a scattering of young white faces, and they were demanding justice for black men and an end to police brutality. The detective's jaw tightened when she read the placards that compared the Portland police to Nazis.

The Reverend Carlos Jones was using a bullhorn to egg on the demonstrators. Jones was frequently involved with civil rights protests and he was willing to disregard the facts when he wanted to get people riled up. Carrie had seen him on the news, where he was telling a reporter that the black community was enraged because Miles Poe, a young black man, had been shot in the back by Arnold Prater, a white cop, shortly after Poe sued Prater for harassment. He had failed to mention that Poe was a drug-dealing pimp and not some young scholar bound for Princeton, but he did tell the reporter that the feud between the two men had started when Poe stopped Prater from beating a black woman. Carrie wondered where he'd gotten that information and the information about the lawsuit. That mystery was solved when she got a phone call from Jackson Wright's attorney.

• • •

Carrie Anders and Roger Dillon ushered Jackson Wright and his lawyer, Elliot Nesbitt, into a conference room, then sat across the table from them. Wright's lawyer had sandy blond hair and blue eyes that were shielded by the lenses of wire-rimmed specs, which kept sliding down his nose. Carrie figured that the attorney was in his mid-twenties and probably only a year or so out of law school.

Jackson Wright was dressed in pressed jeans, a black turtleneck, and a black leather jacket and still resembled the muscular tight end he had been in high school before being expelled for assaulting a teacher. Several of her contacts in Vice had told Anders that Jackson provided muscle and sold dope for Miles Poe.

There had been an APB out for Wright as soon as Arnold Prater identified him as the prime suspect in Miles Poe's murder. Until this morning, all attempts to find Wright had failed. Then Nesbitt had phoned Carrie and told her that Wright wanted to tell what he knew to the police.

"Thank you for coming to see us, Mr. Wright," Carrie said.

Wright scowled. "Miles was my friend, and that fucker Prater . . ." He shook his head. "I want justice for Miles. No offense, but there have been too many good young black men murdered by the police."

Carrie restrained herself and addressed Wright civilly. "Just out of curiosity, Mr. Wright, were you the person who told Reverend Jones that Miles Poe was suing Officer Prater?"

"Before Mr. Wright says anything, we need to reach an agreement," Nesbitt said. "Jackson has come forward in good faith. He's willing to tell you what happened inside the warehouse when Mr. Poe was shot and he will testify for the state before a grand jury and at a trial, but, as I mentioned on the phone, he wants assurances that he won't become the scapegoat for police brutality."

"And what does Mr. Wright want for his cooperation?" Roger Dillon asked.

"Immunity from prosecution for any and all crimes that may have been committed at the time that Miles Poe was murdered."

"And what might those crimes be?" Carrie asked.

"There's murder and assault, in which he was not involved, and there may have been narcotics in the area."

"We can't give your client immunity for a crime of violence, but we can for crimes involving drugs," Carrie said. "And we're going to want a proffer before we give Mr. Wright a get-out-of-jail-free card."

"I figured you would," Nesbitt said, "so here it is. If you give Mr. Wright immunity, he will tell you that Arnold Prater shot Miles Poe."

"And how does he know this?" Carrie asked.

"Because he saw him do it," Nesbitt said.

"You know that Officer Prater says that your client most probably shot Mr. Poe?" Dillon said.

"No, I didn't. I have no idea what Officer Prater said. But I find it interesting that you said that Prater said my client 'most probably shot' Poe. Isn't he sure?"

Carrie suppressed a smile. Nesbitt was sharp.

"Before I tell you what we know, why doesn't Mr. Wright tell us what he knows," Dillon said.

Carrie showed Nesbitt and Wright a document she had prepared as soon as the meeting had been arranged.

"This is our assurance that nothing said at this meeting will be used against Mr. Wright in any way and that we will not arrest him today."

Nesbitt took the notarized document and went over it with his client.

"Okay," Nesbitt said when they finished conferring. "Jackson, tell them what happened at the warehouse."

"I know you won't believe me, because you got me pegged as a pimp and dealer, but you probably don't know about the relationship between Miles and Prater. So I'm gonna fill you in on that before I tell you about the killing."

Wright leaned forward and made eye contact first with Dillon, then Carrie.

"Arnold Prater is a bent cop. Miles used to

pay him off so he wouldn't hassle him about his business. Sometimes he paid him cash, but sometimes he let Prater fuck his girls for free. Now to understand what brought all this about, you got to know that Prater ain't right in the head and he's an animal with women."

"What do you mean?" Carrie asked.

Wright looked directly at the detective. "He gets off on hurting them, and that's how the trouble started. 'Bout a month or so ago, Prater told Miles he wanted to fuck— Well, I ain't gonna name her 'til we have a deal, but it was one of Miles's women. Anyway, Miles agreed, but he seen what Prater done to another one of his girls and he warned Prater not to beat them up no more 'cause they ain't no use if they got their faces beat in. And after what happened to Tonya, he couldn't afford to have another girl out of commission."

Alarm bells went off. "Tonya?" Carrie asked.

"Yeah, the girl who got murdered by that lawyer."

"Are you saying that Tonya Benson worked for Miles Poe?"

"Yeah."

"Did Officer Prater have any contact with her?"

"I got no idea. Miles dealt with Prater, not me."

"What about Alex Mason? Did he have anything to do with any of Miles's women?"

Wright's brow furrowed for a moment. Then

he shook his head. "That name ain't ringing no bells."

"Sorry to interrupt," Carrie said. "Why don't you continue telling us what happened after Mr. Poe told Officer Prater that he couldn't beat up his women."

"He done it anyway. Miles hears this woman screaming and he busted into the motel room and pulled a gun on Prater to get him to stop."

"Did you see this?" Dillon asked.

"No, but Miles told me what happened right after. He was really shook."

"Okay," Dillon said. "Go on."

"By the time Miles got inside the room, Prater had already busted up the girl's face. The problem was, Prater hadn't gotten his rocks off yet and he was pissed. So he wanted revenge and he got it by hassling Miles with traffic tickets every time he saw him. And he got some of his police buddies to give him tickets. Then he had some of his other buddies go to Miles's pool hall and arrest the girls for all kinds of shit they weren't doing. Just generally making a nuisance of hisself. So Miles hired Mr. Nesbitt and sued Prater for violating his civil rights. And that's why Prater killed Miles."

Carrie sat back and studied Wright. "This is a lot to take in, Mr. Wright."

Wright jabbed his thumb at his lawyer. "Ask him if you don't believe me."

Carrie looked at Nesbitt, who nodded. "Miles was killed shortly after I served Prater. We were suing for several million dollars and there was definitely a pattern of harassment."

Nesbitt took the complaint in Poe's civil suit out of his attaché case and pushed it across the table. Dillon leaned over Carrie's shoulder to read it.

"So you're saying Prater had a motive to kill Poe?" Dillon said when he was through.

"A million reasons."

Carrie turned back to Wright. "And you're saying that you saw him do it?"

"I'm an eyewitness."

"Go ahead," Dillon said.

"Okay, so Miles and me do business occasionally. You know what I'm saying?"

"You're a drug dealer, just like the late Mr. Poe," Dillon said.

"Yeah, hypothetically. And, hypothetically, we might have been meeting at the warehouse where I work so I could give Miles some merchandise."

"Let's forget about the drugs, Mr. Wright," Carrie said. "We're Homicide, not Narcotics and Vice. So how did the shooting start?"

"Prater must have followed Miles to the warehouse because, all of a sudden, he popped up and he was pointing his gun at us. Me and Miles jumped inside the warehouse. Then we both took off down the aisles in the dark.

"Seconds later, Prater came through the door. I knew I couldn't make it to the other side of the warehouse, where there's another door, so I ducked behind some shelves. They're high. They go up almost to the ceiling and there are boxes and merchandise in them, so I knew Prater wouldn't be able to see me if I stayed quiet. But Miles kept running. I could hear him. Prater must have, too, because he took off after Miles. I followed them. That's when I heard the shot. Miles grunted and Prater said, 'I got you, motherfucker.'

"By this time, I was a row away and a little bit behind Prater. There was a gap in the boxes I could see through. Miles was lying on the floor, rolling around in pain. Prater kicked him and said something I didn't catch. Miles begged him and put up his hand and Prater told him to roll over and face the floor so he could cuff him. Miles rolled over and that's when Prater shot him in the back of the head.

"When I seen that, I got on my stomach and crawled toward the far door. I heard Prater looking for me. After a while he must have gotten tired of looking, because I heard him head toward the way we came in. That's when I snuck out."

"Mr. Wright, when Prater ran after Mr. Poe, why didn't you run away from him and out the door you came in?"

"I didn't know if he'd called for backup and there was cops waiting out there."

"And you're telling us you actually saw Officer Prater shoot Mr. Poe to death?"

"Yes, ma'am, I did."

Three hours after they'd escorted Jackson Wright and his lawyer to the elevator, Carrie Anders and Roger Dillon finished telling Kyle Bergland about the meeting with Miles Poe's associate.

"What do you want to do?" Carrie asked.

"You checked his story?" the DA asked.

"I got a cop who knows Prater to talk off the record. He says Prater is dirty. We know Poe sued Prater and several cops for violating his civil rights by, among other things, giving him traffic tickets every time he drove downtown. My source says that Prater told him to ticket Poe even if he didn't violate any of the traffic laws. He said he'd do it, but he never did because he didn't think it was right."

"So Prater had a strong motive to shoot Poe," Bergland said.

Carrie and Dillon nodded.

"What do you two think we should do?" Bergland asked.

"It'll be Prater's word against Wright's," Dillon said, "but Poe was shot in the back and in the back of the head with Prater's gun, Prater had it in for Poe, and Prater didn't ask for backup when he went to the warehouse. The whole thing stinks, if you ask me."

"What do the surveillance tapes show?" Bergland asked.

"The cameras inside the warehouse weren't working, but the shots we got from outside back up Wright. Prater had the drop on them when Poe and Wright ran into the warehouse. Prater was holding his gun when he followed them."

"What does the lab say about ballistics?" Bergland asked.

"Poe was definitely shot with Prater's gun," Dillon said.

"Did they print it?"

"Yes, but it was wiped clean," Dillon replied.

"Wright is definite about seeing Prater shoot Poe?" the prosecutor asked.

Carrie nodded. "He claims he saw Prater shoot Poe in the back, then shoot him again in the head. Forensics says blood spatter supports the story. Wright says that Prater searched for him, then left the warehouse when he couldn't find him. Wright says he ran out the back when Prater went out the side door and that he didn't see anything after that. He also says that Poe told him he paid Prater with money and sex to look the other way when he dealt drugs or sold sex. He wasn't there when Poe stopped Prater from beating one of Poe's women, but he says that Poe told him about the incident right after it happened. He says Poe was pretty shook up because Prater told Poe he'd be sorry for interfering."

Bergland had been making notes with a pen while Dillon and Carrie spoke. Now he stared into space and absentmindedly rapped the pen on the edge of his desk. The detectives let him think. After a minute, Bergland sighed and focused again.

"This could turn into a real clusterfuck if we don't do something. Carlos Jones is stirring everyone up and he's got the mayor's ear. The mayor already called the boss, who told me to get moving before we have a riot on our hands."

"There's something else, Kyle," Carrie said. "The Mason case."

"What about it?"

"Wright told us that Tonya Benson was in Miles Poe's stable. If we give Wright immunity, he might be able to help us with the Mason case."

Bergland swore. Then he sighed.

"Let's get Prater in here and see what he's got to say."

CHAPTER TWENTY-ONE

The day after Anders's and Dillon's meeting with Jackson Wright, Robin Lockwood walked into Regina's office and shut the door.

"Arnold Prater's back."

Regina's brow furrowed. "Who?"

"The cop who's in the news for shooting that drug dealer, Miles Poe," Robin said. "Remember, he was in here a few weeks ago. He wanted you to represent him in a lawsuit Poe filed against him."

Regina looked blank, but then she said, "Oh, yes. Does he have the retainer?"

"I don't think he's worried about being sued anymore, what with Poe being deceased and all. I'm guessing he's worried about grand juries and murder charges. Do you want to see him? I know you weren't thrilled about representing him in the civil suit."

"No, I wasn't, but I'll see him. Why don't you sit in."

Moments later, Robin led Prater into Regina's office and took a seat on the sofa. Prater hadn't shaved, he was sweating, there were dark circles under his eyes, and his pupils were dilated. Robin wondered what pharmaceutical he'd ingested before coming to the office.

"How can I help you, Mr. Prater?" Regina asked.

"I have friends in the DA's office. One of them warned me that Jackson Wright is saying that I shot Miles Poe and he's going in front of a grand jury."

"Who is Jackson Wright?"

"He worked with Poe. He's a pimp and a drug dealer, a real piece of shit."

"And Mr. Poe was shot?"

"Don't you watch the news?"

"Yes, I do, but I'm unfamiliar with this case."

"I saw Poe and Wright with drugs and I chased them into a warehouse. Someone knocked me out, took my gun, and murdered Poe, and Wright is saying I killed him."

"Are you presently under indictment?"

"No, but I got called into the chief's office about testifying, so I need a lawyer. I have money for a retainer and I want you to represent me."

"We're talking a minimum retainer of one hundred thousand dollars. That's a lowball estimate if you're indicted for murder and the prosecutor seeks the death penalty."

"Yeah, well, I emptied my piggy bank. I can do one hundred thousand. I'll get you a cashier's check by the afternoon."

Robin thought that was interesting. It suggested that Prater's money was not in a savings account and that his stash was probably not income he'd reported to the IRS. She imagined that Prater would be spending the afternoon running from bank to bank with cash, buying cashier's checks in amounts smaller than the banks were required to report to the IRS.

"Do you have any idea who knocked you out and who shot Poe?" Regina asked.

"It had to be Poe or Wright who coldcocked me. I'm guessing it was Wright and that he's the one who took my gun and shot Poe."

"I can see why he would knock you out, but why would he kill Poe?" Regina asked.

"Business. With Poe dead, Wright can take over Poe's territory."

Regina nodded. "Can I assume that you deny killing Poe?"

"That's right. But Wright says he saw me shoot him."

"And why would they take the word of a pimp and drug dealer who had a motive to kill Mr. Poe over your word?"

"Me and Poe, we have a history." Prater sounded nervous and he shifted in his chair. "Wright's claiming I beat up one of Poe's whores and threatened Poe when he interfered. And there's the lawsuit Poe served on me just before he was killed."

"He was suing you?" Regina said.

Robin frowned. She and Regina had just talked about the lawsuit and Regina had read the complaint during Prater's previous visit.

Prater looked confused. "You saw the complaint."

Regina's face lost all expression for a moment. Then she smiled. "Yes, I did, but why don't you refresh my memory."

"Poe said I was giving him traffic tickets for no good reason and harassing his whores."

"Did you beat up one of Poe's women?" Regina asked.

"I was arresting her for prostitution. She resisted. When she attacked me, I had to subdue her. I was acting in self-defense."

Regina nodded. "And the traffic tickets?"

"Yeah, about them. Poe thought he was hot shit and didn't have to obey the traffic code. I did give him two tickets when I saw him breaking the law, but different officers gave him the other tickets. I had nothing to do with that. He was just a bad driver."

Regina studied Prater for a moment. Then she looked over at Robin.

"Find out which DA is handling the case and see if you can get the police reports."

"Will do."

She returned her attention to Arnold Prater. "Give Robin your contact information, and I'll need a copy of the complaint Poe filed. When I've talked with the district attorney, we can discuss whether or not you should testify before the grand jury."

"Okay," Prater said.

Robin showed Prater out. As soon as the door to her office closed, Regina leaned back in her chair and shut her eyes. Her mouth was dry and she felt panicky. Prater had talked about Poe's lawsuit. He seemed so certain that she'd read the complaint, but she had no memory of it. None whatsoever.

CHAPTER TWENTY-TWO

Robin was in turmoil the rest of the day. She didn't want to believe that something was wrong with her boss, but how else could she explain Regina forgetting about Miles Poe's lawsuit? Regina had read the complaint, and Robin had mentioned it moments before Prater had entered her office.

Robin was no stranger to short-term memory loss. She'd been really scared after Kerrigan knocked her out in her last fight as a professional, because there had been parts of the previous day that were complete blanks. But Regina hadn't suffered a head injury, so what could have caused her to forget about the lawsuit? The word *dementia* kept sneaking into her thoughts. Robin had no medical training or real-life contact with anyone suffering from this condition. And she hadn't been around Regina long enough to tell if she was showing signs of mental deterioration or was merely being forgetful.

Robin left work early and went to the gym in hopes that a rugged workout would relax her. Several MMA fighters worked out there in the afternoon and she'd found a few who wanted to spar once they found out who she was. The workout was exhausting, but it didn't stop her from obsessing about Regina's inability to remember who Miles Poe was or the fact that she'd read the complaint in his lawsuit.

Robin bought some Chinese takeout on the way home. After she ate, she booted up her laptop and did a Web search for dementia.

The first thing she learned was that there were roughly seventy types of disorders that could cause or simulate dementia, and some were curable. Depression and misuse of sedatives could cause behavior that could present as dementia. And Alzheimer's wasn't the only type of dementia. Brain tumors, infections, and strokes could also cause it.

There were warning signs she should look for. If memory changes disrupted daily life, it was something to worry about. Forgetting something that was recently learned or asking for the same information over and over was a sign that there was a problem. Was someone experiencing challenges in planning or solving problems, having trouble following a recipe, or keeping track of bills? Regina had evidenced some of these behaviors, but she'd also been incisive and insightful when she'd discussed complex legal issues with Robin.

Robin learned that problems could occur in the early stages of dementia when a person was presented with unfamiliar tasks or navigating less familiar places. Old memories tended to be preserved and old procedures that had been repeated were more likely to still function. So a person could log in to their computer easily, since they'd done this a thousand times, but change the software slightly so the menus were in a different order or give them a new password and the person could run into trouble.

When the condition progressed, a person might have difficulty reading or judging distances. An article discussed a patient who had hardwood floors with a pattern in the wood. There was also a rug in front of her bathroom. She suddenly refused to go to the bathroom in her home, although she would go into other bathrooms. It turned out that she saw the rug as a gaping hole and was afraid of falling into it. The problem was solved by removing the rug. Robin hadn't seen any evidence that Regina was experiencing these types of problems.

A person with dementia might also have trouble following or joining in conversations or might forget words. They might also misplace common objects like keys and accuse others of stealing them. Showing poor judgment was another serious problem. Robin learned that people with dementia were easy prey for con men and would send large amounts of money to telemarketers. They might also withdraw from social activities that were once important to them by giving up hobbies. Later on, they might forget to root for their favorite sports team or stay away from family gatherings. And they might experience mood or personality changes or become fearful, suspicious, or agitated. These were things she should look for, but the articles warned that normal people also forget their keys or act anxious.

When Robin stopped reading, she was no closer to deciding if Regina had a problem. She had been troubled by some of the things Regina did, like forgetting the code to the copying machine. But Robin had also forgotten telephone numbers and misplaced files. She decided to keep her thoughts to herself but to watch her boss carefully.

CHAPTER TWENTY-THREE

Jeff Hodges had a lot to do in Alex Mason's case, but Regina had emphasized that interviewing Meredith Fenner, the state's star witness, was of the utmost importance. Fenner was living in a four-story brick apartment house two blocks off of Burnside Avenue. The apartment house was old and there was no elevator. A faint odor of Indian food accompanied Lockwood and Hodges up the stairwell. Jeff stopped in front of one of the apartments on the third-floor landing. They could hear a television inside.

"This is it," he said. "Why don't you talk to Fenner? She might respond better to a woman."

Robin rapped her knuckles on the door. After a few seconds, she knocked again. Someone turned down the television and they heard footsteps approaching. There was a peephole in the flimsy wooden door. Robin stood in front of it and smiled.

"Who's there?" Meredith asked. She sounded frightened.

"Hi, Miss Fenner. I'm Robin Lockwood. Jeff Hodges is with me. We work with Regina Barrister. Can you spare us some time?"

"I don't understand," Meredith said.

"Ms. Barrister is representing Alex Mason."

"Why do you want to talk to me?"

"Can you please let us in, so we don't have to shout through the door?" Robin asked. "We won't stay long."

It was quiet for a few seconds. Then Jeff and Robin heard the chain being removed and several locks turning. The door opened and Robin got her first look at the key witness against their client. Meredith looked small, frail, and frightened and seemed to have been swallowed by the faded large-size sweatshirt she was wearing.

"How did you know where I live?" Meredith asked when she'd shut the door behind her visitors.

"We have reciprocal discovery in Oregon," Robin said. "We sent the DA our list of witnesses with their addresses and phone numbers and he sent us his list. Everyone talks to everyone so that we can get a true picture of what happened."

Meredith shook her head. "I . . . I really don't want to talk about it. I have nightmares. I get very upset when I think about what . . . what he did to me."

"That's just it," Robin said. "Mr. Mason says there's been a mistake. That he wasn't the one who hurt you. You don't want an innocent man to go to prison, do you?"

Meredith worried her lip.

"One of the worst things that can happen to a human being is to be sent to prison for something

145

he didn't do," Jeff said. "You don't want to be responsible for that."

"I . . . I think he did do it."

"If you convince us of that, we'll talk to Ms. Barrister and recommend that she tell Mr. Mason to enter a plea. That way, there won't be a trial and you won't have to relive what happened," Robin said, in hopes that would convince Meredith to talk.

Meredith was quiet for a moment. Then she shook her head.

"I don't want to talk to you. Please go."

"We understand why you're upset," Robin said.

Meredith shook her head. "No, you don't. You have no idea what I went through. I know you're just doing your job, but I want you to go."

"You'll have to answer Ms. Barrister's questions in court if the case goes to trial."

"Please," Meredith pleaded. "I can't talk about it. I've told the police what I know. They must have given you a report. I don't have anything to add."

"There might be something you didn't say— something you've remembered since—that will help us get to the truth," Robin said.

Meredith shook her head from side to side. "No. There's nothing. I want you to leave."

Jeff touched Robin's elbow. "Thank you for seeing us," he said as they handed Meredith their cards. "I can see how awful this has been for you. Think about what I said about sending an innocent man to prison. You don't seem like the type of person who would want to be responsible for something like that. If you have a change of heart, please call. We'll meet with you anywhere you choose."

As soon as Robin and Jeff were back in the hall, the investigator turned to the lawyer.

"That is one scared rabbit," he said.

"Can you blame her? You read her statement."

Jeff frowned. "Alex Mason is in big trouble if she points the finger at him."

"Yeah," Robin agreed, but secretly she didn't care what kind of trouble Mason faced if he was the person who had tortured Meredith Fenner.

"Detective White," Harry said when he picked up the phone.

"They were at my apartment. They tried to get me to say he's innocent."

"Calm down, Meredith. Who was at your apartment?"

"They work for Mason."

"Did someone threaten you?"

"No. Not exactly. But they wanted me to say it wasn't him. But it was."

"Okay. Take some deep breaths. Now, who visited you? Did they tell you their names?"

"It was a man and a woman. They work for that lawyer, Barrister, the one who's trying to get Mason off."

"So they were investigators?"

"The card says that Robin Lockwood is a lawyer."

"That's normal. There are always two lawyers in a death-penalty case."

"I'm afraid, Harry. They know where I live."

"You're not in any danger. Lawyers are supposed to interview witnesses," Harry said.

When Meredith spoke, he could tell that she was on the edge of panic.

"I don't want to be alone, Harry. I'm scared."

"Do you want me to drive up? I can be there by five-thirty."

"Would you?"

"Sure."

"Thank you, Harry. Thank you."

Harry White parked in front of Meredith Fenner's apartment house and carried a bag of Chinese takeout up the stairs to the third floor. Meredith answered her door after one knock and greeted Harry with a wide smile. She was wearing a short sky blue dress decorated with yellow flowers. The dress had spaghetti straps and Meredith's shoulders were bare.

"Let's chow down," Harry said as he held out the take-out bag.

"Thank you so much," Meredith replied. "As soon as I hung up, I thought about calling you back and telling you not to come."

"Well, I'm glad you didn't. I was going to spend the evening alone with a baseball game and a frozen dinner. This is a much better plan."

Meredith had showered and washed her hair. When she took the Chinese food from him, Harry caught the faint summer scent of her shampoo.

Meredith walked into the kitchen/dining area in her small apartment. She'd put out plates and silverware. Then she divided the fried rice, kung pao chicken, and pork lo mein between them.

"Do you want some tea?" she asked.

"Water is fine. I'm glad to see you're feeling better."

"I shouldn't have panicked like that," she said as she ladled wonton soup into two bowls. "I feel really stupid."

"You should never feel stupid, Meredith. After what you've been through, it was natural for you to get upset. Someone should have warned you that Mason's people would try to interview you."

"I read the articles in the paper about Regina Barrister. Is she as good as they say? Can she . . . Is there a chance he won't go to jail?"

"Kyle Bergland is good, too."

"But do they have enough to convict him?"

"Yes, thanks to you. You're the star of the show, Meredith. Women who might have been kidnapped and tortured by Alex Mason are going to be safe because of you."

Meredith looked down. "I'm not that important."

Harry smiled. "Don't kid yourself. Alex Mason made a big mistake when he tangled with you. You're one tough cookie."

Meredith looked across the table and returned the smile. "Thank you, Harry."

Harry felt his heart beat faster. Then he caught himself. Meredith was a witness in a murder case. Nothing could happen between them while the case was active. If he got romantically involved with a witness, it could destroy the case against Mason.

"How's work?" the detective asked, wanting to change the subject.

Meredith cast her eyes down. "I quit. The people who own the coffee shop were nice. They said I could come back. I tried. I worked for one day, but I was too frightened. When I went to my car after work . . . I know Mason is locked up, but I could feel him there. I couldn't do it."

"I can understand that. Are you looking for work?"

"Just around here. There's a restaurant looking for a waitress. I put in an application."

"What about moving out of Portland? Have you thought about that? Maybe a change of scenery—getting away from where all the bad things happened—would help."

"I have thought about moving, but I should stay here to help the police until the trial is over. When it's over, when . . . that man is . . . gone, I'll think about what I want to do."

Harry thought about what he wanted to say and whether he should say it. He knew it probably wasn't the right thing to say, but he decided to say it anyway.

"I think you're very brave, Meredith, but it's natural for you to be frightened after what you've gone through, and anytime you're scared, you can call me and we can talk. Don't ever think you're imposing or wasting my time. I'm here for you."

"Thanks, Harry." Meredith hesitated. "There is something."

"What do you want?"

"I'd feel a lot better—a lot less frightened—if I knew Mason was going to be convicted. I don't know if you can, but I'd like to see the evidence they have. Is there some way I could do that?"

Harry's brow furrowed. "Do you mean the physical evidence?"

"Oh, no. But don't you write police reports? Isn't there a record of what the witnesses say or if he made a confession?"

"Sure, but you probably shouldn't see those."

"I don't want to get you in trouble, but I keep on thinking that Regina Barrister will get him off. If I knew that Mr. Bergland's case was strong . . ."

Her voice trailed off and Meredith looked down again. "Forget I asked."

Harry could see how scared she was.

"Let me see what I can do," he said.

When Meredith raised her head, the fear was gone. "Thank you so much. I don't know if I could have gotten through this without you."

"Yeah, well, our motto is 'Protect and Serve,'" Harry said, glad that he'd been able to make her smile. "I'm just doing my job, ma'am."

"How did you get into police work?" Meredith asked.

"Process of elimination," Harry said, grateful for the change of subject.

"I was the big man on campus at Whisper Lake High," Harry said with a wistful smile. "Prom king and the star of the football, basketball, and baseball teams. Unfortunately, our high school played in the smallest league in the state. I was a superstar at that level, but I didn't stack up to the studs in the other leagues. So no college was beating down my door with a scholarship offer. My folks were just scraping by and my grades weren't so hot. Without a scholarship, college was just a dream, so I enlisted in the marines and got my first taste of police work as an MP.

"When my hitch ended, I returned home with no job and no plans. One night, when I was nursing a beer in the Golden Elk Tavern and feeling sorry for myself, Greg Fadley, an old high school teammate, told me to apply for a position at the Hammond County Sheriff's Office." Harry shrugged. "The rest is history."

"Well, I'm glad you didn't get that scholarship. If you had, I'd never have met you."

Meredith smiled and Harry blushed.

"How do you like the food?" he asked, because he was afraid of where the conversation might go.

"It's good." Meredith held his gaze for a moment. Then she stood up and walked to a kitchen drawer. "I think we need some napkins."

As soon as her back was to him, Harry took a deep breath.

CHAPTER TWENTY-FOUR

Carrie Anders went to the address Jackson Wright had given her and parked her car. The apartment was over a grocery store in a run-down area of Portland on the east side of the river. Two men came out of the store. They were carrying beer and their clothes were ragged. When Kyle Bergland got out, they eyed him suspiciously. When Carrie got out, the men smelled cop and hurried down the street.

"What's her name again?" Bergland asked.

"Mordessa Carpenter."

"And she'll talk to us?"

"That's what Wright said."

Mordessa lived in apartment 3A on the third floor of a three-story walk-up. There were buzzers for each apartment and hand-lettered last names in the slots above some of the buttons. There was no name in the slot for 3A. Carrie pushed the buzzer twice before she heard a click and the front door opened.

The sour smell of cigarette smoke, canned soup, and garbage permeated the stairwell. A tall black woman, her hair in cornrows, was standing in the doorway of 3A when the detective and the DA got to the third-floor landing. She was wearing tight jeans and a red tank top. Carrie figured she was in her late teens or early twenties. She had large breasts and a full figure, and her face would have been pleasant-looking if it weren't for the reminders of the beating Arnold Prater had administered.

Mordessa had tried to disguise the scars and bruises with makeup, but that hadn't worked that well. The damage reminded Carrie of Meredith Fenner's wounds.

"Miss Carpenter?" Carrie asked.

The woman nodded.

"I'm Detective Carrie Anders," she said as she held up her ID. "This is Deputy District Attorney Kyle Bergland."

"Jackson said you'd be coming," Mordessa said. "Step inside. I don't want nobody to hear my business. They's some busybodies on this floor."

Mordessa leaned back to let the detective and prosecutor enter. Her small apartment was spotless. The furniture was cheap but well cared for. Their host gestured toward a sofa and sat in a straight-backed chair. A romance novel and copies of *Us Weekly* and *In Touch* were stacked neatly on an end table next to the sofa.

"So, what you want to talk about?" Mordessa asked.

"Mr. Wright told us that you had a problem with Arnold Prater."

Mordessa burst out with a humorless laugh.

155

"That's what he called it, 'a problem'? The motherfucker beat me senseless. If Miles didn't stop him, I could be dead now or brain-damaged."

"Can you tell us what Prater did to you?" Kyle asked.

Mordessa shook her head. "I told Miles I didn't want no part of that man, but he said I got to go with him. He said he'd talked to him and there wouldn't be no violence." She shook her head again. "I shoulda put my foot down."

"Had you met Prater before?" Carrie asked.

"No, but he's got a reputation."

"Oh?"

"He gets off on beating women." She shook her head again. "He sure lived up to his rep."

"What happened?" Carrie asked.

"Miles brought him up to the motel room. He was real pleasant and gentlemanly when he come in. Then Miles left and he changed. First he ordered me to get naked. Then he told me to get on the bed on my back. I did what he said. Then he took out his handcuffs. That scared me. I asked what he was planning to do and he said to shut up and lie back down. I started to tell him I wasn't into that shit, and that's when he hit me in the stomach. I couldn't breathe and I flopped back on the bed. He slapped me hard and said I should do as I was told and stop talking.

"Now I was real scared, but I was weak from lack of air and I couldn't fight him when he wrestled my hands to the headboard and snapped on the cuffs. I got my wind back and screamed for Miles, and that's when he hit me in the mouth."

Mordessa opened wide and showed them the gap where one of her teeth had been.

"He said there would be more of that if I didn't keep my mouth shut, so I stopped talking. As soon as I was cuffed, he got naked. I figured I'd let him fuck me and get it over with. I hoped he'd stop hurting me once he was done. But he didn't get on the bed."

Mordessa stopped and took a breath. Carrie could see that reliving the experience had shaken her.

"What did he do to you?" Carrie asked gently.

"He . . ." Mordessa licked her lips and looked down. When she spoke, her voice was only a shade higher than a whisper. "He burned me."

"With what?"

"A cigarette. When he took it out of the pack, I hoped he was gonna smoke, but he got the tip real hot and jabbed it onto my nipple. I shrieked and he busted my nose. Then he did it again and I screamed again and that's when Miles come in, pointed his gun at Prater's balls, and said he'd shoot him if he didn't stop."

"What did Prater do?"

"Miles been paying him off. That's what I was, a payoff, a free fuck so he would let Miles do his business. Anyway, Prater said he'd shut Miles

157

down, and Miles said Prater couldn't afford that shit 'cause he paid him too much money to look the other way. So they reached an agreement. Miles gave Prater two hundred bucks to leave."

Mordessa lost her composure and started to cry.

"That's how Miles saved me." She wiped her eyes. "And now that bastard went and killed him." She looked at Bergland. "I hope he dies and goes to hell. He's a bad, evil motherfucker."

Mordessa took several deep breaths. "I'm sorry," she said, "but Miles always been good to me."

"You have nothing to apologize for," Carrie said. "It sounds like Prater put you through hell. Do you want some water? Do you want to take a break?"

Mordessa looked into Carrie's eyes, anger replacing despair. "I want that motherfucker dead for what he done to Miles. And I was there when he said he was gonna do it."

"Prater said he was going to kill Miles?" Carrie asked.

"Oh yeah. He did. Not in so many words, but I heard him tell Miles he was gonna be sorry for busting up his fun. He said Miles gonna regret what he done."

"And you'll tell this to a grand jury?" Carrie asked.

Mordessa hesitated.

"We can't get him without your help. Your

158

testimony provides the motive for the murder."

Mordessa looked torn. Then she nodded.

"I have a question for you, Miss Carpenter, that has nothing to do with the murder of Mr. Poe," Kyle Bergland said. "Did you know a woman named Patricia Rawls or another woman named Tonya Benson?"

Mordessa's shoulders slumped and her eyes teared up again.

"That poor girl didn't deserve that."

"Who didn't?" Bergland asked.

"Tonya."

"So you knew her?"

Mordessa nodded.

"Do you know anything that might help us figure out who killed her?"

"Ain't it that lawyer?"

"We think so, but we can use any help you can give us."

Mordessa hesitated.

"If you know something, please tell us," Carrie said. "We want to get the person who killed Tonya as much as we want to get Prater for killing Miles."

"I might know something."

"Go ahead."

"I might have seen the person who took her."

"Why haven't you said something?" Bergland blurted out.

"I don't have nothing to do with no police. I'm

only talking to you because Jackson says I got to."

"Okay," Carrie said, "I get that. But we're talking now. So what did you see?"

"The night Tonya disappeared, we was working our area. It was dark and I was on another corner when this car drove past me and stopped by Tonya. She leaned in the passenger side. Then she got in and the car drove off."

"Do you know what kind of car Tonya went off in?" Carrie asked.

"It was black and foreign. A fancy car. But I can't tell you who made it."

Carrie remembered that Alex Mason drove a black BMW.

"Why do you think this is connected to Tonya's murder?" Bergland asked.

"I didn't say it was. But I got a customer soon after Tonya left in the car, and when I got back to my spot, she wasn't there, and she never came back. Then I come down with something and I was in bed for a day. When I went back to work, I heard Miles swearing about Tonya, telling Jackson he was furious with her 'cause she hadn't brought him no money for two days and he thought she run off. I didn't see her no more after that, and then I heard she got killed."

"Could she have finished up with the customer in the fancy car, returned while you were gone, and been picked up by someone else?" Carrie asked.

"Yeah, there was enough time. And also, I didn't think that customer done anything to Tonya, because I seen her for a second when she drove by me."

" 'She'?" Carrie said.

"Yeah, that's the other reason I didn't think I knew nothing about Tonya's killer. A woman was driving that car."

Mordessa was relieved when the cop and the DA left. She didn't trust cops and she was worried about having to testify against Prater. When she heard the knock on her door ten minutes later, she figured Bergland and Anders had returned to ask her something else.

She opened the door. A man was standing in the doorway. Mordessa opened her mouth to scream and Arnold Prater hit her in the stomach. Mordessa doubled over. Prater shut the door with one hand and used the other hand to deliver a blow to Mordessa's chest that knocked her down. Her head bounced off the floor, dazing her. Prater dropped onto her chest and slapped a strip of duct tape over her mouth. Mordessa was already having trouble breathing and her eyes grew wide with panic.

"Breathe through your nose, bitch," Prater said as he gripped her chin with gloved hands. "I want you sharp so you can hear every word I say."

Mordessa sucked in air through her nostrils.

161

Prater waited until she was still, her terrified eyes focused on him. He gave her cheeks light slaps.

"You okay?" he asked. Mordessa didn't move.

"Nod if you understand the question, or I'll hurt you."

Mordessa snapped her head up and down.

"Good girl. So, I saw Anders and Bergland leaving. You buddy-buddy with the authorities all of a sudden? You going to help your local police by testifying?"

Mordessa shook her head from side to side. Prater hit her in the solar plexus again.

"That's for lying, cunt."

Mordessa spasmed as she strained for air. Prater waited patiently until she caught her breath. Then he pulled a thick envelope out of his back pocket.

"Now listen up. There's a thousand dollars in this envelope and a bus ticket to New York City. I really don't give a fuck what you do when you get there, but you're gonna go or you're gonna die. Got that?"

Mordessa was paralyzed with fright. When she didn't nod, Prater squeezed her nostrils until she almost blacked out.

"I want an answer, bitch," he said when he let her breathe again. "Are you gonna run today?"

Mordessa nodded.

Prater patted her cheeks. "Good girl. Now here's the deal. You go away and stay away. I don't care where. You can peddle your ass on the

East Coast as well as you can here. But you don't tell anyone where you are. In fact, you never call anyone in Oregon ever again. If you talk to the DA, I'll know and you'll die, but it won't be quick. You'll suffer for a long, long time and you'll beg for death by the time I'm through with you. Do you understand?"

Mordessa nodded vigorously.

"Okay. I'm gonna let you up. You're gonna pack and go to the bus station. If you don't get on the bus to New York, you're dead."

CHAPTER TWENTY-FIVE

When Robin walked into her office, she found a pile of new police reports in the Prater case sitting on her desk. She nibbled her scone and sipped her latte while she scanned them. When she was halfway through one of the reports she paused, her scone inches from her lips, and reread a paragraph. She put the scone down and raced through the other documents in the pile. Then, before walking down the hall to Regina Barrister's office, she reread the report that had gotten her attention.

"Did you go through the new discovery we got in Prater?" Robin asked as she waved the police report.

Regina dipped her chin toward a several police reports that were stacked on her desk.

"Do you mean these?" she asked.

"Yes."

"Why do you ask?" Regina said.

"Did anything strike you as interesting in the report of the interview with Mordessa Carpenter?"

Regina hesitated. Then she smiled. "Why don't you tell me what's got you excited and we'll see if it's the same thing I saw."

Robin was certain Regina was bluffing, but

164

instead of challenging her boss, she handed Regina a copy of the interview Carrie Anders had conducted with Mordessa Carpenter. She put her finger on the paragraph that had caught her attention.

"Carpenter may have been the last person to see Tonya Benson before she was abducted. And she may have seen the person who kidnapped and killed her."

Regina read the paragraph Robin had pointed out. "But this says thc driver was a woman," Regina said.

Robin had to work hard to keep from showing surprise when she realized that her boss didn't get it.

"Mr. Mason thinks his wife is setting him up. Allison Mason could have been the woman in the car who pickcd up Tonya Benson."

"Meredith Fenner says a man abducted her."

"If Allison Mason did set up her husband, she had to have had a male accomplice. Allison could have helped abduct Benson while Alex was tied up at home, and the male could have abducted Fenner."

Regina thought for a moment. "I think you should interview Carpenter and show her a photo of Allison," she said.

"My thought exactly."

"Take Jeff with you."

"Will do," Robin said.

As soon as she closed the door to Regina's office, Robin walked down the hall and knocked on Jeff Hodges's doorjamb. The investigator looked up from his computer.

"What's up?" he asked.

"We need to interview a witness," Robin said as she handed Hodges the report of the Carpenter interview.

"Interesting," he said when he was finished. "Give me half an hour to finish this and we can head out."

Regina had kept her features bland when Robin asked her if she'd read the new reports in Arnold Prater's case, but she'd felt sick. She had read through the discovery, but she had no idea who Mordessa Carpenter was or what Robin had been getting at until Robin spelled out her theory.

Regina stood up and walked to her window. Everything outside was so beautiful: the river, the lush green foothills, the snowcapped mountains. But inside her were gray swirling clouds. What was happening to her? Regina's chin dropped and she turned away from the view. A mug of coffee was sitting on her desk. When she reached for it, her hand trembled.

CHAPTER TWENTY-SIX

"She ain't in," said a voice from a doorway across the hall.

Robin stopped knocking on Mordessa's door and turned around, to find a heavyset African-American woman in a housedress sizing up her and Jeff.

"Do you know when Miss Carpenter is coming back?" Robin asked.

"My guess is never. She was toting two suitcases and hustling down the stairs last time I saw her. The landlord been up complaining about rent past due. I think she skipped."

While Robin and the neighbor were talking, Jeff opened the door. "It's not locked," he told Robin.

"You can't go in there," the neighbor said.

"We're just going to peek inside to see if Miss Carpenter is really gone. You can come with us to make sure we don't take anything."

The woman thought for a minute. "Ain't none of my business," she said, and went inside her apartment.

One look around convinced Robin and Jeff that Carpenter was not coming back. Drawers and closets were open and empty in the bedroom, trash was sitting in the can under the sink, and the milk in the refrigerator smelled sour.

"It's a big break for our client if Mordessa's disappeared," Jeff said. "Jackson Wright's claiming that Poe told him that the feud between Prater and Poe started when Prater beat up Mordessa. With Carpenter gone, there's no way to corroborate Jackson's hearsay."

"Do you think the police will find her?"

Jeff shrugged. "That's not our problem. Let's go back and tell the boss the news."

On the way to the car, Robin thought about the Sorceress.

"How long have you been working for Regina?" she asked as soon as they pulled away from the curb.

"A little over three years."

"So you know her pretty well?"

"Yeah, why?"

Robin hesitated. Then she took the plunge. "Have you noticed anything strange about her behavior recently?"

Jeff's brow furrowed. "Strange like how?"

"I don't know," she said, starting to feel silly. "Last week she had to have me help her with the copier because she couldn't remember her code."

Jeff laughed. "It took me two days to figure out how to run that damn machine."

"Yeah, but there have been times that I've asked her about stuff she should know and I've had the distinct impression she had no idea what I was talking about."

"Like when?"

"Okay, I'll give you an example. Arnold Prater came in right after Miles Poe sued him. He wanted Regina to represent him in the civil suit and he showed her the complaint. She read it. They discussed it. But when he came in about his criminal case, she had to ask him to explain why he'd been sued. It was like she didn't remember anything about the first meeting."

Jeff shrugged. "Regina can be absentminded at times, but if there's one thing you can be sure of, it's that Regina Barrister's brain is working on more cylinders than any other attorney's in this state."

If Robin had doubts about how sharp Regina was, they disappeared as soon as she saw her boss's reaction after hearing that Mordessa Carpenter had disappeared.

"Well, well," she said as her lips spread into a big grin. "This couldn't happen at a better time. Arnold Prater just called. He's been arrested on a murder charge. I'm going to set a date for an expedited bail hearing. I think we can blow the state's case out of the water if we act quickly."

CHAPTER TWENTY-SEVEN

As she fought her way past the pickets parading in front of the courthouse, Robin felt a surge of adrenaline like the rush she used to feel when she entered the Octagon. The protesters were carrying placards that read justice for miles and stop killer cops and they were chanting like the crowds in the arenas where Robin had fought. When the protesters spotted Regina, the decibel level increased and a protester tried to hit Regina with her placard. Jeff knocked the protester back and Regina hurried inside.

When they got off the elevator on the fifth floor, Robin shielded her eyes from the bright lights of the TV cameras and followed Jeff and her boss to the courtroom where Arnold Prater's bail hearing was going to be held.

"Why did you demand an immediate bail hearing?" one reporter asked.

"Because Officer Prater, a decorated member of the Portland Police Bureau, is innocent of these charges, which have been brought for purely political reasons."

"Why do you say that politics is behind the murder charge?" another reporter shouted.

"The mayor is beholding to Reverend Jones for delivering the African-American vote in the last election. These charges are a blatant attempt to appease and court black voters. If you were at my motion for a bail hearing in this case, you saw the district attorney object to a speedy bail hearing even though he knows that any policeman in any jail in this country is in great danger. The mayor and the district attorney don't want the flimsy nature of this case exposed to public scrutiny. And now, ladies and gentlemen, I've got to get to work."

Robin followed her boss down the aisle and through the gate that separated the spectator section from the area where counsel sat. Jeff took one of the few unoccupied seats in the spectator section. Moments after Regina settled in at the defense counsel's table, the guards brought her client out of the holding area. Regina had arranged for Prater to wear a suit to the bail hearing, and he looked professional.

"Are you going to get me out?" Prater asked. Robin could see that he was very worried.

"We've got a shot," Regina said. "Let's see how it goes."

The bailiff rapped his gavel and the Honorable Albert Stein walked out of his chambers and took his seat on the bench. Stein was a middle-aged former prosecutor who had been a circuit court judge for several years. His round, pleasant face contrasted with his sharp, no-nonsense temperament.

"The State calls Detective Carrie Anders," Kyle

Bergland said as soon as both sides told the judge they were ready to proceed.

Regina stood as Carrie walked to the witness stand to take the oath.

"We're familiar with Detective Anders and I believe she has appeared before Your Honor."

"Several times, counselor."

"For purposes of this hearing, Officer Prater will not require the State to establish her expertise or that she is the lead detective in this case," Regina said.

"Mr. Bergland?" the judge asked.

"I appreciate the courtesy," Bergland replied.

"Very well," Judge Stein said.

"Detective Anders, can you please summarize the case against Arnold Prater for Judge Stein?"

Anders turned to the judge. "I'll do this chronologically, Your Honor. The defendant is a Portland Police officer. Our witnesses will testify that the victim, Miles Poe, was a pimp and drug dealer. Mr. Poe was bribing Officer Prater with cash and sex with his prostitutes so that the defendant would let him run his criminal enterprises."

"Question in aid of objection, Your Honor," Regina said.

"Go ahead, Miss Barrister," the judge said.

"Detective Anders, are the witnesses you are referring to Jackson Wright and Mordessa Carpenter?" Regina asked.

"Yes."

"Has Mr. Wright been convicted for various crimes?"

"Yes."

"And Miss Carpenter?"

"Yes."

"With regards to Mr. Wright, will he testify that he saw Mr. Poe pay off Officer Prater with cash or sex?"

"No."

"So this is something he will say he learned from Miles Poe?"

"Yes."

"Your Honor, this testimony would not be admissible at trial because it is hearsay. So I object to your considering it when you are deciding whether the State has met the criteria for denying bail."

"Mr. Bergland?" the judge said.

"We believe it is admissible as a statement against Mr. Poe's penal interest. He was admitting that he was committing a criminal act, bribery."

"To a fellow criminal who, the evidence will show, is a pimp and drug dealer with convictions that would call into question his truthfulness," Regina argued. "I don't believe the penal interest hearsay exception would apply in this instance. Mr. Wright is not someone in law enforcement who could use Mr. Poe's alleged statements to prosecute Mr. Poe."

"What about the other witness, this Carpenter woman?" the judge asked.

"Miss Carpenter would testify that she had sex with the defendant as a payoff for the defendant not arresting Miles Poe for promoting prostitution."

"Miss Barrister?" the judge asked.

"May I ask another question in aid of objection, judge?"

"Go ahead."

"My investigator tried to interview Miss Carpenter and he learned that she is not at the address you gave me in discovery. That apartment is vacant and the drawers and closets have been emptied. A neighbor told Mr. Hodges that she saw Miss Carpenter leaving the apartment house with suitcases."

Anders mouth opened in surprise for a moment. Then she clamped it shut, and Regina suppressed a smile of satisfaction.

"Do you know where Miss Carpenter is living or how to get in touch with her at this moment?" Regina asked.

Anders looked at Bergland.

"Do you know, Mr. Bergland?" the judge asked.

"I . . . we . . ." the DA began. "This is news to me."

"Detective?" Judge Stein asked.

"Me, too. I spoke to Miss Carpenter in person a few days ago at her apartment."

"Well, it seems she's no longer there," Regina said. "Can you assure the Court you can find her?"

"No. I mean, we'll have to investigate," Bergland said.

"Then I object to any testimony about what Miss Carpenter might say, since it appears she has run away," Regina said. "That indicates that she is unwilling to testify. I also object to the Court considering anything she may have told the police, because her criminal convictions call her veracity into question."

Bergland looked furious. "If Miss Carpenter has fled, it's probably because she's afraid of the defendant," he said.

"Or because she doesn't want to commit perjury," Regina shot back.

"Enough," Judge Stein said. "Sit down, both of you. I'm going to hear what Detective Anders thinks Wright and Carpenter will say; then I'll decide what weight to give it in light of the circumstances."

"Very well, Your Honor," Regina said.

"Please continue with your testimony," the judge told Carrie Anders.

"Miss Carpenter would testify that Mr. Poe told her to have sex with the defendant at a motel as a payoff for not interfering with his criminal activities. She would testify that she was afraid of the defendant because she'd been told that he liked to beat up women. When she was alone with the defendant, he handcuffed her to a bed and began to beat her and burn her with a cigarette."

Robin frowned as Carrie Anders described how Arnold Prater had tortured Carpenter. She'd read the report of the interview with Mordessa Carpenter, but she'd been focused on what Carpenter had said about Tonya Benson and had not paid attention to the manner in which Prater had abused Carpenter.

"When Miss Carpenter screamed," Anders continued, "Mr. Poe came into the motel room holding a gun and ordered the defendant to stop beating her. After some resistance, the defendant stopped beating Miss Carpenter and left, but not before telling Mr. Poe that he would regret saving Miss Carpenter.

"I talked with Elliot Nesbitt, Mr. Poe's attorney. He would testify that Mr. Poe sued the defendant for several million dollars shortly after the incident with Miss Carpenter. Mr. Poe claimed that the defendant and several other Portland police officers were engaged in a conspiracy to harass him by giving him traffic tickets almost every day and arresting women who worked at his pool hall for no legitimate reason."

Bergland rose. "I'd offer State's exhibit two, the complaint filed by Mr. Poe."

"For purposes of this hearing, I have no objection," Regina said.

"Very well," Judge Stein said. "The exhibit will be accepted. Go ahead, Detective."

"Jackson Wright told me that he and Mr. Poe were outside a warehouse in Portland when the defendant threatened them with a gun. Mr. Wright and Mr. Poe ran into the warehouse. Mr. Wright hid and saw the defendant shoot Mr. Poe in the back. Then the defendant forced Mr. Poe onto his stomach and shot him in the back of the head. The medical examiner will testify that the shot in the head was the cause of death. Ballistics tests have identified the defendant's gun, which was found next to the victim, as the murder weapon."

"That's our offer of proof, Your Honor," Kyle Bergland said.

"Any cross, Miss Barrister?"

"Yes, Your Honor."

Robin had heard that Regina was famous for conducting both her direct and cross-examination without notes and for being able to quote from cases from memory. In Officer Prater's case, Regina had written out her questions and had gone over them with Robin.

"When Officer Prater was interviewed by you about the incident at the warehouse, didn't he tell you that he pulled his gun after seeing Mr. Poe hand Mr. Wright what Officer Prater believed to be a kilo of heroin?"

"Yes."

"Isn't it also true that Mr. Wright told you that

he was at the warehouse doing a drug deal with Mr. Poe?"

"Yes."

"Did you or your officers conduct a search of the warehouse in which Mr. Poe was killed?"

"Yes."

"Did you find any heroin?"

"No."

"Wouldn't the reasonable assumption be that Mr. Wright took the heroin when he fled?"

"I guess," Anders said reluctantly.

"Now, as far as you know, only Mr. Wright, Mr. Poe, and Officer Prater were in the warehouse when Mr. Poe was killed."

"Yes."

"That means that most probably either Mr. Wright or Officer Prater killed Mr. Poe."

"Yes."

"Detective, is it correct to say that Jackson Wright is your star witness?"

"Yes."

"Officer Prater is a decorated Portland police officer, is he not?"

"Yes."

"And Officer Prater told you he was knocked unconscious when he went inside the warehouse and that he woke up after Mr. Poe was murdered."

"Yes."

"When he was found at the scene, did Officer Prater have a head wound?"

"Yes."

"If I told you that a doctor who examined that wound on the evening that Officer Prater was struck on the head concluded that it was reasonable to assume that a person sustaining such a wound would be rendered unconscious and that it was most probably not self-inflicted, would you be able to produce any testimony that would call that determination into question?"

"Not at this time."

"Mr. Wright has arrests and convictions for possession and sale of heroin, does he not?"

"Yes."

"If I told you that we have spoken to officers in Portland Vice and Narcotics who have told us that Mr. Wright worked for Mr. Poe while he was alive and has taken over Mr. Poe's business now that he is dead, would you disagree with them?"

"I don't have that information."

"If it's true, wouldn't Mr. Wright have had a strong motive to kill Mr. Poe and frame Officer Prater for the murder?"

Anders hesitated and looked at the DA.

"This is not a difficult question, Detective Anders. In criminal enterprises, isn't one way an underling can take over from his boss is by killing him?"

"I don't know if that's common."

"Mr. Wright has been convicted of assault, has he not?"

"Yes."

"So he's no stranger to violence?"

"One conviction for assault doesn't make him a killer."

"But the money he would make by taking over his boss's business might."

Regina looked at the judge. "No further questions, Your Honor."

Robin grabbed Regina's sleeve. "You didn't ask about the gun," Robin whispered.

Regina gave her a blank look. Robin turned the page with Regina's cross-examination questions and pointed to writing on the second page. They had gone over these questions less than twenty-four hours ago.

"There were no prints on the gun, remember. A smart cop wouldn't have wiped off the prints, then left the gun behind," Robin whispered.

Regina read her prepared cross about the prints on the gun and flashed a quick smile.

"Yes, of course. Thanks for reminding me."

Regina turned to the judge. "I do have one or two more questions for the detective, if I may."

"Go ahead," the judge said.

"Detective, you testified that Officer Prater's gun is the murder weapon?"

"Yes."

"Were his prints found on the gun?"

"No."

"In fact, no prints were found on the gun, were they?"

"No."

"Do you want the Court to believe that a veteran police officer with knowledge of the way a murder case is investigated would kill a man in cold blood with his own gun, wipe his prints from the gun, then be stupid enough to leave the weapon—which could be connected to him easily—next to the body of the man he murdered?"

"I don't know what may have motivated the defendant. He may have panicked after shooting Mr. Poe."

"Let me see if I understand you. Officer Prater follows Mr. Poe and Mr. Wright inside the warehouse and murders Mr. Poe in cold blood. Then he calmly wipes his prints off the gun. Then he panics and drops the murder weapon by the body. Then he stops panicking and proceeds to fake a head injury by beating his head against something until his wound hopefully is sufficient to fool a doctor. Is that what you want the Court to believe?"

"I don't know what was in the defendant's mind when he murdered Miles Poe," Anders replied, but it was obvious that the detective was unable to respond intelligently to Regina's question.

Regina's witnesses were the physician who treated Prater for his head wound; a dean at the medical school, who testified that Regina's client had suffered from a significant blow to the head that could have been self-inflicted but probably was not; and a detective from Vice and Narcotics, who testified that Jackson Wright had taken over Miles Poe's business. When all the evidence was in, Judge Stein ruled.

"I am compelled to set bail in a murder case if, after hearing a proffer of the State's evidence, I cannot conclude that the State's proof of guilt is evident or the presumption is strong that the defendant is guilty. In this case, the evidence indicates that two people were inside the warehouse when Mr. Poe was murdered. Allegedly, Jackson Wright and Mordessa Carpenter would produce evidence that could lead the jury to conclude that Officer Prater wanted revenge on Mr. Poe because Mr. Poe interrupted him when he was beating Miss Carpenter, and there is the lawsuit Mr. Poe filed, which supports the State's position that Officer Prater was harassing Mr. Poe. But Miss Carpenter has apparently fled and Mr. Wright, the alleged eyewitness, also had a strong motive to murder Mr. Poe, since he is now running Mr. Poe's prostitution and narcotics businesses.

"I am also troubled by the evidence that the officer was hit on the head hard enough to knock him unconscious and the fact that no prints were found on the murder weapon, yet it was left at the crime scene.

"Now, much can change between now and a trial, but I don't feel the State has met its burden today. I am also concerned about the danger a police officer can face when he is in jail. So I am going to grant bail for Officer Prater."

"Yes," Prater said after expelling the breath he'd been holding.

The judge spent several more minutes discussing the terms of the release before adjourning court. As soon as the judge was off the bench, Anders and Bergland left the courtroom. Robin could tell thcy were upset.

Prater turned to Regina. "How soon can I get out?"

"It will take a few hours, but you should be released sometime today."

"They say you're the best, and you sure lived up to your reputation."

"Thank you," Regina said.

Robin walked through the bar of the court just as the guards came up to lead Prater away. Prater nodded to her. Robin realized that it was the first time he'd paid her any attention.

"What did you think?" Regina asked Robin.

"If I were prosecuting, I'd take a very hard look at my case," she replied.

"Nice work, boss," Jeff said.

"Thank you."

"Can I make a suggestion?" the investigator asked.

"Go ahead."

"I talked to some of the courthouse guards. The protesters just learned that the judge granted bail, and the scene outside is getting ugly. I think we should go out the back entrance and avoid the crowds."

"Good idea."

"I'll get a couple of guards to accompany us in case somebody figures out what we're doing."

"Okay. Let me talk to the reporters. Then we can head for the back stairs."

Regina packed her attaché case and Robin followed her and Jeff up the aisle and into the corridor outside the courtroom, where she fielded questions from the reporters. Robin admired the way Regina managed to emphasize the weakness in the State's case every time she answered a question, knowing her answers would be on TV and radio and in the newspaper, where potential jurors would hear and read them. And she was impressed by Regina's devastating cross-examination of Carrie Anders, but one thing nagged at her. Why had Regina forgotten to grill Anders about the lack of prints on the gun?

CHAPTER TWENTY-EIGHT

A strange idea had wormed its way into Robin's brain during the bail hearing. After leaving the courthouse, she picked up a triple-shot latte. When she was in her office, Robin sipped her drink as she reread the police report of Mordessa Carpenter's interview, the interview with Meredith Fenner, and the autopsy reports of the dead prostitutes. Then she looked at the photographs of the battered faces of Meredith Fenner and the prostitutes. When she was done, Robin put her feet up on her desk and stared into space. Five minutes later, she dropped her feet to the floor, leaned forward, and shuffled frantically through the police reports concerning Carol Richardson, one of Alex Mason's ex-wives. When she finished scanning the report, she whispered, *"Yes,"* and felt the thrill she'd experienced when she'd knocked out an opponent in the Octagon. Then she grabbed several police reports and sped down the hall to Jeff's office.

Jeff was working on his computer when she rapped on his door.

"Do you have a moment?" Robin asked.

"Sure, what's up?"

"I've been thinking about the Mason case."

"And?"

"Alex Mason's and Allison Mason's stories are

so at odds with each other that one of them has to be lying."

"That's obvious."

"If Alex Mason is telling the truth, there's a strong possibility that Allison Mason set him up."

"I've thought about that, too, but the setup would have involved long-term planning and great complexity."

"I think Allison is pretty smart," Robin said. "I met her at a cocktail party at the Hilton after I spoke at a CLE. I was arguing with Alex Mason about whether death by lethal injection was cruel and unusual punishment. The U.S. Supreme Court had ruled that Oklahoma could use a specific drug when they executed an inmate. Mason was trying to remember the name of the drug, but he couldn't. Allison chimed right in with midazolam. A dummy wouldn't know that.

"Also, Mordessa Carpenter saw a woman at the wheel of a dark foreign car that Tonya Benson got into on the night she disappeared. The Masons own a black BMW. If Allison is framing her husband, she could have been driving the car while Alex was tied up in their house."

"Where is this going?" Jeff asked.

"Meredith Fenner says that she was kidnapped and tortured by a man. If Allison is involved, the only way to reconcile the evidence is if she had a male accomplice. The possibility that Allison was working with a man got me thinking."

Robin put the autopsy pictures of Tonya Benson, Patricia Rawls, and the photos taken of Meredith Fenner's face on Jeff's desk. Then she handed Jeff the report of the interview with Mordessa Carpenter.

"In bulky clothes, Arnold Prater and Alex Mason would have similar builds, and both men have New York accents. And look at the similarities in the way Meredith Fenner and Mordessa Carpenter were tortured. They were bound to a bed, beaten around the face, and burned with a cigarette."

"Are you suggesting that Arnold Prater and Allison Mason are in cahoots?" Jeff asked.

"It would explain how Prater would know about the Masons' cabin and when no one was using it so he could take his prisoners there."

"I see a few problems with your theory. There are similarities in the way Fenner and Carpenter were tortured, but the person who killed Rawls and Benson and kidnapped Fenner used duct tape, not handcuffs like Prater used on Carpenter, and burning people with cigarettes as a method of torture is not unique."

"Prater wouldn't use his handcuffs. That would suggest that a policeman was involved."

"The killer didn't think Fenner would escape. And you can buy handcuffs a lot of places. And there's something else you're missing. Allison wouldn't ask a police officer to join in a plan that involved serial murder unless she was absolutely certain that Prater wouldn't arrest her. Why would she even think of approaching him with her plan?"

Robin frowned. Jeff had made some pretty good points.

"I can see another problem with your theory," Jeff said. "Allison and Arnold don't exactly run in the same circles. Mason is a member of a country club and lives in a mansion in the West Hills. If Prater and Allison were conspiring to frame Alex, how did they meet?"

Robin couldn't help grinning as she slapped a police report on Jeff's desk.

"Read that. As soon as I thought about the possibility that Prater was working with Allison Mason, I went through all the reports in the Mason and Prater cases again and I came across a report of Carrie Anders's interview with Carol Richardson, Alex Mason's ex-wife. Carol said she called the police when Alex hit her. I found the report of the incident. It was written up by Officer Arnold Prater. Prater responded to the call! That's when he met Alex Mason."

"Now that's interesting," Jeff said when he finished reading the report.

"Prater kidnaps women and tortures them," Robin said, "but Meredith Fenner escapes and he gets scared, so he beats up Poe's women to relieve his urges."

Jeff thought for a moment. Then he shook his head.

"Your theory is that Prater and Allison are working together to frame Alex Mason, but Alex didn't meet Allison in New York until over a year after he met Prater."

"Maybe Alex and Prater bonded."

Jeff laughed. "Are you suggesting a bromance?"

Robin blushed. "It's not so far-fetched," she replied defensively.

Jeff held his hands up to form a frame. "I can picture it. They go bowling together and watch football at sports bars. Then Alex remarries and introduces the little woman to his best pal."

Robin's enthusiasm waned. "Laugh if you want to. But think about it. Allison was in New York four years ago and Prater moved here from New York four years ago."

"New York is a pretty big place, Robin."

Robin looked frustrated. "We know almost nothing about Allison's past. What if she did know Prater in New York?"

"Your theory is based on a lot of pretty unbelievable what ifs."

Jeff had burst Robin's bubble and she started to deflate.

"Hey, buck up. I'm not saying your theory is completely wrong. If Allison is framing her husband, she had to have had a male accomplice. Arnold Prater just might not be that person."

"Who else could it be?"

"Maybe the man she met on the nights she disappeared."

"A lover?"

"It would have to be. Who else could she convince to become an accomplice in these horrible crimes?"

Robin frowned. "That makes sense. Do you think she'd risk seeing him now that Alex has been arrested?"

"Probably not, but maybe I should start following her in case she screws up."

CHAPTER TWENTY-NINE

Gabriella Winter practiced law across the freeway in a Victorian home that had been converted into offices. A psychologist and an Internet consultant occupied the first floor and Winter and an accountant shared the second floor. A nonprofit had an office above Winter's suite.

Robin had scheduled her appointment for lunchtime so she would have an excuse for disappearing for an hour. As soon as she hung up, she felt like a traitor and thought about canceling the appointment, but the stakes were too high. At eleven-thirty, Robin mustered her courage, fought the sick feeling in the pit of her stomach, and walked across town to meet the top Oregon practitioner of elder law.

Winter walked into her waiting room moments after Robin was announced. Robin had imagined a severe older woman in a gray business suit, but the lawyer wore a colorful peasant dress, her short white hair was spiked, and she flashed a contagious smile as she extended her hand.

"Come on back," Winter said as she led Robin down a short hall decorated with American Indian art.

"Utah and Arizona," Winter said when she caught Robin looking at the photographs of the

Southwest that brightened her walls. "That's where I was raised."

"It's beautiful country," Robin said. "I did some hiking in Bryce, Zion, and some of the other parks when I was in college. Why did you leave?"

"It's an age-old story. I followed my man when we graduated from college, then stayed after the divorce. I paid my way through law school by working as a nurse in several assisted-living facilities. That's where I developed my passion for helping the elderly. But enough about me. How can I help you, Robin?"

Robin felt very uneasy about what she was about to say. Even though she knew Winter was forbidden to reveal her confidences, she had decided to disguise her boss's identity and the incidents that bothered her.

"I have a friend and I'm worried about him."

"What's worrying you?" Winter asked when Robin hesitated.

"He's not that old. I mean, he's in his late fifties, and he's extremely smart—way above average—but he's forgetting things and acting odd."

"In what way?"

"I'll tell him something and he won't remember I told him a few minutes later. Recently we discussed a magazine article at great length. Then another friend brought up the article a week later and my friend acted like he'd never heard of it.

And he has trouble remembering simple number sequences like a four-number alarm code."

"And you're worried your friend is showing signs of the onset of dementia?" Winter said.

"Yes, exactly."

"What do you know about dementia?"

"I did a little reading on the Internet, but, honestly, not a lot."

"Okay, then, as you get older, you experience changes that may make you think there's something wrong but which are quite normal. The speed with which you process information may decline and your memory won't be what it used to be. For instance, you'll be talking about an old movie and you'll be able to visualize the face of the star, but you won't be able to recall her name. It's on the tip of your tongue, but it's as elusive as smoke. Then, two hours later, the name will come to you. That type of memory problem is worrisome, but it's quite normal in older people and should not interfere with their ability to function normally. It's only when changes do interfere with normal functioning that an individual is experiencing a medical problem."

"What about the situations I just told you about?"

"I can't give an opinion in a vacuum."

"Can you tell me the common symptoms of dementia so I can try to figure out if my friend has a problem?"

"You should not be diagnosing your friend's condition. You need a professional to do that. There are tests designed to distinguish a serious problem from problems associated with normal aging. But I can tell you what to look for so you can decide if your friend might need professional help."

"Go ahead," Robin said as she took out a notepad and started writing.

Winter repeated a lot of the information Robin had picked up during her Web search.

"If I come to the conclusion that my friend really needs help," Robin asked when Winter was finished, "what should I do? Should I confront him or get a doctor to talk to him?"

"Is this person involved in important work that can affect other people?"

Robin hesitated. Then she nodded.

"Do you think his condition could affect these people adversely?"

"It . . . That could happen."

"There are several approaches you can take. You can partner with people your friend trusts who have seen his odd behavior and are worried about his competence. You should consider having a nonconfrontational meeting with your friend and the other concerned people. It's very important that you avoid confrontation. You might tell your friend you're concerned and hope he won't think you're interfering but that you're worried about him. Or you could say you've noticed that he hasn't been himself lately. Get your friend to talk and do not lecture. Be gentle and respectful and tell him about specific instances where his behavior worried you."

"What if my friend isn't persuaded?"

"It's not unusual for people in the early stages of dementia to be in denial, so you might suggest an assessment by a specific professional and have contact information ready. He might reject the help initially, but remember that trying to help is a process and not a onetime event. Is this useful?"

"Very. You've given me a lot to think about," Robin said as she stood up.

"Good. Please get back to me if you have any other questions."

"I will."

Robin felt overwhelmed as she walked back to her office. Was Regina showing signs of dementia or was she just being forgetful? Robin hadn't known her for long. Jeff had, and he didn't seem concerned. Robin decided to wait and continue observing Regina's behavior before doing anything rash. If she started talking to her boss about her concerns and she was wrong, she could be fired. But she also had an obligation to Regina's clients to make certain that they had competent representation. If Robin's worst fears about Regina turned out to be true, Alex Mason could die.

CHAPTER THIRTY

Jeff Hodges hated stakeouts even when he was a cop. They usually led nowhere and the bad coffee he'd drink to stay awake gave him heartburn and made him have to pee. If you were with another cop, you could run to a bathroom, but his stakeout of the Mason estate was solo, so he'd had to bring a jug to pee in.

Jeff had been prying into Allison's life and had concluded that it was pretty boring. She'd kept working even after marrying Alex, and her life outside of work consisted of trips to her gym, the Westmont Country Club, and the places she shopped. Allison did go for drinks with a few women from work, but when she went to the Westmont or to parties, it was usually with Alex's friends and associates.

Allison stopped going to work when Alex was arrested and had left only a few times during Jeff's surveillance. When she went out, she wore dark glasses, jeans, and a baseball cap to hide her identity. All the publicity generated by her husband's arrest had brought a hoard of reporters to the entrance of her estate. They disappeared after a few days, but Jeff imagined that it would be an ordeal for her each time she went anywhere in public.

Jeff was starting to think the stakeout was a bad idea, when Allison drove out of her driveway a little after ten at night. He kept his lights off and followed her taillights until she drove onto the freeway. She got off near the airport and parked in the shadows of a hotel parking lot. Jeff pulled in after her and parked. Then he waited until she was walking toward the hotel to follow her. Allison went in a side door. She avoided reception and went straight to the elevators. Jeff hung back and watched the lights, which told him that the elevator was stopping on the third floor.

Jeff raced up the stairs and was just in time to see Allison disappear into a room at the end of the hall. When the door closed, he got the room number and went to the lobby. It was late and there was no one at reception except for a sleepy clerk.

"Hi," Jeff said. "I'd like a room and a four a.m. wake-up call. I've got a six o'clock flight."

Jeff registered and started to leave. Then he stopped and turned back.

"I almost forgot. There's a guy flying with me. He wanted a call, too."

Jeff looked embarrassed. "We're both with Nike, but I only met him two days ago. I think his first name is Ralph, but I don't remember his last name. He's staying in three twenty."

The clerk checked her computer and frowned.

"I don't show anyone named Ralph staying in three twenty."

"I'm sure he said three twenty, and we can't afford to miss this flight. Maybe I got the first name wrong, too. Who has that room?"

"It's registered to Jacob Heller."

"No, that's not his name."

Jeff sighed. "I feel like an idiot. I'm going to have to call my boss and get the right name. He's going to be pissed, but we have to be on that flight."

Jeff pretended to go up to his room. When he was certain that the clerk wasn't looking, he went back to his car and turned on his laptop. He was certain that he'd heard Heller's name before. A search for the name Jacob Heller revealed that Heller was a lawyer, and Jeff recognized him as soon as he saw his photograph. Jeff had been in the spectator section at Alex Mason's bail hearing and Heller was the attorney who had approached Regina to tell her that he was representing Allison Mason in her divorce.

Why was Allison Mason meeting her divorce attorney in a hotel instead of in his office? The obvious answer was that they had more than an attorney-client relationship.

Jeff settled in for a long night, but the sound of a car motor starting jerked his heavy eyelids open. He checked his watch. Allison and Heller had been together for an hour—definitely enough time for some extramarital hanky-panky. Jeff waited until Allison was halfway out of the lot before following her back to her house. He watched her car disappear around a curve in the driveway before heading home.

CHAPTER THIRTY-ONE

Robin was working on a brief that was due in the Oregon Court of Appeals when Jeff walked into her office.

"I have an idea that I want to test out. How do you feel about taking a trip to the scene of the crime?"

"Whisper Lake?"

"Yup."

"Why do you want to go there?"

"I'm not gonna tell you because I don't want to prejudice you."

"Won't you even give me a hint?"

"Nope, but I will give you the photographs of the cabin. Study them and see if you see what I see."

During the two-hour trip from Portland to Whisper Lake, the scenery morphed from urban sprawl to thick, verdant forests and views of majestic snowcapped mountains. It turned out that Jeff had wrestled in high school and was a big fan of boxing and MMA, so they talked sports for a while. Each time Robin looked toward Jeff, she noticed his scars. One time, Jeff's hair moved away from his ear when he turned his head and she saw the remnants of what she supposed was plastic surgery.

During a lull in the conversation, Robin mustered her courage.

"Do you mind if I ask you how you were injured?"

Jeff smiled. "I was wondering how long it would take you."

Robin blushed, and Jeff laughed.

"Don't worry. I'm used to the question. I joined the Washington County police after college and I took part in a raid on a meth lab. There was an explosion that put me in the hospital for quite a while. The doctors repaired most of the damage, but my leg was really busted up and I had to retire. Shortly after I finished rehab, I learned that Regina was looking for an investigator. I've been with her ever since."

"Thanks for telling me."

Jeff shrugged. "It's not a big secret. I've adjusted to my physical limitations and the scars. It's other people who have a hard time with it."

Robin smiled. "You don't look so bad."

Jeff laughed again. "Well, thanks, ma'am. Some of the ladies actually think it's sexy."

It was Robin's turn to laugh.

"So, since we're getting personal," Jeff said, "what do you do besides work and work out?"

"Not much," Robin replied with a sigh. "Law school, MMA, and my clerkship haven't left me much time for socializing."

"So no boyfriends?"

"My, we *are* getting personal."

"Don't worry. I'm not hitting on you. I'm just making small talk."

"No boyfriends at the current time," Robin said. "There was a guy from my gym in New Haven and a law professor."

Jeff turned his head.

"Don't look so surprised. I was never in any of his classes."

"What happened?"

Robin shrugged. "I moved west and he wanted tenure. It wasn't that serious anyway."

Before Jeff could reply, they passed a road sign that said that Whisper Lake was fourteen miles away.

"We're almost there," Jeff said.

"And you still won't tell me why we're making this trip?"

"Nope. I don't want to spoil the surprise."

Alex Mason's summer retreat stood under a clear, sunlit sky on the shore of a deep blue lake rimmed by towering evergreens. Robin found it difficult to reconcile the idyllic setting with the horrific crimes that had been committed inside Mason's cabin.

"I've looked at the crime-scene photos and I still don't understand what we're looking for," Robin said when they got out of Jeff's car.

The investigator flashed a wicked grin. "You're

not going to let a community college grad one-up an Ivy Leaguer, are you?"

Robin gave Jeff the finger. Jeff laughed as he opened the door with the key Regina had given him. Robin followed Jeff through the front door into a large living room. To one side were steps leading to the second story. Then there was a hall that separated the living room from the kitchen. Robin knew what was midway down that hall and her gut tightened.

After exploring every part of the house but the places Jeff wanted her to see, he led Robin into the hall and pushed open the door to the room where Meredith Fenner had been held. The curtains were up and the sun's rays shone on an empty space where the bed had been. The evidence in the torture room had been transported to the crime lab along with the other physical evidence found in the house, so there were no bloodstained sheets on the floor or any other furniture in the room. Even though the room was sterile, Robin still hesitated. Then she took a breath and walked around it, searching for some clue that would tell her why Jeff wanted her at Whisper Lake.

"I don't see anything that helps Alex's case," Robin said when she had studied every inch of the room.

"Then let's look at the closet where Meredith was held before she escaped."

Jeff walked to the end of the hall. The lock on

the closet door had been broken by Meredith's kick and the door was halfway open. Jeff walked into the closet and tugged at a string connected to a lightbulb. Dim light illuminated a claustrophobic interior. Jeff fanned the closet with the beam from his flashlight, finally bringing it to rest on a jagged nail that protruded from the floorboards.

"Do you remember the crime-scene photos of the floorboards?" Jeff asked.

"Sort of," Robin replied as she leaned over Jeff's shoulder.

"What do you see?" he asked her.

"I assume that this is the nail that Meredith used to cut through the duct tape that had bound her wrists."

"Yes. Do you see anything interesting?"

Robin scrutinized the nail for a few minutes before giving up.

"Look at the other nails," Jeff said as he pointed the beam from the flashlight at the other nails that had secured the floorboards to the wall. All Robin could see was the flat tops.

"I still don't get it," Robin said.

"The nail Meredith used to escape was jimmied, so the sharp end was sticking out."

Jeff straightened up and pointed at the lock. "Now look at the lock itself. This door is pretty frail, but someone made it easier to kick out the lock by chiseling away at the area around it."

"What are you getting at?"

"What did the first two victims have in common?"

Robin thought for a moment. "It wasn't race. It would have to be their profession."

Jeff nodded. "They were both ladies of the night. What does Meredith Fenner have in common with them?"

Robin concentrated but came up blank. "Nothing."

"Exactly! She's a clean-cut young woman with a steady job and no criminal record. Do you see what that means?"

Robin thought for a moment, then shook her head.

"If Alex Mason is innocent, would you agree that there is a high probability that Allison Mason set him up?"

"That's how I'm leaning."

"So what would she need to frame him?"

"Oh shit!" Robin said.

Jeff grinned.

"She would need a clean-cut young woman with a steady job who would be an unimpeachable witness," Robin said.

"You get a gold star," Jeff said. "Here's what I think. Allison needs Alex to be a horrifying serial killer. She and her male accomplice kidnap two prostitutes and torture and kill them at the cabin so that the police will have evidence that incriminates the owner. Then they kidnap Meredith. They torture her, but they don't leave her tied to the bed, where she would have no chance to escape. Instead, they leave her with her wrists loosely duct-taped in a closet next to a sharp nail she can use to cut through her bonds and they weaken the door so she can break out and flee to the police. Once she identifies the cabin, Mason's goose is cooked."

Robin thought for a moment. Then she frowned.

"Something about the idea that Allison has been conspiring to frame Alex for murder bothers me. This scheme seems pretty elaborate. Why didn't she just kill him?"

"She'd be the prime suspect."

"That's true, but if she is after Mason's money, she didn't even have to kill anyone to get it. All she had to do is what she's already done, file for divorce. She's going to get a healthy chunk of his dough when the divorce is final."

Jeff's shoulders slumped. "I never thought about that."

"I'm not saying you're wrong, but committing murder and kidnapping seems like a lot of trouble to put yourself through to get money you can get anyway with no risk. If Regina proves that Allison is really the bad guy, Allison could end up on death row."

"You're right. But, if Allison didn't frame Alex . . ."

Robin nodded. "Alex could be guilty after all. And if he isn't guilty, who is Allison's male accomplice? You've told me that you don't think it's Arnold Prater. Do you have a viable alternative?"

"Actually, I might. I used my contacts at the phone company to get the records for Allison's cell phone."

"That's legal?"

Jeff answered with a raised eyebrow and a smug grin.

"All right, I don't need to know."

"You are wise beyond your years. It must be all that ninja training."

"Go on, asshole."

Jeff grinned. Then he sobered. "Allison made several calls to Jacob Heller, her divorce lawyer."

"What's so odd about that?"

"Heller is not only Allison's divorce attorney; he's also a member of the Westmont Country Club, the son of old Portland money, and close to Allison's age. Oh, and by the way, I followed Allison to a hotel near the airport two nights ago. She stayed for an hour. Want to guess who was registered in the room she stayed in?"

"Heller?"

"Bingo. I work with some local PIs when I need help, and one of them is watching Heller. It will be very interesting if he and Allison meet up again."

CHAPTER THIRTY-TWO

Regina was scared. She was used to being in control, but right now she didn't know what to do and she was getting more panicky by the minute. She had been driving home from her gym and had to make a detour because of a street closure. As soon as she deviated from her normal route, she had gotten disoriented and couldn't figure out how to get home. Then she saw a large shopping mall. She parked and went into a restaurant to ask directions to the freeway. Someone had drawn a crude map on a napkin for her and she'd left the restaurant. That's when she realized that she didn't remember where she had parked.

"Ma'am?"

Regina turned. Standing behind her was a teenager, who was watching her with kind eyes that radiated concern. The girl was dressed in a waitress uniform and looked familiar, but Regina could not remember where she'd seen her before.

"Are you okay?" the girl asked.

"Of course I'm okay," Regina snapped, furious that this child was questioning her competence.

The girl stepped back, startled. "I didn't mean to upset you, but you've been standing here for half an hour and you looked lost."

Fear coursed through Regina. How could it have been that long?

"I'm sorry," she said. "I shouldn't have yelled at you."

"That's okay. It's just that I drew you the map a while ago. Then I came up front to clean a table and I saw you were still out here. Is everything okay?"

Regina faked a smile. "This will sound ridiculous, but I don't remember where I parked."

"You told me you drove into the mall to ask directions. Your car should be near our restaurant, don't you think?"

"Yes. That makes sense."

"Do you have your key?"

"My key?"

"You can press a button on a lot of them and the car will beep or flash its lights. It helps you find it if you forget what floor you parked on in one of those big garages."

"Of course." Regina forced a laugh. "I should have thought of that."

"Here, let me have the key and let's see if we can find your car."

Regina gave the girl the key and they started walking along the line of cars near the sandwich shop. The girl pressed a yellow button several times before they heard a noise. The girl turned in a circle as she continued to press the button. Then she stopped.

"Is that yours?" she asked, pointing at Regina's Mercedes.

"Yes!" Regina said as the tension drained out of her. "Thank you so much."

They walked to the car and the girl looked inside. Then she smiled at Regina.

"You have a GPS. I can help you punch in your address and it will guide you."

"Would you? I can never get the hang of the thing."

The truth was that she could not remember the steps she would have to take to make the GPS work.

"Sure. Where's home?"

Fifteen minutes later, Regina found the freeway ramp and got back on a familiar route. She wiped away the tears that had started as soon as she was out of sight of the young waitress. She had never been so scared and had never felt so lost. Aside from her marriages, Regina had never failed at anything. She had always been first in high school, college, and law school, and she rarely lost any case if there was a chance she could win it. One reason that she excelled was her sky-high IQ and another was her incredible memory; only now she was having trouble remembering the simplest things and figuring out the easiest problems. She had to confront the possibility that something was wrong. There had to be a rational explanation for what had happened in the mall. But what if the explanation was . . .

"No, goddamn it!" Regina swore as she shut down that line of thought. Getting lost happened. The detour had just confused her. That was all. Everyone got confused or lost from time to time. Regina laughed. She *was* almost sixty. She shook her head. She'd never imagined herself at sixty. It seemed so old. But she didn't look or act sixty. She still enjoyed sex and she had the energy of much younger women. She was doing great for someone her age. And what had happened today was certainly an aberration.

And if it wasn't? whispered a voice in her head. Regina's poise deserted her for a moment because there was no one she could talk to if what was happening wasn't normal—not Stanley, not anyone at work, certainly not anyone at the Oregon Bar. Revealing what she feared could only lead to a future where she could no longer practice law.

But that was not going to happen because she was just fine and today was just . . . something that could happen to anyone. Everyone got lost from time to time, Regina reassured herself. Everyone.

CHAPTER THIRTY-THREE

Jeff dropped Robin at her apartment a little after six. While she whipped up a quick meal out of leftovers, she thought about Jeff. He treated her as an equal even though she was totally inexperienced, and she appreciated the fact that he'd included her in the trip to the crime scene. They definitely got along, and she'd enjoyed his company when they went to interview Meredith Fenner and Mordessa Carpenter. The bottom line was that she felt comfortable with him. Of course, office romances were hideous, horrible ideas, but she still found herself wondering what he would be like in bed.

Robin didn't have a ton of experience with men. There had been two boys in college, but that was adolescent experimentation. She'd had a lover who trained in mixed martial arts at her gym in Iowa. He'd been exciting, but she'd never seen a future with him, especially after getting accepted at Yale. And the law school professor was more in love with himself than with her. So, what about Jeff? She bet he would be a considerate lover, something, she decided with a sigh, she would never find out.

The microwave dinged and Robin fixed some tea to drink with her meal. While she ate, she thought about what she'd seen in Mason's cabin. Was Jeff right? Had Meredith Fenner's kidnapper put her in the hall closet because he wanted her to escape? If that was the plan, Alex Mason was the victim of a sick and twisted plot. Allison was the obvious suspect if Alex was innocent, but she had to have had a male accomplice, because Meredith had been kidnapped and brutalized by a man. Jeff had made a case for Jacob Heller. At a minimum, it looked like he and Allison were lovers.

After she ate, Robin ran a Web search for Heller. Someone as beautiful as Allison could seduce a man and get him to do things for her, but getting someone to commit the crimes of kidnapping, torture, and murder was a little different from convincing a guy to buy a girl diamonds. Nothing she read hinted that Heller was so twisted that he would commit heinous crimes in return for sex, no matter how good the sex might be. Heller's parents had been married for forty years, he had no criminal record, he'd been an excellent student in college and law school, and he was on the board of two charitable nonprofits—hardly the profile of a serial killer, although Ted Bundy had seemed like Mr. Clean.

If Heller wasn't Allison's accomplice, who was? Robin couldn't stop thinking about Arnold Prater, who was definitely sick and twisted. There were too many similarities between the way he beat up Mordessa Carpenter and the way the victims had been tortured at the cabin. And Tonya Benson worked for Poe, so Prater could have known her. Robin decided that she had to learn more about Prater. Jackson Wright was someone who might be able to help her.

As soon as she finished dinner, Robin drove to the address listed in the police report of the interview with Wright. Robin was new to Portland and she expected a drug dealer/pimp to live in a slum, but Wright lived in a condo in one of the new, hot neighborhoods that had been gentrified by an influx of young professionals.

The streets were crowded with people who were going into or hanging out around the taverns, restaurants, and shops that lined the streets near the condo. Robin searched for a parking spot and was just about to pull in when a car pulled out of the condo's garage. Jackson Wright was behind the wheel.

Robin made a U-turn and let another car get between her and Wright's car. She had no trouble following him onto the freeway. A few miles later, Wright exited and headed toward an industrial area near the river. The neighborhood stores had shuttered hours before and it was dimly lit. Robin had to hang back because the streets were deserted. She turned off her headlights and followed Wright's taillights.

Wright pulled into a driveway that led to a parking lot behind a deserted strip mall. Robin parked down the street and jogged to the drive-way. It was empty. She worked her way up to the far corner. When she looked around it, she saw Wright standing next to his car. Robin was about to turn the corner, when a man stepped out of the shadows and paralyzed Wright with a Taser. Robin stifled a gasp as she watched Wright collapse on the asphalt and twitch like a hooked fish.

Wright's assailant knelt beside the drug dealer and handcuffed his hands behind his back. Then he stood up and watched Wright shake his head to clear it.

"I know that hurts like a motherfucker, because we had to get Tased as part of our training."

Robin couldn't see the face of Wright's assailant, but she recognized Arnold Prater's voice as soon as he spoke.

"I bet you were expecting Rasheed," Prater said, "but Rasheed isn't coming. I busted Rasheed and he just worked off his beef by luring you here. He's also looking forward to taking over from you. Sort of like what happened when you killed Miles."

"Hey, man, I'm sorry I got you in trouble," said Wright, who was starting to recover his wits. "You understand how it was. If I didn't say you shot Miles, I woulda gotten stuck with the murder rap."

"I accept your apology, but it doesn't do me any good unless you confess."

215

"Yeah, yeah, I'll go to the DA," Wright promised. "Just don't do anything crazy."

"Crazy? Like framing an innocent man for murder?"

"I feel real bad about that, Arnie. Honest, I do. So why don't you let me up and we can go to the police together so I can make it right."

"That would be nice, Jackson, but, unfortunately for you, I can't trust you to keep your word. What other solution can you think of that will help me avoid prison? I'll give you a hint. You're the only witness who can pin Poe's murder on me. If you disappear, the state has no case."

"Hey, man, don't do this."

Prater shrugged. "Sorry, bro, but you leave me no choice."

Prater Tased Wright again. Then he took Wright's car keys and opened the trunk of the drug dealer's car. Prater put the Taser on the ground and grabbed Wright with both hands.

Robin was terrified. She wanted to turn and run, but she couldn't let Prater murder Wright. Robin closed her eyes and let her MMA training take over. She was always nervous before a fight, but she knew how to focus and become calm.

When Prater had his hands full with Wright, Robin walked into the parking lot. Prater heard her and turned, startled. Robin knew Prater wouldn't expect a girl to hit him, so she flashed a disarming smile and walked forward until she was within striking distance.

"It's me, Mr. Prater, Miss Barrister's associate." Robin said.

"What are—" Prater started to say just as Robin drove her foot into his knee. Prater dropped Wright and fell back against the drug dealer's car. Robin maneuvered to hit Prater again, but Wright's body was in the way. As she stepped around Wright, Prater gritted his teeth and swung. Robin rolled with the punch, but it caught her on the shoulder and pushed her back.

Prater stepped over Wright. Robin flicked a jab at Prater's face. When he raised his hands, she drove a roundhouse kick into his thigh. Prater took a step back, and Jackson Wright sank his teeth into Prater's calf. Prater screamed and tried to wiggle free, but Wright ground into Prater's leg like a dog protecting a bone. Prater looked down for an instant, giving Robin the opening she needed. She smashed her foot into Prater's jaw with all the force she could muster. Prater sagged and Robin drove the edge of her foot into Prater's knee, forcing it to move in a direction it was never intended to go. Then she spun behind the policeman, leaped on his back, and wrapped her arm around his neck.

Robin's weight and the lack of support from his crushed knee made Prater topple over. He clawed at Robin's arms as she cut off his air. He tried to gouge her eyes and punch her in the face, but she tightened the choke hold. Prater's strength ebbed. In the Octagon, this would have been the time for Prater to tap out, but this was the street and Prater was a violent criminal. Robin kept the pressure on until she was convinced that he was unconscious. Then she looked at Wright and made a decision. She shoved Prater in the trunk and flipped the lid shut. Then she grabbed the Taser for safety's sake and dialed 911.

"Hey, what are you doing?" Wright asked.

"Calling the police," Robin said as she waited to be connected.

"Yeah, that's good. You gonna tell them Prater tried to kill me?"

"This is nine one one," the dispatcher said. "How can I help you?"

"I just stopped a man from murdering someone. He's subdued, but I need an officer quickly."

"That's right," Wright said.

Robin gave the dispatcher the address. As soon as the dispatcher told her that a patrol car was on the way, Robin called Jeff. Wright backed against his car and started to stand. Robin pointed the Taser at him.

"Sit the fuck down," she said. "I heard you confess to killing Miles Poe, so I'll have no qualms about electrifying your ass. Understand?"

"I didn't kill Miles. I just said that so Prater wouldn't kill me."

"Tell it to the judge," Robin said at the same moment Jeff picked up. "And shut your mouth. I'm not going to warn you again."

"What?" Jeff said.

"Not you. I have a situation here and I need you to bring Regina with you."

Robin told him the address and where he would find her.

"That's way across town," Jeff protested. "Can't this wait until morning? Regina will be asleep."

"I don't give a shit, Jeff. I just stopped Arnold Prater from killing Jackson Wright after Wright confessed to killing Miles Poe."

"What?"

"I locked Prater in the trunk of a car, Wright is handcuffed and Tased, and the cops are on the way. So get Regina here ASAP, because I'm probably going to need a lawyer."

Two patrol cars appeared within minutes of Robin's 911 call and an ambulance showed up a few minutes later. Then Roger Dillon and Carrie Anders arrived. Jeff and Regina walked into the parking lot shortly after the ambulance left with Arnold Prater. Jackson Wright was in the back of one of the patrol cars.

Robin's boss talked to Carrie Anders for a few minutes. Then the detective pointed across the parking lot toward Robin, who was sitting in the other patrol car, her head back and her eyes closed. The door to the car was open. Regina stuck her head in.

"You've certainly had a busy night," she said.

Robin opened her eyes. When she saw her boss, she flashed a weary smile.

"I solved Arnold Prater's case for you, but you're going to have to drop him as a client."

"How did you solve the case and why will I have to get off Prater's case?"

"I'm going to testify that I heard Jackson Wright confess to murdering Miles Poe, so Bergland will have to drop the murder charges against Prater. I also saw Prater assault Wright and threaten to kill him because Wright was the only witness who could testify against him. Then I saw Prater start to throw Wright in the trunk of Wright's car after Tasing him for a second time. That makes me a witness for the State in a case against Prater for attempted murder. I see more conflicts of interest for our firm than you can shake a stick at."

Regina sighed. "You're right."

Carrie Anders walked over to the patrol car. "Miss Lockwood, are you ready to tell me why you locked a policeman-slash-client in the trunk of a car owned by a handcuffed drug dealer?"

"I'd be glad to, now that my lawyer is here," Robin said. "Will you represent me, Regina?"

"You did that to Arnold Prater all by yourself?" Roger Dillon asked, clearly awed.

220

Robin blushed. "I surprised him."

Dillon shook his head slowly.

"And you're certain you heard Wright confess?" Carrie asked.

"Yeah."

"You know he's going to say he confessed under duress. He'll swear he didn't know what he was saying because he had been Tased and that he confessed to something he didn't do because he was afraid of Prater."

"I'd expect nothing less, but he had no idea I was listening when he confessed, and he never protested when Officer Prater accused him of setting him up."

"Okay. You look pretty tired, so I'm going to release you. You'll probably have to give a more detailed statement tomorrow."

"I'll be at work. Call and I'll walk over."

"You look all in," Jeff said. "Let me drive you home. Regina can follow in my car."

"Thanks, Jeff," Robin said, "but I'm good to go. It's not that long a drive."

"You're sure?"

"Yeah, but if it's okay with you, Regina, I may come to work late?"

"Get a good night's sleep. I'll need you fresh so we can figure out what to do about this mess."

CHAPTER THIRTY-FOUR

Robin usually woke up early so she could work out before going to the office, but the next morning she slept until eight and had to pass on the gym. After she dressed, she realized that she was ravenously hungry, so she dropped into a local café for an unhealthy breakfast of pancakes and bacon. When Robin walked into the law office, Susan, Regina's receptionist, gave her an odd look, which let Robin know that the story of last night's adventure had made the rounds.

Mark Berman saw her as she passed by his office.

"Hey, Robin, hold up."

Robin stopped and Mark walked to his doorway.

"Did you really put one of our clients in the hospital last night?"

Robin blushed. "I didn't have much choice. He was trying to kill someone."

Mark grinned, did a fist pump, and sang "Go Rockin' Robin," an old rock song her fans chanted when she fought in the Octagon.

Robin turned a brighter shade of red. "You know about that?"

"Sure. I'm a big MMA fan. I didn't mention it because I wasn't sure if you wanted everyone to know about your sordid past."

Robin smiled. "I'd appreciate it if you kept it that way."

"No problem," Mark said. Then he flashed an impish grin. "However, as a quid pro quo, there are a couple of DAs I wouldn't mind seeing in an arm bar. Can I count on you?"

"Absolutely not!" Robin said as she went to her office. She had just turned on her computer when Jeff walked in.

"How are you feeling?" he asked.

"A little sore but pretty good over all. I slept like a log."

"I bet you did. Are you ready to see the boss so we can try to straighten out this mess? Prater has been calling all morning."

"What did you tell him?"

"I didn't talk to him, but I was sure he'd call, so I told Susan to say that Regina was unavailable. We have to give her time to figure out what to do."

Robin followed Jeff down the hall to Regina's office. Regina smiled when they walked in and motioned them to set across the desk from her.

"So, what's up?"

"Prater's been calling from the hospital," Jeff said.

Regina frowned. "What does he want?"

"Probably for you to represent him in his attempted-murder case," Robin said. "But we can't have anything to do with Prater anymore. This is as clear a conflict of interest as you're going to see. A member of your firm—me—put him in the hospital and is the key witness to his attempt to murder Jackson Wright."

Regina nodded. "Yes, that does present a problem."

"I also heard Jackson Wright confess to murdering Miles Poe, so I'll be a key witness for Prater in his murder case."

Regina nodded again. "You've convinced me."

"You should go to the hospital and tell him that you have to get off his case," Robin said.

"I'll check with the hospital to see if Prater can have visitors," Jeff said.

"You should be there when Regina talks to Prater," Robin said. "I don't think he's going to take it well."

"Good idea," Jeff agreed. "Our client doesn't seem to have great anger-management skills. But before I find out when we can visit Prater, I want to tell you about a few things I've discovered that should help in Alex Mason's case."

"Don't keep us in suspense," Regina said.

"I sent our lab the glass I took from Allison Mason's bathroom and they lifted a print. When they ran it, they turned up a five-year-old Florida arrest for prostitution under the name Alexis Cooper."

"That's great!" Robin said. "Was there a conviction?"

"I'm trying to find out."

"Does she have any other crimes on her record?" Regina asked.

"Not that I've been able to find, but I'll keep digging. I did find something else you can use. Allison told the police that Alex Mason paid for her plane ticket to Portland, but the airline records show that Allison paid for the ticket with her credit card. That calls into question her story that he was the one who wanted to continue the relationship. If she flew here on her own dime, you can use that fact when you argue that she was trying to trap Alex into marriage. I also have a theory about why she came here in such a hurry.

"I've been suspicious about the timing of Allison's move to Oregon ever since you told me about the attorney fees Mason's firm received when it settled the case with the company represented by the firm where Allison worked as a temp. I had a New York PI ask some of the secretaries and attorneys at the firm about Allison. There were rumors that she was screwing one of the senior partners. What if she learned about the settlement? She'd have known that Alex was going to come into a lot of money as soon as the case was settled, and that could have been her motivation to move here to try to rekindle their romance."

"Good work, Jeff," Regina said.

"There's one more thing. It looks like Allison may have a lover. His name is Jacob Heller and he's handling Allison's divorce. It's interesting that she never mentioned she's been screwing a lawyer who can advise her on how to get the most out of her hubby in a divorce."

"Is there anything else we can use to call Allison's truthfulness into question?"

"Not that I've turned up. Hopefully, we'll know more when I learn the facts of Allison's prostitution arrest."

Regina looked puzzled. "Allison has a record for prostitution?"

Robin felt sick, and Jeff had to work at keeping his composure.

"Remember, I ran her prints and found the old Florida case?"

Regina had a blank look on her face for a moment. Then she recovered.

"I thought you meant that there was more than one case," she said.

"No. There's just the one."

"Okay. Well, it looks like Mason's case is starting to shape up nicely. Why don't you check with the hospital."

Jeff stood up. "I'll let you know what they say."

When Robin and Jeff left Regina's office, Robin was very worried. Why had Regina asked Jeff about Allison's prostitution case when he had just told her about it?

"When you get back, let's get together," Robin said to Jeff.

CHAPTER THIRTY-FIVE

Jeff called Robin when he and Regina left the hospital, and they agreed to meet for lunch at a coffee shop near the courthouse. Robin found a table in a corner where they wouldn't be overheard and waited for Jeff, getting more anxious with each passing minute.

Jeff walked in twenty minutes after Robin. He searched the room, then smiled when he saw her.

"How did things go at the hospital?" Robin asked.

"Not well. Prater is threatening to sue everybody and he's also going to report you to the State Bar for beating him up. Regina doesn't think he has a leg to stand on—and that pun was intentional. Anyway, he's hopping mad."

"Cut that out." Robin laughed.

Jeff smiled. "I think some of his bad mood has to do with getting the shit kicked out of him by a girl. You did some real damage to his self-esteem."

"Good. It couldn't have happened to a nicer guy. Maybe he'll start to understand how Mordessa felt."

"I doubt it. Prater doesn't strike me as someone whose strong suits are empathy and self-analysis."

"Did Regina resign from Prater's case?"

Jeff nodded. "She refunded his entire retainer and gave him a list of attorneys. He crumpled it in a ball and threw it at her. I was tempted to tell him I was going to send you over to teach him some manners, but I restrained myself."

A waitress came over and took their order. "You wanted to talk about some other stuff?" he said when she left.

Robin nodded. She felt sick as she pulled out the notes she'd been keeping on Regina's behavior.

"You were in Regina's office this morning. She forgot what you told her about Allison's prostitution arrest minutes after you'd mentioned it."

"She said she thought we were talking about a second conviction."

"That's not how I heard it. I'm pretty sure she was bluffing. And do you remember Prater's bail hearing?"

"Yeah, I thought she was brilliant."

"Jeff, she forgot to cross-examine Anders about the fact that there were no fingerprints on the gun. I had to remind her. We went over that line of questioning right before court."

"Everyone forgets stuff."

"I don't take this lightly, Jeff. I've done my homework."

Robin handed him a typed record of Regina's behavior.

"As soon as I suspected that Regina was acting oddly, I started taking notes. Earlier this week, I met with an expert on dementia."

"Jesus, Robin, you didn't—"

"I never mentioned Regina. I said there was a man I was concerned about and I disguised the incidents so the person I consulted wouldn't know Regina's sex or that she's a lawyer. And the expert is also a lawyer, who I consulted as a client, so everything we discussed is covered by the attorney-client privilege. She can't talk about it, but what she told me is disturbing."

The waitress brought their food. While they ate, Robin told Jeff everything she'd learned from Gabriella Winter. Then she went over her notes. When she finished, Jeff looked troubled.

"I'm not saying I'm buying this, but you've got me thinking."

"I'm totally out of my depth here," Robin said. "I'm not a doctor and I've never tried a case. You've known her for years. Is this normal behavior, or is something wrong?"

"Fuck" was all Jeff could manage.

"What about doing what the person I consulted recommended? We could approach Regina in a nonconfrontational way and say we're worried about her. You could explain why, since she knows you better and trusts you more than she does me."

Jeff put his head in his hands. "I can't do it. The law is Regina's life. It's who she is."

"There's a chance that Alex Mason is innocent. How are you going to feel if he's sentenced to death because Regina is too impaired to try his case competently?"

Jeff was quiet for a while and Robin waited. She knew what she had told him was a lot to take in.

"You've convinced me that Regina *could* be showing signs that she's . . . losing her edge," Jeff said, unable to use any of the terms that defined Regina's possible condition. "But we can't confront her now—not this close to trial."

"This is the point where we *have* to confront her—before she goes to court and makes a mistake that sends Mason to death row."

"What if you're wrong? Confronting her would really upset her, and she has to be sharp to win this case."

"Then what do you suggest?"

"You'll be at Regina's side every minute of the trial. You have to admit that she did great in Prater's bail hearing, even though she did forget to cross on the lack of fingerprints on the gun. If she does have dementia, it's in the early stages. You can be her safety net. Regina at her best is Mason's best chance to win. She's still his best chance, even if she's lost a step, especially with you there to help her."

"We're taking a huge risk if we don't get this right.

"I agree, but let me ask you this. Are you one hundred percent certain that Regina has Alzheimer's, that her forgetfulness isn't normal for someone her age?"

"I . . ." Robin shook her head. "No. I don't have the medical background to make that call. Winter told me we would need a specialist to make the diagnosis."

"Then I say we wait and watch."

They talked a little longer. Then Jeff said he had to get back to the office. Robin was too upset to go back. She asked Jeff to use the fight with Prater as her excuse if Regina asked where she was.

Robin decided to walk home to clear her head, but it didn't work. Regina Barrister was an icon in the State Bar. Robin had never tried a case, and Jeff was asking her to baby-sit one of the nation's best defense attorneys. It was insane and she didn't know if she could go through with it.

But what was the alternative? Confronting Regina without a professional's opinion would just upset her and could cost Robin her dream job. And Regina's career could be ruined if even a hint of what she was thinking leaked. This was a no-win situation. Alex Mason's life would be in Regina's hands, but his death might be on Robin's head.

CHAPTER THIRTY-SIX

Regina, Robin, and Jeff had worked at a fever pitch during the weeks leading up to Alex Mason's trial, and Robin felt like she'd been a student in an upper-level seminar on death-penalty litigation by the time the team went to court to pick the jury.

Citizens usually receive a summons to report for jury duty on a specific day to a room reserved for them. During the day, a clerk sends jurors to courtrooms, where they are questioned by the attorneys for the parties. The jury selection process is called voir dire, after the French verbs for "see" and "tell." After a lawyer questions a potential juror, he or she can reject the person for cause or use a set number of peremptory challenges to dismiss the juror for no specific reason.

Jury selection in death-penalty cases is different. Potential jurors for Alex Mason's case were summoned to Judge Martha Herrera's courtroom and not to the room where all other jurors reported. The judge's bailiff handed each of them a questionnaire that had been specially prepared for death-penalty cases. It was twenty pages long and it asked the jurors to answer questions about their jobs, families, education, military service, religion, politics, physical condition, their views on capital punishment, and many other topics that the attorneys for the defense and prosecution needed to know about in order to make an informed decision on whether or not to keep a juror on the panel. As soon as they were completed, the questionnaires were sent to the defendant's attorney and the DA so that the lawyers could decide what jurors they wanted to keep or dismiss.

Regina, Robin, and Mark Berman spent a day going through the questionnaires, looking for the most desirable and least acceptable candidates. Then Regina and Kyle Bergland spent two contentious days in Judge Herrera's courtroom before settling on twelve jurors and six alternates. The alternates sat through the trial but did not vote unless they took the place of a juror who was dismissed after the trial started.

When the jury was in place, Judge Herrera recessed court. The next morning, Kyle Bergland gave his opening statement. Bergland's presentation had been understated and business-like, punctuated for contrast with graphic photos of the victims and the torture room in Alex Mason's cabin. The prosecutor laid out his evidence in chronological order, starting with Tonya Benson's disappearance and the discovery of her body and ending with an account of the testimony he expected from Meredith Fenner.

When Regina walked to the jury box to give her

opening statement, Robin was as tense as she'd been at the start of any of her fights. Even though Regina radiated confidence, Robin worried that she would lose her train of thought or forget a key point. She also knew that the case against their client was very strong and the arguments for acquittal they had discussed in the conference room at Regina's office were weak.

The defense team had agreed that Regina's opening should be brief and should emphasize the fact that Alex did not have to present any evidence or examine any of the State's witnesses because the State alone had the burden of proving the accusations against her client. In the end, there were no missteps, but Robin knew that Regina's vague opening and lack of facts had given the first round to Kyle Bergland.

Robin slept fitfully the night before the State was going to call its first witness. At 6:00 a.m., she finally gave up trying. She did calisthenics for half an hour and took a freezing cold shower, but she still had cobwebs wrapped around her brain. A pancake breakfast and several cups of black coffee helped a little, but she was feeling dull when she arrived at the courthouse.

The previous night, she'd called her mother to tell her that she was helping Regina try a big case, but she'd been depressed when the call ended.

"Who did this Mr. Mason murder?" Robin's mother had asked.

"He says he didn't murder anyone."

"Then why did the police arrest him?"

"Three women were kidnapped and tortured and two of them were killed. The crimes occurred at Mr. Mason's cabin, but he says he doesn't know anything about it."

"And you're going to help him?" Robin's mother asked. The question sounded like an accusation.

"Defend him, Mom. I told you: He says he didn't do it and the law presumes that he's innocent."

"What if he isn't? What if he really tortured those women?"

Robin could see where this was going. "Everyone is entitled to a fair trial, even a murderer. A jury will decide if he's guilty."

"I see."

"Mom, this is what defense attorneys do. We make sure that every American gets a fair trial and we protect people who are falsely accused. You read the papers. Look at how many people are released from prison after spending years in a cell for something they didn't do."

"But this man . . . I know you're doing important work, but, if he did what they say and you get him off . . ."

"I don't get anyone off, Mom. A jury or judge

will decide if Mr. Mason is guilty. Miss Barrister just keeps the State honest and presents Mr. Mason's side of the story."

"Well, okay," her mother had said before they'd changed the subject, but Robin could tell that she hadn't convinced her.

Robin had been through this before. Her mother had been proud of her law degree, but she'd hoped Robin would pursue one of the more "respectable" areas of law. Robin had tried everything to get her mother to accept the fact that representing people accused of a crime could be a noble profession, but she had yet to succeed.

Regina had already fought her way through the reporters and spectators who crowded the corridor outside Judge Herrera's courtroom when Robin walked in. At the prosecution's table, Kyle Bergland was engaged in a whispered conversation with Vanessa Cole, a middle-aged African-American who was a veteran in the DA's office and had been lead counsel or second chair in over a dozen death cases.

Just as Robin walked through the gate that separated the spectator section from the bar of the court, the guards brought Alex Mason into the courtroom. When he was at the defense table, the guards unlocked his handcuffs and leg chains. Mason was dressed in an expensive charcoal gray suit, white silk shirt, and red-and-blue-striped

Hermès tie, and the manacles looked strange on him.

"Good morning, Mr. Mason," Robin said. Mason looked harried and he only nodded. He had been cold and distant during jury selection and opening statements and Regina had had to remind him frequently to appear to be engaged in his own trial.

Robin and Mason were just sitting down on either side of Regina when Judge Herrera called the court to order and had the jurors brought in.

"Are the parties ready to proceed?" she asked when the jurors were seated in the jury box.

"We are," Regina and Bergland replied.

"Then call your first witness, Mr. Bergland."

During the morning session, Bergland put on Carrie Anders, who gave an overview of the investigation into the deaths of Patricia Rawls and Tonya Benson and Meredith Fenner's kidnapping that included the dates on which the three victims had been abducted. She also told the jurors about Meredith Fenner's identification of Alex Mason's cabin as the place where she had been held and about the arrest of Alex Mason. Regina elicited the fact that Alex Mason had denied any involvement in the crimes when questioned.

When Detective Anders was through testifying, Bergland called several more witnesses. Harry

White described Whisper Lake and the cabins around it, Caleb White testified about how he found Meredith Fenner, and Dr. Nicholas Hayes told the jury about Meredith's condition when she arrived at the hospital.

After lunch, Bergland called the cook who had discovered Tonya Benson's body in the Dumpster behind his restaurant and the dog walker who had found Patricia Rawls's corpse in the woods at the rest stop. Dr. Sally Grace described her autopsy findings and testified to the similarities in the injuries to Rawls, Benson, Meredith Fenner, and Allison Mason before Judge Herrera recessed for the day.

"How do you think it went?" Alex Mason asked anxiously as Regina and Robin packed away their papers after court recessed.

"Very little the witnesses said implicated you," Regina told him.

"Who is Bergland calling next?"

"Allison Mason," Regina replied.

And that's when your troubles begin, Robin thought.

CHAPTER THIRTY-SEVEN

On the way back from court, Robin grabbed some sushi to go for supper, then headed for her office to work on other cases she had put on hold. Susan stopped her as soon as she entered the waiting room.

"You got a call earlier from Jackson Wright. He wanted to talk to you about Mr. Mason's case."

Robin's brow furrowed. "What would he know about Mason?"

"He just said that you should go to the jail, that it was important and that he wasn't going to ask his lawyer to be present."

While Robin ate her sushi, she tried to decide what to do about Jackson Wright. She was the key witness in his murder case, the one person who could put him behind bars for life. Could this be a setup? She couldn't figure out how it could be. And she would ask for a noncontact visit so that he couldn't attack her.

There was still the ethical problem of meeting with someone who was represented by counsel without the lawyer present. But it looked like Wright had made a conscious choice to speak to her without his lawyer.

Should she tell the DA who was prosecuting Wright? They'd try to stop her from talking to him. And Wright said he wanted to talk about Alex Mason, so involving a prosecutor was out of the question.

The more Robin thought, the more she realized that she had to go, if for no other reason than to satisfy her curiosity. Probably nothing would come of the meeting, but she would be violating her duty to Mason if she didn't explore the possibility that Wright knew something that could help Mason's case.

The noncontact visiting room at the county jail was separated into two identical spaces by a thick plate of bulletproof glass that was framed by a concrete wall. Each space was just wide enough for a folding chair.

As soon as Jackson Wright entered his side of the room through a metal door that opened into the holding area in the jail, Robin passed a sheet of paper through a narrow slot and signaled the guard to give Jackson a pen.

"What's this?" Wright said through the telephone receiver that was attached to the wall. Robin spoke to the inmate through an identical receiver.

"That's a statement that you've waived the presence of counsel and you've asked me to speak to you about matters that have nothing to do with the incident in the parking lot."

"Don't you trust me?"

"I trust you to try to use this visit to set me up at your trial."

"You must have a bad opinion of me," Wright said as he flashed a toothy smile.

"That is one hundred percent true, Mr. Wright." Robin placed her phone on the narrow ledge in front of her. "And that is why I'm going to record this conversation."

"Feel free. I'm not trying to trick you."

Wright signed the document and passed it back through the slot. The guard took back the pen and closed the door to Wright's cubicle.

"So, Mr. Wright, why am I here?"

"Call me Jackson."

"Let's keep this formal for now," Robin said. "I am, after all, the witness who is going to put you in prison."

"You're also the person who saved my life and beat the shit out of that cocksucker Prater."

"There is that," Robin said.

"So I don't hold a grudge against you for helping the DA. And if what I tell you helps Mr. Mason, maybe you can put in a good word for me."

"Let me make this clear. You can tell me what you want to tell me, but don't do it with any expectation that you'll get any benefit for talking to me."

Wright nodded his head up and down. "No, no. I'm talking to you because I hate Prater. I'm not expecting anything in return." Wright flashed

Robin a wide smile. "But, later, if *you* decide to do something for me—of your own free will and not as a quid pro quo—it would be appreciated."

"Let's cut to the chase, okay? I've had a long day in court and I'm beat. What do you want to tell me?"

"You know who Mordessa Carpenter is, right?"

"We tried to interview her, but she skipped town. Do you know where she is?"

"She wouldn't say."

"You talked to her?"

"The same day Prater tried to murder me."

"What did she want?"

"Revenge for what Prater done to her."

"What did Prater do to her?"

"He beat her up, gave her some money, and told her to get out of town. He said he'd kill her or have someone kill her if she came back. So she took the money and ran."

"Why did she call you?"

Wright smiled. "Why do you think? She spent all Prater's money and wanted me to send her some more."

"Did you?"

"Hell no! The bitch would just shoot it up her arm."

"Why are we talking about Mordessa?"

" 'Cause she knows about Tonya Benson."

"One of the women Alex Mason is supposed to have killed."

"Exactly."

"What does she know about that?"

"She said I should tell you to call her because she knows that Mason didn't kill Tonya. Prater did."

Robin waited until she was in her office with the door shut before calling the number Jackson Wright had given her. Robin let it ring until it went to voice mail. Then she left her name and the number of her cell phone and told Mordessa to call her anytime. The phone rang two minutes after Robin ended her call.

"Miss Lockwood?"

"Yes. Is this Miss Carpenter?"

"Yes."

"Thanks for calling. Mr. Wright gave me your number."

"Are you the one who put Prater in the hospital?"

"I am."

"How'd you do that?"

"I worked my way through college and law school fighting in mixed martial arts contests. Prater wasn't expecting a girl to give him a hard time."

Robin heard a hearty laugh on the other end of the line. "I hear you really fucked up Prater's shit."

"That I did."

"Man, I wish I was there." Then Mordessa tone became somber. "You know he hurt me bad."

"I do know that, and it was a real motivator when I was smashing his knee and choking him out."

"Thank you." There was silence on the phone. Then Mordessa asked, "Is Prater locked up?"

"Yes."

"Will he get out?"

"He shouldn't. I saw him try to murder Jackson and I'm going to say so in court."

"If he really did murder someone, would that help keep him in prison?"

"If the prosecutor can prove the charge. Why, do you have evidence that he killed someone?"

"Not something I saw. But I know he killed Tonya."

"Tonya Benson?"

"Yeah. She's one of the ones the DA says your client killed, right?"

"Yes."

"Well, Prater had a history with her."

"What kind of history?"

"The same kind he had with me."

"You mean he beat her?"

"And tied her to the bed. And burned her with cigarettes. Just like they saying Mason done."

"How do you know this?"

" 'Cause I untied her and took her to the ER."

"There's a police report of your interview with

Detectives Dillon and Anders. In it you told them about being with Tonya on the night she disappeared, but you didn't say anything about Prater beating her up."

"This was about a month before she went missing. I didn't know about her killer tying her to a bed and doing what Prater done to her and me until I read about what the DA said in his opening statement about what that white girl was gonna say. That's when I got to thinking."

"If it was necessary, would you come back to Portland to testify?"

"I ain't got no money to get back."

"That's not a problem. I'll get you a ticket."

"Why don't you send me the money and I'll get my own ticket."

"I'm going to be up front with you, Mordessa. I know you have a drug habit. I know you mean well, but I also know you'll spend the money on dope."

"No, no. You can trust me."

"I'd like to believe that, but I've known people with drug habits, and they make promises their bodies won't let them keep. If you decide to come to Portland, I'll send you a ticket that is nonrefundable. Then I'll help you get into rehab. But you've got to come. Alex Mason is facing the death penalty. You have his life in your hands."

The line was silent for a while. Robin could hear Mordessa breathing.

"I'd need to know for sure that Prater couldn't get to me," Mordessa said.

"His bail is sky-high and I could arrange for protective custody."

The line went silent again.

"You still there, Mordessa?"

"Yeah. Let me think about it."

"We don't have much time. You have my cell number. I'll give you my number at my law office. Let me know if you'll testify for Mr. Mason as soon as you decide. This is literally a matter of life and death."

CHAPTER THIRTY-EIGHT

Robin got to work at six-thirty the next morning and walked right to Regina's office, where Jeff and her boss were already discussing trial strategy.

"We have a problem," Robin said.

"Oh?" Regina replied.

"You may have to get off of Alex Mason's case because of a conflict of interest."

"What's the conflict?" Jeff asked.

"I have a witness who will say that Arnold Prater tied Tonya Benson to a bed and tortured her with cigarettes about a month before Tonya was murdered. Prater has a build similar to Mason's and a New York accent. And he was the officer who went to Carol Richardson's house when she reported Alex for domestic violence."

"That's great!" Regina said. "That testimony will definitely raise a reasonable doubt about Alex's guilt."

"We can't call the witness," Robin said.

Regina looked puzzled. "Why not?"

Robin stared at her boss. Regina didn't understand the conflict, and that was very troubling.

"Prater was our client."

"He isn't anymore."

"That doesn't matter. Mordessa Carpenter is the witness. She heard him threaten to get even with Miles Poe. She was a key witness in the case against Prater for—"

"Poe?" Regina's brow furrowed. "Who is Miles Poe?"

Robin thought she might throw up, and Jeff's face lost color.

"Poe was the pimp and drug dealer who was paying off Prater," Robin said slowly, using the same tone she might if talking to a very slow child. "Poe sued Prater for harassing him. Then Prater was charged with shooting Poe, and Prater hired you to defend him."

Regina stared for a moment. Then she flashed a wide grin and shook her head.

"Yes, I know. My brain is mush this morning. I didn't get much sleep last night."

"So you see why we can't represent Mason. To win his case, you would have to argue that another of your clients is guilty."

"Where is this Mordessa person?"

"I don't know. She wouldn't tell me. She's terrified of Prater. He beat her up and told her to get out of town or he'd kill her."

"So she might not testify or she may be making this whole thing up. Did she see Prater torture Benson?"

"No, but she says she untied Benson from the bed and took her to the hospital right after Prater tortured her."

"Why did she call you? Why didn't Carpenter call me?"

"Last night, Jackson Wright called from the jail and said he wanted to talk to me. He thinks he owes me for saving his life, and he hates Arnold Prater. I went to the jail and he told me Mordessa wanted me to call. He said she wanted revenge on Prater for beating her up. She heard I beat up Prater. That's why she wanted to talk to me. She'd read about Mr. Mason's case and learned that he's accused of killing Benson. When she read the way Benson and the other victims were tortured, she realized it was the way Prater tortured her and Benson."

"Do you have any assurance that Carpenter will testify for us or that she's not lying to get back at Prater?" Regina asked.

"No."

Regina thought for a moment before shaking her head. "If Kyle objects to her testimony on relevancy and hearsay grounds, Herrera won't let her on the stand. That's assuming she'll even show. Right now, I don't see the conflict."

"I've always thought that Prater was a viable suspect in these murders," Robin said. "A case can be made against him with Mordessa."

"Through hearsay from an unreliable witness. I don't think we can get over the threshold for introducing evidence that someone else committed these crimes. No, until we know Carpenter is coming to testify and has admissible evidence, there is no conflict."

CHAPTER THIRTY-NINE

Robin didn't get a chance to talk to Jeff until Regina left for the courthouse.

"Did you catch the bit with Poe?" Robin asked.

"Yeah."

"She had no idea who he was. I'm really worried."

"I'm starting to worry, too," Jeff said, "but I don't know what we can do. We're right in the middle of the trial and she's been doing a decent job so far."

"There hasn't been a chance for her to screw up. Allison Mason is on today, and this is her first chance to raise doubt. What if she blanks?"

"That's why you're here. You'll have to make sure she stays on track."

"What if I can't?" Robin asked.

"We'll have to talk to her."

"And if that doesn't work?"

When court resumed, Kyle Bergland called forensic experts, who testified that DNA connected Alex Mason to the duct tape that had bound Meredith. Then Bergland called Allison Mason to the stand.

Allison was dressed in a simple black dress and a minimum of jewelry and makeup. Alex glared at her when she walked by him, but Allison didn't look at him.

Robin waited for Regina to make the legal motion they had briefed, but Regina didn't say a word when the clerk started to swear the witness.

"Regina, you should object to her testimony on the grounds that it would violate the husband-wife confidentiality privilege." Robin pushed the memo and copies for the Court and DA across the table to her boss. "We've got it all briefed."

Regina stared at her for a second before looking at the memo. "Of course. I was waiting for Allison to be sworn."

Regina stood, the memo in her hand. "I have a motion for the court that should be heard out of the presence of the jury."

Robin tensed. Regina should have brought this up before the jury came in. Now the jurors would think Mason had something he wanted to hide from them.

"What's your motion, Miss Barrister?" Herrera said as soon as the jurors had left.

Regina handed a copy of the memo to Kyle Bergland and a copy to the judge.

"I am assuming that Mr. Bergland is going to ask Mrs. Mason about the Masons' sex life, but that testimony is barred by the husband-wife privilege."

"We anticipated this motion, Your Honor. The defendant's actions, such as tying Mrs. Mason to the bed and burning her with cigarettes, are not communications, so they aren't protected," Bergland said.

"Furthermore, Mrs. Mason can consent to waive the privilege under ORS section 40.255(3) in a criminal proceeding where she has been called as a witness. Also, *State v. Lindley*, 11 Oregon Appellate Reports 417, a 1972 case, held that the doctrine of marital privilege doesn't prohibit the testimony of third persons as to information volunteered by a defendant's wife. Mrs. Mason voluntarily told Detective Anders everything to which she will testify."

"What do you say about that, Miss Barrister?" the judge asked.

Robin waited for Regina to make several arguments they had discussed at the office, but Regina looked lost.

"Well, I'll . . . We'll take this up on appeal if you deny my motion," she managed after a few seconds of silence.

Robin clenched her fists in frustration.

"Okay, well I am going to deny the motion and let Mrs. Mason testify," Judge Herrera said.

"Mrs. Mason," Bergland asked when the jury was back and the witness had been sworn. "Are you married to Alex Mason, the defendant?"

"I am."

"How did you two meet?"

"Alex was in New York for depositions in the firm where I was working as a temp."

"Did you have any contact during the depositions?"

"Do you mean in the law office?"

"Yes."

"Not that I remember."

"What about later in the evening, at the hotel where the defendant was staying?"

When his wife told the jury that he had approached her in the bar of his hotel, Alex leaned over to Regina.

"That's a lie," he whispered.

"Don't interrupt while Allison is testifying," Regina told him. "I need to concentrate. Write that down. We'll go over your notes before I cross-examine her."

Robin concentrated on Allison's testimony, making her own notes of points she thought were important. She also watched Alex write furiously when his wife testified about their sexual encounters, his profession of love, and his request that she move to Portland. When she testified that Alex bought her a ticket to fly to Oregon, Alex almost bored a hole in his paper with the tip of his pen.

Kyle Bergland moved the testimony through the early months of their relationship and Allison's decision to marry Alex. Then the DA focused his examination on the couple's sex life.

Robin watched their client out of the corner of her eye as Allison testified that it was Alex who had convinced her to try S and M. His hands curled into fists and he couldn't contain himself any longer when Allison told the jury that she had agreed to be bound and burned with cigarettes even though she didn't enjoy pain.

"You have to do something," Alex begged Regina. "Her testimony is a complete lie."

"I'll expose her during cross."

"You have to. She's burying me."

"If you didn't like sadomasochistic sex, why did you agree to participate in it?" Bergland continued.

Allison looked down. "I . . . I loved Alex and these . . . things made him happy. I wanted him to be happy. I wanted the marriage to work."

"When the defendant bound you to your bed, what did he use?"

"Duct tape."

"Did he tear the tape off the spool with his teeth on occasion?"

"Yes."

"And he used cigarettes to burn you?"

"Yes."

"Did he ever try to cut you?"

"Yes, but I told him I wouldn't have sex with him if he did that, and he didn't go any further."

"Did the defendant always have intercourse with you during these sadomasochistic sessions?" Bergland asked.

"No. There were times where he masturbated while I was in pain from the burns."

Alex leaned over to Regina. "That's a lie. We always had intercourse. I never masturbated."

"No further questions," Bergland said.

Regina stood up and walked to the witness box without conferring with Alex. Alex started to stand, but Robin put a hand on his forearm. Alex turned to her.

"What about my notes?" he asked. "There are several points she has to make."

"Let Regina do her thing, Mr. Mason. That's why you hired her."

Mason looked like he was going to protest. Then he sank down onto his chair. Robin had calmed down their client, but she was as worried as he was by the fact that Regina had dived into her cross-examination without taking time to confer with her or Alex.

"The hotel where Mr. Mason stayed when he was in New York to take depositions was near the firm where you worked, wasn't it?" she asked.

"Yes."

"And every once in a while you and some of the other women in the office went to the bar at this hotel after work for drinks?"

"Yes."

"And on the evening you met Mr. Mason, the other women left, but you stayed?"

"Yes."

"Then you saw Mr. Mason at the bar and went over to talk to him."

"No. He came over to my table when the other women left."

"You're saying, under oath, that you didn't go to the bar and sit next to Mr. Mason and start a conversation with him?"

Allison's eyebrows arched up in surprise. "No! I wouldn't have had the nerve to do that. I mean, he was an important lawyer and I was just a temp. It would have been inappropriate and I could have gotten in trouble if he complained, especially since he was suing the firm's clients."

When Regina said, "Let's talk about your sexual preferences" and didn't pursue her previous line of questioning, Robin saw Alex's shoulders sag.

"You suggested these S and M games because they brought you sexual satisfaction," Regina said.

"No. I just went along with Alex because he wanted to do this, not me. I didn't want anything to do with getting tied up or hurt. If Alex said I had anything to do with that, he's lying, because I'd never do that."

"Why is that?"

Robin couldn't believe Regina had asked that question. The prime rule of cross-examination was that you never asked a question if you didn't know the answer.

Allison licked her lips. She seemed to be in great distress.

"I'd rather not say," she replied, her voice almost a whisper. "Can we discuss something else?"

Robin was terrified that Regina was walking into a minefield, but there was no way she could stop her.

"Your Honor," Regina said, "please instruct the witness to answer my question."

Robin looked at Kyle Bergland. He had not objected and he looked like he was fighting hard to keep from smiling.

"Yes, Mrs. Mason, you have to answer the question," the judge said.

Allison hunched her shoulders and seemed to shrink. She was either an excellent actor or her distress was real.

"My . . . my father . . . he was in the army and he died in a car accident on his base. My mother remarried, but I was raised in foster homes because my . . . my stepfather . . . he molested me, and my mother didn't stop him, so Children's Services took me away.

"And the molestation, it didn't stop there. Another stepfather did it, too. That's why I ran away. I couldn't stand those men forcing themselves on me. That's why it's so hard for me to have sex."

Allison looked at her lap. The courtroom was completely silent.

Robin looked at Regina. She didn't look fazed, even though the answers had been devastating.

"How did you support yourself after you ran away?"

"Any way I could. I was a waitress. I taught myself to type and I did temp work. I modeled. I did get my GED and I wanted to go to college, but it's very expensive."

"Where did you live before you moved to Manhattan?"

"All around."

"Where specifically?"

"Texas, New Mexico, Chicago. Like I said, all over."

"Chicago is one of my favorite cities," Regina said. "How did you like it?"

"I didn't. It was too cold."

"What did you do there?"

"This and that. I was a waitress."

"Oh, anyplace I may have heard of?"

"I doubt it. I can't even remember the name. I only stayed two months."

"Did you ever live in Florida?"

Allison hesitated for a beat. "Yes."

"Can you remember any place you worked in Florida?"

"It's been a while and they were all short-term, low-paying jobs."

"So you didn't make a lot of money as a prostitute?" Regina asked.

Allison's mouth opened and she turned bright red.

"Objection!" Bergland said as he sprang to his feet.

Regina held up a document.

"I have a copy of a five-year-old Florida arrest record for prostitution for an Alexis Cooper and a mug shot that clearly shows that Alexis Cooper and Allison Mason are the same person. I can also call witnesses who will testify that Alexis Cooper and Allison Mason have identical fingerprints."

"An arrest can't be used for impeachment," Bergland insisted.

"Your Honor, Mrs. Mason gave a list of jobs she held down and failed to mention this job. Additionally, she has testified that she didn't like having sex. I think the fact that she worked as a prostitute contradicts that statement."

"I'll allow the question," the judge said.

"I . . . I did work for an escort service a few times. I'm not proud of what I did, but I was desperate. I couldn't get a job and . . . and I was going to be evicted."

Robin could barely contain herself. Regina was letting Allison run on with all these excuses when she should have been objecting.

"I didn't want to be homeless. That's why I did it."

Allison dipped her head and it looked like she was going to cry. She took a sip of water. When she raised her head, she looked pathetic.

"Now, you've told the jury that Mr. Mason told

you he loved you when he was in New York."

"Yes."

"And he asked you to move to Oregon, but you had to think it over?"

"Yes."

"Then you called Mr. Mason and said you'd fly out and he bought you a ticket?"

"Yes."

"But he didn't, did he?"

"I don't understand the question."

"Mr. Mason never bought you a ticket to Oregon, did he? You bought the ticket and flew to Oregon to try to trap him into marriage."

"That's not true."

Regina handed the witness several documents.

"This is a record of your flight to Portland. The ticket was purchased with your credit card, was it not?"

Allison studied the paperwork. "Yes, I used my card, but Alex told me to. Then he reimbursed me when I got to Portland. So, you're right. Technically, I bought the ticket. But I did it at Alex's request and he paid me back."

Regina stared at Allison for a few seconds. Then she turned to the judge.

"I have no more questions of the witness."

"Any redirect, Mr. Bergland?"

"No, Your Honor."

"Then I think we'll take our lunch recess. Please be back at one."

Regina returned to the table and stood while the judge left the bench.

"I thought that went well," she told Robin.

Robin nodded and forced a smile, when what she really wanted to do was scream.

CHAPTER FORTY

Jeff's phone rang the next morning just as court was about to resume. The caller ID told him that Sean O'Hair, the PI Jeff had hired to keep an eye on Jacob Heller, was trying to reach him. Jeff stepped out of the courtroom and took the call.

"He's on the move," O'Hair said.

"What does that mean?"

"He's driving south and he just turned off the highway, headed east at the Salem exit."

"In the direction of the Masons' cabin?" Jeff asked.

"That's why I called. Of course, there are hundreds of other places he could be going."

"Yeah, thanks. I'm on my way. Keep me posted if he goes to Whisper Lake."

Two hours later, Jeff parked behind O'Hair's car on the road that led to the Masons' cabin and walked over to the PI. O'Hair was a short, thickset man with a barrel chest and a beer gut. He had curly gray hair and a bushy mustache.

"He's been inside for half an hour," O'Hair said.

"Do you know what he's doing?"

"I didn't want to risk being seen."

"Okay. You packing?"

O'Hair pulled aside his jacket to reveal a holstered .38 Special.

"Is this guy dangerous?" O'Hair asked.

"Only if he's Allison Mason's serial killer accomplice," Jeff replied as he started walking toward the cabin.

The two men had just walked into the yard when Heller walked out. He was making notes on a legal pad and didn't see Jeff and O'Hair right away. When they registered, he stopped, startled.

"Can I help you?" the lawyer asked.

"Jacob Heller, right?" Jeff said.

"Yes. Do I know you?"

"You know my boss, Regina Barrister."

Heller looked back and forth between the two men. He seemed confused.

"You know this is a crime scene, right?" Jeff said.

"It's also property belonging to Alex Mason. I represent his wife in their divorce and I came out to take a look at it."

"Let's be honest, Jake. You're not just Allison's lawyer."

Heller's brow furrowed. "What do you mean by that?"

"Isn't it against the State Bar's ethics rules to sleep with a client?"

"What!" Heller said.

"Care to tell me what you and *your client* were doing in your room at the Holiday Inn airport hotel, last week?"

"You've been following me?"

"Not you. Mrs. Mason."

"And you think we're . . . lovers?"

"That's what it looks like."

Heller stared at Jeff. Then he started to laugh.

"What's so funny?" Jeff asked, genuinely confused.

Heller caught his breath. "I met Mrs. Mason at the hotel to go over some issues in her divorce because I had to fly to Los Angeles on short notice."

"You were together for over an hour."

"Yes, we were, but it was strictly business."

"We'll see if the jury believes that when Regina gets you on the stand."

Heller smiled. "She's not going to want to go there," he said confidently.

"And why is that?"

"My boyfriend is an actor in L.A. He's the understudy for the lead in a new play and the lead was hospitalized when a motorist ran into his bike. I flew down to catch opening night."

CHAPTER FORTY-ONE

Meredith Fenner was wearing a conservative blue dress that looked a little large on her slight frame. The dress, her pale complexion, and the haunted expression she had worn since Caleb White found her made her look childlike. Kyle Bergland knew that the jurors would be horrified at what had been done to someone so vulnerable and that Regina Barrister would be a villain if she was too hard on his witness.

"Thanks for helping with Meredith," Carrie Anders told Harry White as soon as the detectives turned Meredith over to the prosecutor.

"Don't thank me. She's been through hell, and anything I can do to make this easier for her . . ."

Harry shrugged, as if accompanying Meredith to court was no big thing, but Harry had been looking for an excuse to see her again. He'd thought that Meredith would call him after she read through the case file he'd put together for her. He hoped it would make her feel better when she realized that a conviction in Alex Mason's case was inevitable. But she had not called. This was probably good because of his attraction to her and the possible impact any relationship could have on the prosecution of Alex Mason. But there was part of him that wanted to keep in contact in hopes that something would happen between them when the case was over.

"She's been scared to death of having to face Mason in court, Harry. Seeing you sitting with Kyle will be a big help."

"What made you think of calling me?" Harry asked.

Carrie smiled. "Meredith talks about you all the time. I think she may have a crush on you."

Harry laughed to hide his embarrassment, but he was elated. Maybe something *would* happen after the case was over.

The door to Bergland's office opened and Meredith, Bergland, and Vanessa Cole walked out.

"Okay, people. The bailiff just called. We start court in fifteen minutes."

"Will Harry be in court when I testify?" Meredith asked.

Harry suppressed a smile.

"Definitely," Bergland told her. "Witnesses aren't allowed in the courtroom when other witnesses are testifying. The Court doesn't want them to be influenced by what the other witnesses say. That's why I called Harry before I called you. Since he's testified already, he can sit at counsel table with me and you'll be able to see him while you're on the stand."

Bergland put his hand on Meredith's shoulder and gave it a quick squeeze.

"Don't worry. You'll do fine. Mason can't hurt you anymore. Not where he's going."

Court recessed and Robin took the opportunity to go to the ladies' room. Just as she headed back, the elevator doors opened and Kyle Bergland and Vanessa Cole stepped into the corridor. They were followed by Detective Harry White, who had testified earlier in the trial. White surveyed the corridor. Then he said something to someone who was still inside the elevator car. When Fenner stepped out, she looked scared to death. She hesitated and White took her hand and led her toward the courtroom. Robin followed and noticed the way Fenner leaned into the detective and the tight grip she had on his hand.

The reporters had gone into the courtroom and the corridor was empty. White and Fenner sat down on a bench at the far end, where they couldn't be seen through the glass in Judge Herrera's courtroom door. Robin cast a quick look at the couple as she passed by. Something about the way they were sitting suggested that there was more to their relationship than witness and detective, but she'd seen them for only a second. Fenner was obviously frightened and White could just have been comforting a skittish witness.

Robin slipped into her seat at the counsel table just as the judge called court back into session and told Bergland to call his next witness. When

Meredith Fenner and Harry White entered the courtroom, Alex Mason swiveled in his seat and stared at her. Meredith hunched her shoulders and looked forward. Then, just before she walked through the bar of the court, Meredith turned her head and looked at Mason for a second before looking straight ahead.

Harry escorted Meredith to the witness stand before taking a seat next to Kyle Bergland. The bailiff administered the oath. Robin noticed that Meredith kept her eyes on Harry when she took the stand and never looked toward the defense table again.

"Where were you born, Meredith?" Kyle Bergland asked.

"Minneapolis, Minnesota."

"And you went through school there?"

"I . . . I didn't finish high school. I had to work."

"Why is that?"

"My parents, they were killed in a car accident and I moved in with my aunt, who was on her own and didn't have much money."

"Have you tried to further your education?"

"Yes. I have a GED and I've taken classes at community college."

"When did you move to Portland?"

"About eight months ago."

"Have you been working since you moved here?"

"Yes."

"What were you doing?"

"I was working at People's Coffee House as a barista."

"Did you like your job?"

"Yeah. It was a good job. Judy—she's the owner—was very nice to me and the other workers were very friendly."

"Are you still working at People's Coffee House?"

"No."

"Why did you stop?"

"I tried to go back. Judy wanted me to. But I just couldn't. Whenever I went to my car . . ." Meredith shook her head. "Being there made me think about what happened to me."

"Besides paying for your rent and food was there another reason you were working?"

"Yes. I want to go to Portland Community College to study nursing and I needed to get money for tuition."

"How was that working out?"

"Okay. I didn't make that much, but I was putting money away. And I'd been checking into loans."

Robin leaned over and whispered to Regina. "This is all irrelevant. He's trying to make her look sympathetic. Shouldn't you object?"

"If I did, I'd look like an ogre and she'd just look more sympathetic," Regina whispered back. "You don't object unless you have to. Fenner isn't lying and there's very little I can cross her on, so the best policy is to get her off the stand as quickly as possible."

"Can you please tell the jury what happened to you after work on the day you were kidnapped?" Bergland asked.

"I helped clean up after we closed."

"Was it late?"

"Yes. We close around nine."

"Was it dark out?"

Meredith nodded.

"You have to speak your answer, Miss Fenner, so the court reporter can get it down and the jurors can be certain of what you're saying," the judge instructed Meredith in a kind voice.

"Sorry. Yes, it was dark."

"What did you do after you left the shop?" the prosecutor asked.

"I walked out back to my car. Employees have a place to park behind the shop."

"Please tell the jury what happened in the parking lot."

Meredith licked her lips and looked at Harry. Robin saw him flash a smile to reassure her.

"There was a man. He . . . he grabbed me and . . . He pressed a cloth on my face. Then I don't know what happened."

"What is the next thing you do remember?"

Meredith swallowed. It looked like she was fighting back tears.

"Would you like some water?" Bergland asked.

Meredith nodded and the bailiff brought her a glass. After she sipped some water, Meredith took a deep breath and looked at the jury.

"I was in the trunk of a car. I was woozy from what he gave me. My hands were tied behind me and my ankles were tied. The car was bouncing. Later I saw the driveway. It was a dirt road."

"What happened when the car stopped?"

"The man opened the trunk and pressed the cloth to my face again and I blacked out."

"You're certain it was a man?"

"Yes."

"Could you see the man's face?"

"No, I never saw it. He always wore a ski mask and gloves and he had bulky clothes."

"Okay. What's the next thing you remember?" Bergland asked.

Meredith's shoulders hunched and she looked back at her lap. She sipped some water and it looked like she was stalling to gather her strength.

"He . . . he tortured me," she managed to say in a voice so soft that the judge had to ask her to repeat her answer.

"Where were you?" Bergland asked.

Meredith described the room where she'd been held.

"Did you still have your clothes on?"

"Just . . . just my . . . my underpants and my blouse, but he'd unbuttoned it."

"What did the man do to you, Meredith?" Bergland asked.

In a halting voice, Meredith told how she had been tortured. She had to stop several times. When the judge asked if she wanted a recess, Meredith shook her head and said that she just wanted to get her testimony over with. When she told the jury about wetting herself, some of the jurors teared up and others flushed with anger.

Robin was trying to be objective and unemotional during Meredith's testimony, but it was a losing battle. She couldn't help feeling drawn to the witness, and one look at the jurors' faces told Robin that Meredith tale of terror was affecting them in the same way.

Bergland elicited the fact that Meredith's kidnapper had a New York accent and she could tell he was white when he took off one of his gloves to masturbate. After Meredith described her escape and told the jurors how she had identified the cabin, Bergland ended his direct examination and the judge called a recess.

When court resumed, Regina rose and walked to the witness box.

"Good afternoon, Miss Fenner."

Meredith looked frightened and didn't respond.

"I'm going to ask you some questions and I want to make sure you understand them. I don't want to trick you. If you don't understand my question, please ask me to rephrase it. Okay?"

"Yes."

"Now, I can see how trying this has been for you, so don't be afraid to ask for a recess or for a chance to drink some water if the stress gets to be too much. Okay?"

"Yes."

Regina gave Meredith a warm smile. "Good. Did your captor always wear bulky clothes and a ski mask?"

"Yes."

"And you never saw his face."

"No."

"The best you can say is that he's a white man and he had an accent that is similar to the accent of some of the New Yorkers you met in Florida."

"Yes."

"Have you had a lot of contact with people from Connecticut or New Jersey or Vermont?"

"No."

"So you can't be one hundred percent positive that the accent wasn't from some other area of the East Coast?"

"I . . ." Meredith shook her head. "No."

"Could it have been foreign?"

"I don't think so."

"But you can't be certain?"

"No."

"So all you can say about your captor is that he could have been from New York but could have been from some other area of the country or even a foreign country?"

"Yes, but . . ." She looked up at the judge. "I don't know if I can say this, Your Honor."

"When Miss Barrister is questioning you, you can only answer her questions."

"But this is about identifying the man who took me."

Judge Herrera frowned. Then she turned to the jurors.

"Let's take a short break," she told them.

As soon as the jurors were out of the room, the judge turned to Meredith.

"Okay, Miss Fenner. What is it you wanted to say?"

"There was one other thing I just remembered. His hand."

Robin had a sick feeling in her stomach.

"I haven't asked about the kidnapper's hand," Regina said.

Kyle Bergland leapt to his feet. "Miss Barrister asked for ways in which Miss Fenner could identify her assailant. Miss Fenner should be allowed to answer that question."

"I agree, Mr. Bergland. You asked the question, Miss Barrister, and the witness may answer. What were you going to say about the kidnapper's hand, Miss Fenner?"

"When . . ." Meredith licked her lips, then sipped some water. "When he . . . When he masturbated, he took the glove off his right hand and one time I saw a scar on his right hand, under his thumb, a crescent-shaped scar."

The color drained from Alex Mason's face.

"May I have a moment, Your Honor?" Bergland said.

"Yes."

The DA shuffled through a pile of police reports. He read something in one of them intently.

"Your Honor," Bergland said, "when the jury comes back, I would ask you to instruct the defendant to show the jury his right hand."

"I object," Regina said. "This is a complete surprise. The witness never said anything like this before."

"Mr. Bergland," Herrera asked, "did you know about this scar?"

"No, Your Honor. This is the first time Miss Fenner has mentioned it."

"I still object," Regina said. "We've had no time to prepare for this. I move for a mistrial."

"Denied," the judge said.

"I want Mason to show the jury his right hand. Either he has the scar or he doesn't," Bergland said.

"Making Mr. Mason exhibit his hand is an illegal search," Regina said as she fished desperately for some way to keep the Court from ordering her client to exhibit his hand.

"That's ridiculous," Bergland said. "Mason is

in custody. He's been arrested. It's like taking fingerprints or having his photo taken when he was booked."

"Nice try, Regina," the judge said, "but any objection you have has no basis in law."

The judge ordered her bailiff to bring back the jury. When the jurors were seated, Herrera looked at Meredith.

"Miss Fenner, did you remember something that might help identify the man who kidnapped you?"

"Yes, Your Honor."

"Please tell the jury what you remember."

Meredith turned to the jury. "One time when he was masturbating, my kidnapper took off his glove and I saw a crescent-shaped scar under the thumb on his right hand."

Every juror turned toward Alex Mason.

"Miss Barrister," Judge Herrera said. "Will you please have your client stand and hold up his hand to the jury."

"This is a setup. The DA coached her," Mason whispered to Regina.

"There's nothing we can do. You saw me object. The judge shot me down. The only thing we can do is use it as a point on appeal if you're convicted."

Mason balled his right hand into a fist. "I won't do it."

"You have to. You're a lawyer, Alex. You know you have no choice."

Mason hesitated. Then he stood, unreeling as slowly as possible. Robin thought he looked like a man facing a firing squad.

"Please show the jury your hand, Mr. Mason," Judge Herrera said.

Mason raised a fist, then slowly unfurled the fingers of his right hand. Directly below his thumb was a white crescent-shaped scar.

All of the jurors leaned forward and some made notes.

"You may retake your seat," the judge said. "Any further questions, Miss Barrister?"

"It has been many months since your escape, hasn't it, Miss Fenner?" Regina said.

"Yes."

"And you've been questioned by the police about the events in the cabin?"

"Yes."

"Several times?"

"Yes."

"And Mr. Bergland and members of his staff have talked to you about those events?"

"Yes."

"And you just testified about them here in court when Mr. Bergland questioned you?"

"Yes."

"And I assume that you've thought about the events in the cabin over and over from the day of your escape until now?"

"Yes."

"Is it fair to say that you hate the person who kidnapped and tortured you?"

For the first time, Meredith turned toward Mason. Then she glared at him.

"Yes, I do. I hate him."

"And you want to put him in prison?"

"Yes."

"Or on death row?"

"Yes."

"Isn't it true that even though you never saw the face of the man who kidnapped you, you have convinced yourself that Alex Mason is that man?"

Fenner hesitated. Then she said, "Yes."

"When you walked from the corridor into the courtroom and to the witness stand, you passed Mr. Mason, did you not?"

"Yes."

"And you had a chance to see him?"

"Yes."

"And when you passed Mr. Mason on the way to the witness stand, you saw the scar on his hand and realized that this scar, which you had never, ever mentioned to anyone, could help you exact your revenge, didn't you?"

Meredith shook her head vigorously. "No, no. It wasn't like that. I just hadn't remembered it."

"So you want this jury to believe that you never remembered this scar during months of questioning and days and nights of thinking about what happened to you. Then, miraculously, while I was questioning you, you had this sudden revelation?"

"Yes."

"How convenient. I have no further questions of Miss Fenner," Regina said before turning on her heel and retaking her seat.

"Any redirect, Mr. Bergland?" Judge Herrera asked.

"No, Your Honor, and the State rests."

"You were fantastic," Harry White told Meredith as he escorted her out of the courtroom. "That scar is going to send Alex Mason to death row."

Meredith looked up at Harry. "I couldn't have done it without you. I was so scared, but whenever I got frightened, I looked at you and you gave me strength."

Harry squeezed Meredith's hand. "You never needed me, Meredith. You are stronger than you know. You're the strongest woman I've ever known."

Harry caught himself and let go of Meredith's hand, but it was too late and he saw the way she was looking at him.

"Look," Harry said, "I wanted to talk to you about, well, us. But I can't. Not while this case is going on."

"I understand. You've done so much for me already."

"If there was even a hint that we . . . It could torpedo the whole case."

"I said I understand. And I can wait, Harry. When Alex Mason is in prison and on death row, I'll be able to start living again. You understand that, right?"

"Yes."

"We should both wait. I still have nightmares and . . . and I'm not sure when I could be, you know, natural with any man."

"No, you're right. I can wait until you're ready."

Meredith squeezed Harry's hand. "Thank you." Meredith smiled. "You are my rock."

And that and the promise of a possible life with Meredith was enough for Harry.

CHAPTER FORTY-TWO

It was almost impossible to project a positive attitude after Meredith Fenner's bombshell, but Regina managed until court recessed and Alex Mason was taken back to the jail.

"That scar killed us," Regina said when they were free of the reporters and headed back to the office.

"Your cross may have saved Mason by making the jurors think Fenner made up her testimony after she saw Mason's hand in court," Robin said.

"I hope so, but Fenner is so damn believable."

"I reread the report of Mason's arrest," Robin said. "There's a section about identifying marks that lists the scar. Do you think Mason is right? Do you think Bergland knew about the scar and coached Fenner to bring it up during cross?"

"I've known Kyle for a long time," Regina said. "He'll bend the rules on occasion, but I can't believe he'd do something that unethical."

"Should we brainstorm?" Robin asked as they rode up in the elevator.

"Not now. I'm wiped. Let's meet tomorrow at six."

"Where's Jeff?" Robin asked.

"He told me he was working on a lead. He may be back by now. Why don't you check on him, then get a good night's sleep."

"Robin," the receptionist called out when they walked into the waiting room.

"Yes."

"A Mordessa Carpenter called for you." The receptionist handed Robin a message slip with a phone number on it. "She wanted you to call her back."

Robin called Mordessa as soon as she was in her office.

"That you, Miss Lockwood?"

"Yes. You wanted to talk to me?"

"I'm in town and I want to help."

"That's great! When can we get together?"

"This evening is okay."

"Terrific. Where are you?"

Mordessa gave Robin the address and Robin hung up. She was about to go to Regina's office, when Jeff walked in.

"Anything interesting happen in court?" he asked.

"Yeah. Our case was blown all to hell."

When Robin finished telling Jeff about the scar, she said, "Regina told me you were working on a lead. I hope it panned out, because we can use some good news after today,"

"Sorry to disappoint you," Jeff said. Then he told her about his encounter with Jacob Heller.

When he finished, Robin tried to suppress a giggle and couldn't.

"Go ahead and laugh," Jeff said as his cheeks colored.

"I'm sorry. I know this is serious, but I gotta tell you, I wish I'd been there."

"It was definitely uncomfortable. He showed me his notes on the house. It seems Heller worked his way through law school selling real estate and he wanted to get a feel for how much the cabin was worth."

"And you checked out his . . . sexual orientation?"

"That's what I was doing all afternoon. He's openly gay and he gave me a list of organizations and friends I could ask if I doubted him. They all panned out."

"So we're back to Prater," Robin said.

"That's what it looks like. Unless Allison's accomplice is someone whose name hasn't come up in the investigation."

"We may have gotten a break. Mordessa Carpenter just called. She's willing to talk to me tonight."

"After what happened with that scar, it looks like our only chance to create a reasonable doubt is by going after Prater as Allison's accomplice."

"There's another upside to Mordessa coming forward," Robin said. "Regina will have to get off the case and we won't have to worry about dementia affecting her performance."

"Let's go talk to the boss," Jeff said.

Regina looked up when Robin and her investigator walked in.

"We have some good news and some bad news," Robin said.

"Give me the good news. I can use some after what happened this afternoon."

"Mordessa Carpenter will meet with me tonight. She can testify that Arnold Prater tortured women the same way Meredith Fenner was tortured. And one of the women Prater tortured was Tonya Benson."

"You're not still on this campaign to bring Prater into this, are you?"

"We have to," Robin insisted. "After the testimony about the scar, Mason has no chance for an acquittal if we don't give the jury a viable bad guy alternative."

"Prater was my client," Regina said. "It would be unethical for me to inject him into the case."

"That's the bad news. If you're convinced that Mason's only chance is to argue that Prater is Allison's accomplice, you'll have a conflict of interest and the firm will have to resign."

Regina shook her head. "Not gonna happen," she snapped. "I'm not deserting my client in the middle of his trial."

"You wouldn't be deserting him. You'd be saving him. Herrera would have to grant a mistrial. A new lawyer would have the transcripts of the trial to work with and time to figure out something to counter the testimony about the scar."

"There's not going to be a new lawyer. Get that through your head."

"But . . ." Robin began.

"Enough! I won't have you questioning my judgment. This conversation is over."

Regina set her lips in a grim line, and Robin could see that she wasn't going to win this argument.

Jeff followed Robin out. "What do you want to do?" he asked as soon as the door had closed behind them.

"We should talk to Mordessa in case Regina changes her mind."

"I'd say that's a long shot."

CHAPTER FORTY-THREE

The morning after Meredith Fenner's devastating testimony, Robin came into Regina's office an hour before court was to begin, carrying two lattes. She handed one to Regina, who raised a skeptical eyebrow.

"What do you want, Robin?"

"What makes you think I want something?"

Regina folded her arms across her chest, leaned back in her chair, and stared at her associate.

Robin sat down and leaned forward. "I talked to Mordessa last night and she told me in graphic detail what Prater did to her. It's so similar to how the victims at Whisper Lake were tortured that I think—"

Regina sat up and raised her hand, palm out, toward Robin.

"Stop right there. I thought I made it crystal clear yesterday that we are not introducing any evidence about Arnold Prater."

"But—"

"There will be no more time wasted on this, Robin. We have more important things to discuss."

Robin wasn't used to giving up in a fight, physical or intellectual, but she held her tongue.

"Do you think we should put Alex Mason on the stand?" Regina asked.

"I think he'll make a terrible impression, but won't the jury think he has something to hide if you don't call him?"

"That's what they teach you in law school's ivory tower, but this is the real world. I called the first two defendants I ever represented to the stand because of that type of thinking. Do you know what happened?"

"No."

"They confessed. So I started thinking that it might be better if my obviously guilty defendants didn't make it easy for the prosecutor."

"So we're not going to call him?"

Regina sighed. "I wish we didn't have to. I agree with you. He'll make a horrible witness. But I've learned that you have to call your defendant in one particular situation, and that's when there is powerful evidence against him and he's the only one who can refute it."

"Mr. Mason, where were you born?" Regina asked as soon as Mason was sworn.

"In New York."

"Did you attend high school and college in New York?"

"Yes."

"Where did you attend law school?" Regina continued.

Robin watched Mason turn to the jury and smile.

"I was fortunate enough to be accepted at

287

Harvard," Mason said as he puffed up his chest.

Robin felt uneasy. When Regina had prepped Mason before court, she had emphasized that he had to be humble. Robin glanced at her boss. If Regina was upset by Mason's deviation from the script they had rehearsed, she didn't show it.

"Did you move to Portland to practice law after graduating?"

"I did."

"Why did you move cross-country when you'd always lived on the East Coast?"

"I married Christine Dickey, a Portland girl, and she convinced me that Oregon was a great place to live."

"You're currently married to Allison Mason, are you not?"

"Yes."

"Why did your marriage to Christine Dickey end?"

As they'd rehearsed, Alex dropped his eyes and stared at his lap. "She passed away from cancer."

"Mr. Mason, are you the senior partner in a law firm that you helped to build?"

"Yes, and we're one of the best in the Pacific Northwest," Mason bragged, forgetting that he was supposed to be sad because he was remembering the death of his first wife.

Robin glanced at the jurors. Several jurors frowned, and Robin worried about Mason's egotism alienating them.

"Did you travel to New York three years ago for depositions in a case you were handling?"

"I did."

"During that trip, did you meet Allison Mason?"

"Yes."

"Tell the jury how that happened."

"She was a temp at the firm where the depositions were held and she was in the conference room, but we didn't have any contact then. When the deposition ended, I went back to my hotel. After freshening up, I went down to the bar. She was there with some friends. When her friends left, she came to the bar, sat next to me, and started talking to me."

"Your wife testified that you approached her at the table where she'd been sitting when her friends left."

Mason turned to the jury box. "That's a lie. And, quite frankly, my wife has lied to you several times. She's the one who got me involved in kinky sex. I never suggested tying her up or burning her with cigarettes."

This was not how Mason's testimony was supposed to go. Robin waited for Regina to do something to stop him, but her boss seemed at a loss as to what she should do.

Kyle Bergland could have objected because Mason was not answering the question Regina had asked and was making a self-serving speech.

But the prosecutor seemed content to let Mason hang himself.

"And I know why she's lying," Mason rambled on. "She knows she'll be rich if I go to prison. She'll divorce me and get half of my money and our house and anything else she can get her greedy hands on."

Robin leaned over and tugged on Regina's sleeve. "You've got to stop him."

Regina stared at Robin.

"Look at the jurors. They're appalled," Robin said.

Regina looked toward the jury box. Then she looked at her client.

"Let's move on, Mr. Mason," she said. "Please tell the jury what happened after you returned to Portland."

The rest of Regina's direct examination went as badly as the first part, and Robin was certain that their case was a lost cause by the time Regina turned the questioning over to Kyle Bergland.

"Mr. Mason, you've spent a good part of your time on the stand telling the jury that Allison Mason is a liar. Do you stand by that position?"

"Most definitely."

"And you are still maintaining that you didn't murder Patricia Rawls and Tonya Benson?"

"Absolutely."

"And you did not kidnap and torture Meredith Fenner?"

"I had nothing to do with that."

"May I assume, then, that you can tell the jurors where you were on the evenings that these women were abducted?"

Mason blanched. "You know where I was. I told you. Allison tied me up and left me for the entire evening."

"She says that the exact opposite situation occurred. She testified that you tied her up and left on those evenings."

"Well, she's lying."

"And she's framing you so she can get your money?"

"Most definitely."

"Wouldn't she get half of what you have if she simply divorced you?"

"I . . . Yes."

"Wouldn't that be simpler than engaging in serial torture and murder?"

"She . . . she's a sick woman."

"Well, she would be if she did what Meredith Fenner says was done to her, wouldn't she?"

"Yes, yes she would."

Bergland looked puzzled. "One thing confuses me, Mr. Mason. Maybe you can clear this up for me. Will you help me?"

Robin could see that Mason knew this was a trap, but he had to answer the question.

"What do you . . . Yes, if I can."

"Is Allison Mason a man or a woman?"

"That's ridiculous," Mason replied.

"Of course it is. But tell me. Does Allison Mason have a New York accent and a crescent-shaped scar on her right hand?"

Mason just gaped at the prosecutor. Bergland stared at him for a moment before turning to Judge Herrera.

"I don't think it's necessary for me to ask Mr. Mason any more questions."

CHAPTER FORTY-FOUR

Regina Barrister stopped in Robin's doorway. "Let's go."

"Do they have a verdict?"

Regina nodded as she headed out of the office. Robin grabbed her attaché case and hurried after her boss.

Neither attorney spoke on the way to the courthouse. There was nothing to say. Within the hour, they would learn if Alex Mason would live or die. As they walked, Robin tried to remember if there was anything that had happened in the case that would have prompted the jurors to show mercy to their client. She couldn't think of a thing.

The defense case in *State v. Mason* had been a disaster. Alex Mason had been arrogant, conceited, and argumentative when he was on the stand. Robin had watched the jurors when their client tried to shift the blame for the murders onto his wife. It was clear that none of them bought his testimony. As bad was the fact that Regina had been unable to rebut any of the scientific evidence, including the most damning piece—the duct tape with Alex's DNA that had been attached to Meredith Fenner's body.

Another problem was the inability of the

defense to produce evidence that a man other than their client had kidnapped Meredith Fenner. Arnold Prater would have been a viable suspect, but Regina had refused to call Mordessa Carpenter. As a last resort, Regina could have asked for a mistrial because of the conflict of interest that implicating Prater presented, but she refused to raise the conflict issue.

Kyle Bergland's closing argument had been brilliant. Regina had done her best to raise reasonable doubt, but she hadn't had much to work with. A verdict of guilty of aggravated murder in the Rawls and Benson cases and another guilty verdict in Meredith Fenner's kidnapping and assault case had been a forgone conclusion.

The day after the verdicts, the jurors had reassembled to hear evidence on the sentencing issue in the Rawls and Benson murder cases. There were three possible sentences for a defendant convicted of aggravated murder: Death, life without the possibility of parole, or life with the possibility of parole. In the sentencing phase of the trial, the jurors were asked four questions: Was the conduct that caused the death of the deceased committed deliberately and with the reasonable expectation that the death of the deceased or another would result? Was there a probability that the defendant would commit criminal acts of violence that would constitute a continuing threat to society? If raised by the evidence, was the conduct of the defendant in killing the deceased unreasonable in response to the provocation, if any, by the deceased? And finally, should the defendant receive a death sentence? In order for the court to sentence a defendant to death, every juror had to answer yes to every question. A single no on any question would save Alex Mason's life.

Kyle Bergland had shown the jurors photographs of the dead women and Meredith's injuries and he had argued that Alex Mason's crimes proved that he was a cold, calculating killer who would kill again without remorse.

Regina put on the few witnesses she could find who had positive things to say about Mason.

Robin knew in her heart that the prosecutor had made an excellent argument for sending Alex Mason to death row and that Regina had lacked the ammunition she needed to obtain mercy from any of the twelve people who held Mason's life in their hands.

As soon as Robin and Regina were seated at counsel table, the guards brought Alex Mason out of the holding cell. Mason was pale and had lost weight since his incarceration. Robin had never liked Mason, but he'd always seemed filled with energy. Now his shoulders slumped and he shuffled toward his seat.

"Are you okay?" Regina asked.

Mason's bravado had disappeared after his conviction and he shook his head slowly instead of answering.

The bailiff rapped his gavel and everyone stood when Judge Herrera took her place on the dais. As soon as she was seated, she had the jury brought in.

"Have you answered the questions in the two cases involving the murders of Tonya Benson and Patricia Rawls?" Judge Herrera asked the jury foreperson as soon as the jury was in place.

"We have, Your Honor."

"Please hand your answers to the bailiff."

Robin watched the bailiff take the verdict forms from the foreperson and hand them to the judge. When she finished reading the forms, the judge turned to the foreperson.

"With regard to the first question, 'Was the conduct that caused the death of Patricia Rawls committed deliberately and with the reasonable expectation that the death of the deceased or another would result,' what is your answer?"

"Yes," the foreperson said.

"And was this answer unanimous?"

"It was."

The answers to the rest of Herrera's questions in the Rawls case were the same and so were the answers to the questions in Benson's case. And with each answer, Alex Mason slumped forward a little more.

When she was finished, Judge Herrera looked grim. Robin could see that the responsibility of condemning a person to death was taking a toll on her. The judge took a moment to compose herself. Then she looked at the defense table.

"Please stand, Mr. Mason."

Alex hesitated. Then he stood. Robin saw his legs tremble and he touched the table to steady himself. Robin and Regina stood with their client.

"Mr. Mason, the jury has found you guilty of aggravated murder in the Rawls and Benson cases. They have also answered the four questions posed by Oregon's death-penalty statute in the affirmative in both murder cases. Therefore, I have no alternative but to sentence you to death for—"

Mason's knees buckled. "I didn't do it," he moaned. "Not any of it."

Regina reached out to steady Mason and Robin walked behind him to assist her.

Mason's head dropped. Then he threw off Regina's hands and twisted around and glared at the jurors.

"It's Allison, you stupid bastards. That bitch framed me. Can't any of you idiots see that? She set me up."

One of the guards grabbed Mason's arm, but he shook off the guard's hand and staggered back.

"Please, Alex," Regina begged. "We'll appeal. We're not through."

Mason whirled on Regina. "You incompetent cunt!" he screamed. "This is your fault. You let that bitch get away with this."

One of the guards got Mason in a hammerlock and forced him to bend toward the table while the other handcuffed him.

"Don't hurt him." Regina said as the guards forced Mason onto his chair.

"This has to stop, Mr. Mason," Judge Herrera said firmly. "This will do you no good. You're an attorney. You know your right to appeal. This display won't help. Please calm down."

Mason looked defiant for a moment. Then the reality of his situation struck him and he sagged forward and began to weep. Regina reached out and touched his shoulder.

"We're not done, Alex. This is just the beginning," she said to soothe him. Robin, however, was an expert at appellate law and she didn't see any light at the end of the dark tunnel that Alex Mason had just entered.

When they left the courthouse, Regina told Robin to go home. Robin felt disoriented during her walk. She hadn't found one thing to like about Alex Mason and he had treated her like a piece of furniture during the trial, never acknowledging any of her attempts to be friendly and addressing any questions to Regina. But he was a human being and she imagined him pacing back and forth in his cage for years while his appeals slowly wound through the courts. She knew the appeals would fail. In the end, Mason would be put down by lethal injection like a dog. Thinking about Mason's awful future made Robin sad even though he deserved every second of his torment if he was really guilty. But was he guilty? Was Mason right when he claimed he had been framed by Allison Mason? Was he a monster or the victim of a cold and calculating killer?

Robin bought a sandwich at a food cart, but she had no appetite and ate only half of it. All she could think about was whether the guilty verdict and death sentence could have been averted by presenting the jurors with evidence about Arnold Prater? Did Regina's refusal to ask for a mistrial stem from her mental problem? But what really kept Robin awake was the possibility that she was equally responsible for sending her first murder client to death row because she'd lacked the courage to confront Regina.

CHAPTER FORTY-FIVE

Harry White knocked on Meredith Fenner's door thirty minutes after Judge Herrera had sentenced Alex Mason to death.

"Whose there?" Meredith asked anxiously.

"It's Harry, and I've got great news."

Harry heard the locks spring open. Then Meredith was standing in the doorway. Harry smiled as he held out the bouquet he'd purchased.

"It's over. Mason got a death sentence. You don't have to worry anymore."

Meredith looked stunned. She stared at Harry for moment. Then she leaped into his arms.

"Thank you, thank you."

Harry held the flowers at arm's length while Meredith clung to him.

"Watch it. You'll crush the roses," he said.

Meredith stepped back and looked confused for a moment. Then she saw the bouquet.

"Oh, Harry," she said as she took it. "You've been so good to me."

Meredith stepped aside to let Harry in. When she turned toward him, she looked sad.

"What's wrong?" Harry asked. "You got him, Meredith. You identified Mason's cabin and your testimony won the case. I thought you'd be happy."

"I know I said that I wanted Mason dead, but

now that I know he really is going to die . . . I guess I'm just relieved, but I can't take any joy in a human being's death, even if he is a monster."

Harry sobered. "You're right. But you should be more than just relieved. You can start living your life again."

Meredith looked away. "That's the other reason I'm not happy. I've given this a lot of thought. I know how you feel about me and I know you've been by my side every step of the way. But . . . There's no easy way to say this, so I'm just going to say it. I'm going away."

"What?"

"I can't stay in Oregon. Every place I go reminds me of what that man did to me." She looked directly at Harry. "I really care about you, but every time I see you, I think about the hospital and the trial." She paused. "I've got to get away from here and go someplace where I can start over. Where it looks different and smells different and—"

Meredith broke off and looked away from Harry.

"I love you," he said.

"I know you do, and that's what makes this so hard. But you live near Whisper Lake. How could I live there?"

"I could move."

Meredith shook her head. "Your home is in Oregon. So is your job."

"I could be a cop anywhere."

"Harry, it won't work. When I look at you, it brings back horrible memories. I know it's not your fault, but that's what happens."

"Time will change all that," Harry said.

"We can't know that and . . . Look, Harry, I'm damaged goods. Making love is part of a normal relationship, but I don't know if I can ever have sex again without thinking about what that man did to me. I know you want to save me, but sooner or later you'd regret your decision and you'd blame me."

Meredith reached up and touched Harry's cheek. "You're a great guy and you're going to meet some great girl who can love you in every way a woman should love a man. That girl is not me."

Harry's chest heaved and he thought he might cry. He tried to speak, but he was too choked up. He took a deep breath.

"Look," he said. "Don't write me off. Move where you want to. Put Oregon behind you. But keep in touch. Then, if someday you change your mind . . ."

"I could never write you off. I would never have gotten through this without you."

"Then you'll keep in touch?"

"Yes, but promise me that you won't ruin your life by waiting for me. Find someone, Harry. Find someone you love and who loves you back. That's what will make me happy, Harry. That's what will make me happy."

CHAPTER FORTY-SIX

Regina was too exhausted to go back to her office, so she went straight from the courthouse to her garage. When she was in the elevator, she looked at the panel with the floor buttons and couldn't remember where she'd parked.

Regina started to panic. It was happening again. There had been more and more of these incidents lately. In desperation, she stabbed the button for the top floor. She'd start there and walk down. There were only ten floors. She'd find her car soon enough. Then she froze. What kind of car did she drive?

The door opened on ten and Regina stepped out of the elevator. She looked at the cars on her right and her left. None of them looked familiar. She felt sick. What if she couldn't remember? But she would. She would see the car and she would know it was hers.

Regina walked by all of the cars on the top floor. Then she wound her way down. None of the cars looked familiar and her fear grew as she drew blank after blank. Tears were trickling down her cheeks by the time she reached the bottom floor of the garage and she felt like she might throw up.

Then she remembered Stanley. She could call Stanley and Stanley would save her. She took out her phone and speed-dialed his number.

"Please Stanley, help me," she sobbed when Justice Cloud answered.

The parking garage was next to a hotel, and Stanley Cloud found Regina sitting in the hotel lobby, her shoulders hunched and her eyes fixed on the floor. Regina ran to Stanley and threw herself into his arms.

"Thank you, thank you. I didn't know who else to call."

Stanley felt desperation in her tight embrace and he let her cling to him for a moment. Then he put Regina at arm's length. Her cheeks were tear-stained and she looked lost.

"Talk to me, Reggie. What's going on here?"

"I don't know," she said. "I don't know."

Stanley was shocked. Regina sounded terrified and pathetic—two emotions Stanley couldn't imagine Regina Barrister experiencing.

"Does this have something to do with the death sentence in Alex Mason's case?"

"No," she said as she swung her head from side to side. "It's . . . it's my car."

"Your car?" he asked.

"I don't remember where I parked and I . . . I can't remember my car."

"What do you mean?"

"I can't remember the car I drive," Regina sobbed. "I've tried and tried, but . . ."

The lobby was fairly empty, but the desk clerk was casting troubled looks in their direction. There was a restaurant with a bar just off the lobby. Stanley led Regina inside and got a booth in the back.

"Okay," he said when they were seated. "Start at the beginning. What's going on?"

"It's not the first time and it's happening more frequently. I can't remember things I should remember, like appointments or where I've put important things like my keys. I'm scared, Stanley. I'm really scared. And it might be affecting my work. I can't trust the decisions I make and . . . And I'm getting funny looks from the people in the office."

"Funny looks?"

"Things I say confuse them. I won't know what they're talking about when I should and . . ." She put her head in her hands. "There's something wrong with me."

Stanley studied Regina, his thoughts spinning. His mother had spent the last years of her life in a nursing home. Toward the end, she had no idea who Stanley was. Her descent into mental oblivion had started with incidents very much like the ones Regina had just recounted.

"You need to go to a doctor," he said, trying to appear calm even though his thoughts and emotions were spinning out of control. He loved Regina with a passion he had never felt for anyone else and he knew he would lose her if he was right about her affliction.

Regina saw the fear in Stanley's eyes. "You think it's . . ." Her stomach clenched and she could not say the words.

"I don't know. I'm not a doctor. That's why you have to go to a professional."

Regina ran a hand across her face. Then she wept silently.

"I'd have to resign from the bar, Stanley. The law is my life. I'd have nothing."

Stanley reached out and squeezed Regina's hands. "You'd have me, Reggie. I won't desert you."

Regina looked at Stanley. "That's what you say now. What will you do when I've lost my mind?"

Stanley found Regina's car. He wrote down the floor and the number of the space and gave the paper to Regina. Then he drove her home in his car. Regina didn't talk during the ride.

"Come in with me," she said when Stanley parked in her driveway. "I don't want to be alone."

When they were inside, Regina gripped Stanley's hand and led him upstairs. In bed, she was wild and desperate, as if she believed that this might be the last time they would make love. When she climaxed, Regina wept and clung to Stanley with a death grip. When she released him, she lay by his side, staring at the ceiling, her hand in his. After a while, Stanley felt Regina's grip slacken and heard her breathing soften. He turned on his side and saw that she was sound asleep.

Stanley tried to sleep, but it was impossible. He loved Regina desperately and he realized that he should have divorced his wife long ago. Was it too late? Would Regina descend into madness, her brilliant intellect fading until there was nothing left of her mind? That thought sapped him of all joy and left him filled with despair.

When the sun woke the chief justice, he heard the shower running. He lay in bed and waited for Regina to come out of the bathroom. He'd hoped that her deep sleep would give her new energy, but she looked broken.

"How are you?" Stanley asked.

"Not good. But I've reached a decision," she said with great sadness. "I know what I have to do."

CHAPTER FORTY-SEVEN

Regina Barrister was usually surrounded by an aura of energy and self-confidence. When Robin walked into her boss's office on Monday morning, Regina's shoulders were slumped and she looked defeated.

"Tell me about your interview with Mordessa Carpenter," Regina said.

"She told me that Arnold Prater handcuffed her to a bed, beat her, and burned her."

"And you think she was telling the truth?"

"You didn't see her. Mordessa Carpenter has been working as a prostitute for years. She's hard as nails and she broke down twice."

"Do you really think that her testimony could have raised a reasonable doubt?"

"I think what happened to Mordessa and what happened to Meredith Fenner could have been the work of one person, but I don't have any trial experience. Jeff thought it would have been worth a try, but he's not a trial lawyer, either."

Regina leaned back in her chair and closed her eyes.

"I thought about what to do all weekend and I've decided that I did have a conflict and should have asked the judge to take me off of Mason's case. A new lawyer might have been able to save him."

"What are you going to do?" Robin asked.

Regina ran her hand across her face. She looked completely lost.

"I'm going to do the only thing I can do and still live with myself."

Regina Barrister had fearlessly faced down Supreme Court justices and rabid DAs and had always held her head high, but she could not look Martha Herrera in the eye when she walked into the judge's chambers on Monday afternoon. With Regina were Robin Lockwood and a compact African-American man with salt-and-pepper hair, wire-rim glasses that framed serious light brown eyes, and thick lips that were set in a grim line. As soon as the man explained why he was accompanying Regina, the judge told her secretary to call the jail and Kyle Bergland.

When Bergland entered her chambers, Herrera looked subdued.

"Why are we here?" he asked.

"Take a seat, Kyle. As soon as Mr. Mason comes down, I'll answer that question."

The judge's court reporter was setting up her machine when two jail guards escorted Alex Mason into Herrera's chambers. The judge told him to take a seat on a sofa that was set against the wall.

"This proceeding is being held at the request of Regina Barrister, Alex Mason's attorney. Present are Mr. Mason, Miss Barrister, Miss Barrister's associate, Robin Lockwood, the prosecutor in Mr. Mason's case, Kyle Bergland, and Dr. Warren Guest. I'll let Miss Barrister explain why we're here."

Bergland turned toward Regina. His opponent was one of the most dynamic attorneys in the state bar, but today she looked used up.

"This is very difficult for me," Regina said so softly that Bergland had to strain to hear her. "Recently I've found that I have trouble remembering things. On Friday, after Mr. Mason was sentenced to death, I went to my garage, but I couldn't remember where I had parked or what kind of car I drive. This wasn't a onetime thing. It's been going on for a while and other people have noticed."

Bergland's brow furrowed. "What does this have to do with our case?"

Regina pointed at the man who was sitting beside her. "This is Dr. Warren Guest. I went to see him Saturday and he gave me some tests."

Judge Herrera saw how difficult this was for Regina.

"Why don't you let the doctor tell everyone about your visit," she said. Regina looked thankful that the burden of revealing her problem had been shifted to someone else.

Dr. Guest was dressed in a dark suit that matched his somber mood.

"I'm a neurologist. My specialty is diagnosing dementia."

Bergland shifted his gaze to Regina, but she was looking at the floor.

"Regina came to my office on Saturday morning because she was worried that she might have Alzheimer's. I conducted a series of tests and I've concluded that she is experiencing the early onset of the disease."

Bergland looked stunned. "I am so sorry, Regina. My God . . . I don't know what to say."

Alex Mason jumped to his feet. "You kept representing me when you knew you were losing your mind!" he shouted before the guards could push him down.

"Control yourself, Mr. Mason. This is very serious and we're going to approach this problem like adults."

"It's my life on the line. You're not going to be locked up in a cell and killed for something you didn't do."

"That's why I'm here, Alex," Regina said. "That's why I'm telling you and everyone else that I'm sick. I want Judge Herrera to set aside the guilty verdict and death sentence. I should have spoken up sooner. I . . . I should have gotten off the case as soon as I . . ."

Regina choked up and tears streamed down her cheeks.

"But you did a very good job," Bergland

protested. "I didn't see anything that led me to believe you weren't presenting a competent defense."

"There's more to this. Mr. Mason did have a defense, but I couldn't present it. I should have asked for a mistrial because of a conflict of interest, so Mr. Mason could have hired another lawyer who could have used the evidence in his trial, but I didn't. Now I think my judgment was impaired."

"What kind of defense?" Judge Herrera asked.

"I want Robin to outline the evidence she discovered," Regina said.

Everyone listened intently while Robin told Judge Herrera the manner in which Arnold Prater had tortured Mordessa Carpenter and what Mordessa knew about Prater's treatment of Tonya Benson.

"Your Honor," Bergland said when Robin was through. "The evidence Miss Barrister wanted to use wouldn't be admissible if she or another attorney tried to admit it."

"Why do you say that?" Herrera asked.

"Our office had this come up recently in a misdemeanor case, so we researched the issue. I can send down for the memo, but the law is very clear. When a defendant wants to create reasonable doubt by pointing the finger of guilt at someone other than the defendant, he must show more than that this third party had a motive or opportunity to commit the charged crime. Miss Barrister would have had to prove with admissible evidence that there was substantial evidence tying the suspect to the actual commission of the murders and kidnappings."

"Arnold Prater tortured Tonya Benson in much the same way that it is alleged that she was tortured by Mr. Mason," Robin argued.

"Prater didn't *kill* Benson or Carpenter. He let them loose after he beat them up. In Carpenter's case, he knew she could send him to prison, but he let her go to New York after threatening her.

"Another point: According to your witness, Prater used handcuffs, not duct tape, and burning a victim with cigarettes is certainly not unusual enough to establish a unique modus operandi. Then there's the fact that Carpenter's evidence about what Prater is supposed to have done to Benson is hearsay and inadmissible. But most important, our forensic experts have been over every inch of Mr. Mason's Whisper Lake cabin and there is not one shred of evidence that Arnold Prater was ever there."

Robin started to speak, but the judge held up her hand. "I agree with Mr. Bergland. Unless you could have shown me admissible evidence that ties Mr. Prater to the incidents at the cabin, I would not have permitted Miss Carpenter to testify or granted Miss Barrister's motion for mistrial. Can you do that?"

Robin looked at Regina, who shook her head.

"No, Judge. What we told you is what we have."

Judge Herrera turned to Dr. Guest. "I do find your conclusion that Miss Barrister may have tried this case with a mental impairment very troubling. As you know, Mr. Mason has been convicted of murdering two women and kidnapping another and he's been sentenced to death. He has claimed he is innocent from the start. Countless hours have been put into prosecuting and defending this case, but I will have to set aside the verdicts and sentence if Regina was so impaired that she didn't present a competent defense. Can you tell me—in your professional opinion—whether Miss Barrister, at this stage of her disease, is so impaired that she was incompetent to represent Mr. Mason?"

Dr. Guest thought before responding. "I can't answer your question. I didn't see any part of the trial and I'm not a lawyer. I can say that Miss Barrister is in the earliest stages of the disease, but I didn't see her when she was making decisions about how to proceed in Mr. Mason's case."

"Would it help if you read the transcript of the trial?"

"I don't think so, but I'd be willing to read it."

Judge Herrera stared into space. When she spoke, she looked very troubled.

"I'm not going to make a decision about this without giving it a lot of thought. I'll have a transcript prepared for you," she told Dr. Guest, "and I'd like a report."

"Okay," the neurologist said.

"I'll take briefs from both sides. You can include arguments on the issue you raised concerning the alternate theory of who committed the crime. But I have to tell you, Regina, I've known you a long time both in court and out. If you hadn't brought Dr. Guest here, I would never have suspected that you have a problem. This was a very tough case for the defense and, given the facts, I thought you did an excellent job."

"How can you say that?" Mason burst out. "She just told you she's so crazy that she can't even remember what kind of car she drives. Someone like that had no business representing me when my life is on the line."

"I understand why you're upset, Mr. Mason," the judge said. "It's very reasonable, and if I conclude that you're right, I'll give you a new trial. And if I don't, then, obviously, your appellate attorney will make Miss Barrister's mental condition the cornerstone of your appeal."

When she got back to the law firm, Regina called Robin, Jeff, Mark Berman, her receptionist, and the secretaries into her office. Dr. Guest stood beside her.

"I have some troubling news for everyone. Some of you may have noticed that I have not been myself lately. I've been forgetful and have reacted in strange ways in certain situations. There is a medical reason for this. This is Dr. Warren Guest. He is a neurologist who specializes in diagnosing people who may have Alzheimer's."

Mark and the clerical staff looked at Dr. Guest, then back to their boss.

"Over the weekend I went to see Dr. Guest because I suspected that I was having trouble. He gave me a series of tests and concluded that I am in the early stages of dementia. Dr. Guest has prescribed medication that will hold the disease at bay for a while, but he has informed me that there is no permanent fix for what I have. At some point, I will not be capable of practicing law.

"Dr. Guest believes that I am probably still functioning well enough to represent clients in a competent manner, but I will need your support and assistance to make sure I don't commit mistakes that will hurt our clients. I will also understand if any of you wish to look elsewhere for work. At some point, all of you will have to. I will write you glowing recommendations because all of you deserve them. And I don't want anyone to stay here out of guilt or loyalty. I called this meeting to make you all aware of my situation and to encourage you to make decisions that are best for you. I want to make it absolutely clear that there will be no hard feelings on my part if you get another job. Now, does anyone have any questions for me or Dr. Guest?"

"Well, that's the shits," Jeff said to Robin. He, Robin, and Mark Berman were huddled over beers at a tavern near the office.

"What are you planning to do?" Robin asked Mark.

"I'm not going to desert Regina, if that's what you're asking. She's gone out of her way to help me build a practice and she's been a great teacher. What about you?"

Robin flashed a sad smile. "I'm going to stand by Regina. Working for her is my dream job and I want to learn as much from her as I can. If it doesn't work out, I'm pretty confident I can get another job. But I don't think my conscience would ever let me leave her now."

"Amen," Jeff said as he raised his glass.

They clinked and sipped.

"You sure nailed it," Jeff told Robin. "I should never have doubted you."

"Nailed what?" Mark asked.

"Robin figured out that something was going on with Regina a few weeks ago, but I wouldn't listen to her."

"Why didn't you tell me?" Mark asked.

"I was never certain," Robin said. "I didn't know what was normal for Regina."

"We've got to be on our toes," Jeff said. "She's going to make mistakes and we have to be there to straighten them out."

"Agreed," Mark said.

"And that may get harder and harder. Someone needs to talk to Dr. Guest and ask about the signs that will tell us when she's got to stop practicing."

"I'll do it," Mark said, "but I'm not looking forward to the day when we have to tell the best trial lawyer in the state that she isn't fit to practice law anymore."

PART TWO
THE FOURTH VICTIM

CHAPTER FORTY-EIGHT

In the summer between her senior year in college and her first year at law school, Robin fought a brutal match against a very good opponent. She knew that a win would vault her into the top ten in her weight class and that a loss could derail her career. When she'd gone to her corner after the final bell, her manager had told her that the fight was too close to call.

Now, three months after the terrible end to Alex Mason's trial, as Robin waited for the foreperson in her first jury trial to read the jury's verdict, she had the same sick feeling in her gut that she'd had when she waited for the referee to announce the decision in her MMA match.

Sitting next to Robin was Esmeralda Washington, a twenty-eight-year-old African-American single mother, who was raising her five children on welfare. Robin had been appointed by the court to represent her when she was charged with shoplifting a box of Band-Aids in a supermarket.

The security guard who had arrested Robin's client said he saw her pocket the box, then fail to pay for it when she paid for her other purchases. Esmeralda testified that she had the box in her hand when her two-year-old took off running.

She claimed that she had pocketed the item so she would have both hands free when she went after her son. When she caught him, he started screaming. Then her other children started acting up, and she testified that she simply forgot to put the box in her cart.

The case was a push until Jeff found a store clerk who heard the white security guard make several derogatory comments about African-Americans to another clerk right after the arrest, including a statement that Esmeralda should have been sterilized.

"Have you reached a verdict?" the judge asked.

"We have," the foreperson answered.

"What is your verdict in *State v. Esmeralda Washington*?"

Esmeralda looked stunned when the "not guilty" verdict was read and Robin exhaled with relief. Then her client hugged her.

"Thank you, thank you," Esmeralda said, and Robin felt better than she ever had after acing a test or winning a fight. Getting a high grade or winning a decision in the Octagon benefited her. By winning her trial, she had changed another person's life.

Jeff waited in the corridor down the hall from the courtroom as Esmeralda's mother and children showered Robin with praise.

"You look pleased with yourself," he kidded when Robin walked over.

"I couldn't have won if you hadn't found that witness."

"Oh, I don't know. I thought you did a great job cross-examining that racist asshole and you did a terrific job prepping Esmeralda. Are you headed back to the office?"

"Yeah, I want to tell Regina about the verdict. Maybe it will cheer her up."

"She can sure use some good news. By the way, have you heard about Meredith Fenner?" Jeff asked.

"No, what about her?"

"She just hired the Reed, Briggs firm to sue Alex Mason for millions."

Living in constant fear was the worst part of Regina's situation. Dr. Guest had prescribed Aricept, a medication he said would keep her slide into dementia in check for a while, but he had emphasized that the medication provided only a temporary fix for an incurable disease. Dr. Guest had also prescribed daily workouts because physical exercise would help keep her disease at bay for a while. But Regina knew that she was eventually going to lose her mind, just like she'd lost her keys. Every time she forgot something—which happened to people all the time—her stomach twisted into a knot because she couldn't be sure if what she was experiencing was normal or a sign that she was on a descent into madness.

There was a knock on her door and Robin walked in. Robin's grin made Regina smile.

"Can I assume you won?" Regina asked.

"With your help. I followed your game plan to the letter and the verdict was unanimous."

"I didn't do anything, Robin. You were at counsel table, not me."

"She was terrific," Jeff chimed in. "You should have seen her take the security guard apart. I almost felt sorry for him when Robin got done."

Regina looked at her watch. "It's almost five o'clock. Let me take you both to dinner to celebrate."

"You don't have to do that," Robin said.

"Of course I do. Winning your first case is a big deal. You get to pick the restaurant."

"Since you're paying, how about the Ringside? I have a sudden craving for meat."

"Done. I'll have Mary make the reservation for six o'clock. And ask Mark to come, too."

When Robin and Jeff left, Regina was still smiling. She predicted a great future for Robin, and Jeff and Mark were excellent. With them at her side, Regina hoped that she would be able to stay in the game for a while more, and that was all she could ask.

Robin went to her office. There wasn't enough time to do any work before they went to dinner, so she called her mother to tell her about her first "not guilty" verdict. Her mother could be very critical about her career choice, so Robin held her breath when she finished explaining what had happened in Esmeralda Washington's case.

"That was a good thing you did, helping that poor woman," her mother said.

"That's why I do it, Mom," Robin said. "Some of the people I represent *are* terrible, but some of them are really good and they need me to stop their life from being ruined."

"Well, you keep on doing good."

Her mother's reaction and the praise from Regina made her victory even more special, but thinking about Regina sobered Robin. She remembered what fate had in store for her boss. What a way to end a brilliant career, knowing that her diminished capacity might have been responsible for Alex Mason's conviction and sentence of death.

It had been three months since Judge Herrera had denied Regina's motion for a new trial. Alex Mason had fired Regina and hired Les Kreuger to handle his case in the Oregon Supreme Court, where all death sentences were automatically reviewed. Robin thought less about the Mason case as time passed. The jury had found Alex guilty—and he probably was—but there were times when Robin wondered if the jury had reached the right verdict. The problem was that there were so many differences between Allison's version of events and Alex's that they both couldn't be telling the truth. The deciding factor had, of course, been Meredith Fenner's testimony about the scar on Alex's hand. A man had kidnapped Fenner, and it didn't seem possible that two men with New York accents would have crescent-shaped scars on their right hands.

Robin was suddenly struck by a bizarre idea. She frowned. No, it wasn't possible. But what if . . .

Jeff poked his head in the door and said it was time to head out for dinner. Robin turned off her computer and decided it wasn't worth spending any more time thinking about her theory. It was pretty ridiculous. She laughed. An idea like that was probably the result of taking too many blows to her head.

CHAPTER FORTY-NINE

The people at the Hammond Sheriff's Department had noticed that Harry White seemed different when he returned to town after the verdict in the Mason case. Harry had always been "one of the boys," someone who could be counted on to join a group going for beers after work or participating in softball games against other police departments. Though serious, he was never moody and he was quick to laugh at a joke. Since his return, he seemed depressed and had taken to going home after work, turning down invitations to fish or go to someone's house for dinner. A few of his fellow cops had asked him if anything was wrong. Harry had said he was fine, so no one pressed him. But the truth was that Harry was lovesick.

On Friday afternoon, Harry was working on a police report when someone walked in. He looked up, saw Carrie Anders, and smiled.

"Hey, stranger. What brings you from the big city to the sticks?"

"It's my mom's birthday tomorrow, so the family is in town."

"How old is she?"

"It's a big one, seventy-five."

"Is Tom coming?"

"Yeah."

"Ask him to give me a ring. I haven't seen him in ages and it would be good to catch up."

"No need to talk on the phone. I'm here to invite you out to the house for a barbecue. Can you do tomorrow at three?"

"I'll be there. Want me to bring something?"

"A six-pack would be good, and a date if you're seeing someone."

Harry stopped smiling.

"What's up?" Carrie asked.

"Nothing."

"Hey Harry, I'm a detective. You can't get anything by me. Now, what's the problem?"

Harry had not been able to talk to anyone he worked with about Meredith because they'd just ride him, but Carrie worked in Portland and she'd always been a good listener.

"Shut the door and sit down," Harry said. As soon as the door was shut, Harry unburdened himself.

"It's Meredith."

"Oh?"

"I thought we had something going, but I didn't do anything because I knew it would screw up the case. But we talked about it. She was straight with me. She said she liked me but that she was still a mess because of what happened. She told me she cared about me but couldn't stay in Oregon because everything she saw reminded her of what Mason had done to her—which I totally understand. But I really like her and, well, I thought we were friends. But she hasn't called or written once, even though she has my number and I gave her my address. Then I read that she'd hired a Portland law firm to sue Mason, which means she was probably up there. But she didn't call when she was in town."

"Did you ever think that you remind her of what happened?" Carrie asked. "You were one of the first people she saw at the hospital and you were with her all through the case."

"But I've always been on her side."

"True, but that doesn't mean she doesn't flash back to that cabin every time she sees you."

"So you think it's hopeless?"

"No, but I do think you have to give her time."

Harry nodded. "What you say makes sense, but I'd still like to stay in touch. Do you have her address?"

"I don't know if writing her is such a good idea. It's probably best if you let her make the first move when she's ready."

"I'm not going to stalk her, Carrie. I just want to drop her a note. I'll be real neutral."

Carrie thought for a moment. Then she nodded. "I don't remember her address, but I'll email it when I get back to Portland."

"Thanks."

"You're a good friend, Harry. I hate to see you sad."

CHAPTER FIFTY

Arnold Prater glared at Robin when she walked past him on the way to the witness stand to testify in Prater's attempted-murder case. Robin ignored Prater until she'd been sworn. Then she turned his way, locked eyes with him and, without saying a word, let Prater know that she was not intimidated.

Robin answered the prosecutor's questions, then withstood the scathing cross-examination conducted by Prater's attorney. When the judge told Robin that she was excused, she walked down the aisle without giving Prater another glance.

Carrie Anders had listened to Robin's testimony from the back row of the spectators' section, and she followed Robin into the corridor outside the courtroom.

"You did great in there," the detective said.

"I just told the jury what happened," Robin said.

"Prater is a scumbag, and you're going to be responsible for taking him off the street."

Robin shrugged. "I won't feel bad if he's locked up. Especially after what he did to Mordessa Carpenter and Tonya Benson."

"Amen."

Robin was about to walk away, when a thought occurred to her.

"Can you do me a favor, Carrie?"

"That depends on what it is."

"Thinking about those women made me remember the similarities between the way they were tortured by Prater and the way Meredith Fenner was tortured."

Anders frowned. "What are you getting at?"

"When we were representing Alex Mason, we thought that Arnold Prater might have been the man who kidnapped and tortured Fenner. He has a build that's similar to Mason's and a New York accent."

"You can forget that," Anders said. "You're not the only person who went down that road. I checked out Prater as soon as I found out what he'd done to Carpenter, but Prater has an alibi for the night Fenner was kidnapped. He was part of a team that arrested a heroin dealer and he was with several other cops all night."

"Oh."

"Don't feel bad. Mason is guilty as sin and where he belongs."

"Yeah. I guess so."

Robin was a little dejected now that she knew that neither Prater nor Jacob Heller was Fenner's kidnapper. That left Alex Mason as . . . Robin froze. What if there was something they had overlooked?

For decades, the Pearl had been a dusty, decaying warehouse district populated by the homeless. Then the developers moved in. Seemingly overnight, the grimy, run-down buildings were replaced by gleaming high-end condos, in restaurants, and chic boutiques. McGill's Gym was on the bottom floor of one of the few old brick buildings that had escaped gentrification. It was dimly lit and filled with the sweat stink you never found in the modern, air-cooled, disinfected workout emporiums patronized by young professionals and those trying to outwit Father Time. Robin had joined McGill's because it was home to boxers and MMA fighters who would spar with her on days she didn't pump iron.

Barry McGill had been a top ten middleweight in his day and he kept up on boxing and mixed marshal arts, so he had recognized Robin when she'd filled out her membership application. Now McGill nodded to Robin when she walked in after work.

"Is Sally around?" Robin asked.

"She's changing," McGill said.

"Thanks," Robin said as she headed for the locker room.

Twenty minutes later, Robin was sparring with Sally Martinez, who had won all-American honors wrestling for Pacific University. Martinez, a CPA, was a few pounds heavier than Robin, but

Robin usually came out on top when they sparred. The women walked to a wrestling mat in a musty corner of the gym and started working. Martinez shot a single leg, swept Robin's other foot, and ended on top after a few seconds of scrambling. Then she caught Robin in a fireman's carry and put her on her back. By the time she took Robin down for the third time, it was clear that Robin's head wasn't in the game.

"I don't think I've ever beaten you up this bad," Martinez joked. "Did you drink some slug juice before you came here?"

"No, I'm just distracted by something I'm working on."

"Workouts are for putting work behind you."

"You're right," Robin said as she shook out her arms and crouched down. "It's time to kick ass."

"In your dreams," Martinez replied as the women began to circle.

Robin did a little better during the rest of the workout, but she couldn't shake the thoughts that had kept her from focusing during her sparring session. She kept going over everything she knew about Alex Mason's case as she walked home, and those thoughts kept her up well after she'd burrowed under her covers.

Early the next morning, Robin rode her bike across town to People's Coffee House, where Meredith Fenner used to work. The shop had just opened when Robin arrived and there were only two customers.

"Is the owner in?" Robin asked the barista when she got to the counter.

"That's her," the young girl said, pointing at a slender middle-aged woman with blue-dyed hair who was stocking a box with napkins in a corner of the store.

Robin paid for her latte and walked over to the woman.

"Are you Judy Molineaux?"

"Yes," the woman said with a smile.

"I'm Robin Lockwood. I'm an attorney."

Molineaux's smile widened. "I'm not in any trouble, am I?"

Robin returned the smile. "No. I'm here to get a little information about one of your ex-employees, Meredith Fenner."

Molineaux stopped smiling. "What kind of information?"

"I'm Regina Barrister's associate. We represented Alex Mason."

Molineaux's features tightened. "I know who Miss Barrister is. I thought Mason's case was over."

"He was sentenced to death and my firm doesn't represent him anymore, but there were a few loose ends we've been trying to tie up."

"If you don't represent Mason, why do you care about his case? Meredith is a sweet girl and what that man did to her . . ."

Molineaux shook her head in disgust.

"You're right. I never felt clean while I was working on his case and I wouldn't bother you now if it wasn't important."

"What did you want to know?"

"If it isn't too much trouble, I'd like to see her employment application."

"That's private."

"I don't need a copy. And it may help her," Robin said, lying. "You know she's suing Mason for all the terrible things he did to her."

"No, I didn't know that. But how can seeing her employment application help her lawsuit?"

"There was a rumor that she had an arrest record, but she said she'd never been arrested. If it turns out she lied to the police, it could damage her credibility."

"If Meredith was arrested, it's news to me."

"Not in Chicago, Texas, New Mexico, Florida, or New York?"

"Not that she told me. And I did a background check before I hired her. I had a problem with another employee, who embezzled money from me, so I'm extra careful now."

"This is very helpful. And she's never lived in any of those places?"

"She lived in Miami before moving here, but none of those other places."

"Okay. Well, thanks."

CHAPTER FIFTY-ONE

Allison Mason and Meredith Fenner had both lived in Miami, where Allison had been arrested for prostitution. Jeff had found out about the arrest, but, as far as Robin knew, he had never gotten the police report. One of Robin's classmates from Yale had been hired by a Miami firm. Robin called her, and a day later she received an email with a copy of Allison's arrest report. A complaint had been made by Daniel Prescott, a salesman with a corporation headquartered in Minneapolis, who traveled all over the South for the company. The report said that Prescott had hired a woman through an escort service and had had sex with her and another woman in his hotel room. After the women left, Prescott discovered that his wallet was missing. Prescott reported the theft. The escort service gave the police Allison's address, and the wallet was found in her apartment. Allison was arrested, but Prescott didn't press charges after he got the wallet back. The report didn't name the other woman, but the fact that there had been two women sparked Robin's curiosity.

Robin called in sick as soon as Daniel Prescott agreed to meet her. The flight to Minneapolis took a little under three hours, so she was able to go to Minneapolis and back and only miss a day at work. Robin had imagined that a traveling salesman who hired prostitutes would be ugly and dumpy, but Prescott was tall, handsome, tanned, and fit.

"Thanks for coming," Robin said when they were seated in a booth in a restaurant near Prescott's office.

"You said a man's life was at stake."

Robin nodded. "Alex Mason was convicted of multiple murders in Oregon and he's on death row, but there's a possibility that he was framed."

"What does what happened in Miami five years ago have to do with an Oregon case?"

Robin placed a photograph of Allison Mason and another of Meredith Fenner on the table. Meredith's photo had been taken at the hospital on the day Caleb White found her.

"Do you recognize either of these women?" she asked.

Prescott studied the photos. Then he pointed at Allison's picture.

"No question. I remember her."

"What about the other woman?"

Prescott frowned. "I can't be certain. She looks familiar, but this woman's face is all marked up and she has brown hair. The woman I remember was wearing a blond wig."

"Can you tell me what happened?" Robin asked.

"Sure," Prescott said, showing none of the embarrassment Robin thought he'd display when discussing his sex life with a woman. "I'm a bachelor and I'm on the road a lot, so I don't have time for serious relationships. I also like the ladies, so I've found discrete escort services in some of the cities I hit regularly. I never use company money, and the people I deal with make certain their girls are clean and high-class.

"When I got to Miami, I called the head of the service I use when I'm there. I like soft-core S and M and she'd sent this redhead over the last time I was in town. I don't remember the name she used. It was Alice or Allie, something like that, but I definitely got my money's worth, so I asked for her again."

"Does Alexis Cooper ring a bell?"

"It could have been. That sounds right. Anyway, the redhead showed up with another woman and suggested a threesome. That sounded great, so I said I was in."

"Did you ask the service to send over two women?"

"No. That was Alexis's idea. She said the other woman was a friend."

"Did you catch the other woman's name?"

"Sure, but she called herself Candi, with an *i,* so I'm guessing that wasn't her real name."

"Did you notice anything unusual about Candi?"

"Not really. Alexis captured most of my attention. When we got down to business, Alexis worked the top half and the other woman disappeared down below, if you know what I mean. Plus, I was wearing a blindfold part of the time."

"Did the other woman say or do anything that you remember that might help identify her? Did anything unusual happen?"

Prescott thought for a moment. Then he laughed. "There was one thing I definitely remember, but I don't know if this will help. S and M can get dicey. I like being teased, but I don't enjoy pain, so Alexis told me a safety word I should say if things got too rough. Anyway, like I said, Candi was down below and she bit me." Prescott laughed again. "That really hurt, so I yelled 'Pumpkin' and she stopped and apologized."

"What happened next?"

Prescott grinned. "Great sex. Then I sent the girls off because I had an early appointment the next day. They left while I was in the shower. When I got out, I noticed that my wallet was missing. That's when I called the cops."

"Weren't you afraid you'd get in trouble?"

"I was pissed off and I had a lot of cash and credit cards in the wallet."

"The police report said you got your wallet back."

"Yeah. Some guy in Vice knew the owner of the escort service. I'm a good customer and they didn't want to get a bad rep, so they gave him Alexis's address. The service said they'd only sent Alexis over and didn't know anything about the other woman. The police found the wallet and credit cards in Alexis's apartment. She claimed that she had no idea how they got there and she refused to give up the other woman. I didn't need the hassle of a trial and I didn't think a woman working for that escort service would boost a client's wallet. I figured her friend Candi was the culprit, so I didn't press charges. My cash was gone, but my credit cards were there." Prescott smiled. "I was out a couple of hundred bucks, but the little thief gave great head, so I figured I broke even."

"This has been a big help. If we needed you to eyeball a woman who could be Candi, would you be willing to do that? We'd pay for the flight and room and meals."

"You say your guy's on death row?"

Robin nodded.

"Yeah, definitely."

CHAPTER FIFTY-TWO

Robin took a red-eye back to Portland and walked down the hall to Jeff's office at eight the next morning. Half an hour later, she and Jeff went to see Regina.

"Do you have a minute?" Robin asked.

"Sure, have a seat."

"The day I won Mrs. Washington's case, Jeff and I were walking back from court and he told me that Meredith Fenner was suing Alex Mason. That got me thinking. Then one thing led to another and I started wondering if we've gotten this case all wrong."

"I'm not following you," Regina said.

"Everyone has assumed that Meredith Fenner was Alex Mason's third victim, so we didn't look into her background. She was so vulnerable and pathetic that we all felt sorry for her. But what if she wasn't a victim?"

Regina frowned. "What are you getting at?"

"What's Alex Mason worth?"

"About fifty million dollars if you take his real estate holdings into account."

"Fenner's lawsuit against Mason is a slam dunk. When she wins, she's going to be a very rich woman. One reason I thought that Allison Mason was telling the truth is the fact that she didn't have to commit serial murder and frame her husband to get his money. She gets a lot of Mason's fortune just by divorcing him. But what if she and Fenner were coconspirators? Between the divorce settlement and the lawsuit, they'll end up with every penny Alex owns."

"Go on," Regina said.

"Without Fenner, there would have been no case against Alex. Fenner led the police to Mason's cabin. She said that a man with a New York accent and a crescent-shaped scar on his hand kidnapped her.

"We considered the idea that Allison set up her husband, but Meredith said that a man kidnapped her. What if there never was a man? What if Meredith was Allison's accomplice and no male was ever involved?"

Regina's mouth opened and she stared at Robin. "That . . . Oh my God."

"Think about it. The person who kidnapped and killed Benson and Rawls didn't have intercourse with them. Meredith said that her kidnapper masturbated instead of trying to penetrate her, which we thought explained why none of the victims showed signs of having been raped. But there would be no signs of intercourse if two women kidnapped Rawls and Benson."

Robin told Regina about Jeff's demonstration at Mason's cabin that showed how easy it had been for Meredith to escape.

"What if there was no escape?" Robin asked. "What if Meredith let Allison beat her up and starve her to make her look like she was a pathetic victim? What if the escape was staged?"

Regina went quiet and stared into space. Then she refocused.

"I'm not saying I buy your idea, and Alex Mason isn't our problem anymore, but I feel responsible for what happened to him."

She turned to Jeff. "I never suggested that you check out Meredith Fenner, even though I usually have you look at all of the witnesses, but, as you know, I haven't been at my best lately. It wouldn't hurt if you ran a background check on Fenner now to see if you can come up with something suspicious."

"I've already done a little investigating," Robin said.

She told Regina about her meeting with Daniel Prescott.

"Meredith lived in Miami around the same time that Allison Mason lived there and met Prescott."

"Do you think Candi is Meredith?" Regina asked when Robin was through.

"Prescott only said she could be. If she is, it proves Allison and Meredith knew each other before they moved to Portland, and that changes everything."

"Let's assume Robin is right," Jeff said. "Allison must have figured that she'd hooked a live one when she saw that Mason was falling for her in New York, so she and Meredith concoct a plan. Allison gets Mason to marry her, then initiates S and M sex with him that mirrors the way they plan to torture their victims. If Mason denies using the duct tape or burning Allison, he'll flunk a polygraph."

"Then Allison starves and tortures Meredith to make her situation seem real. She saves a piece of duct tape that has Mason's saliva on it and attaches it to Meredith when she makes her phony escape," Regina said.

"All Meredith has to do after that is wait until a driver comes along, lead the cops to the cabin, and—voilà!—Mason is screwed," Jeff said, summing up.

"It would be great if we could get Prescott and Fenner in the same room," Regina said.

"How do we do that?" Robin asked.

Regina smiled. "I may know a way. Cyrus Benfield is representing Alex in his divorce and defending Mason in Fenner's civil suit. He'd be very interested in finding out if Meredith and Candi are the same person. Cyrus and I go way back. Robin, why don't you stick around while I give him a call."

The conversation with Cyrus Benfield had been very productive and Regina was excited by the time it ended. Robin left to work on other projects and Regina swiveled her chair so she could look out at the mountains and the river. The medication Dr. Guest had prescribed was helping, but she was definitely not herself anymore. In fact, she felt as if she was losing pieces of herself every day.

Regina's excitement waned as she came to grips with the fact that in the near future she would no longer know who she was. A tear formed and she began to choke up. It had felt so good conceiving her plan of attack and putting it into action. For a short time, she'd felt like her old self. But that feeling was gone now. Robin and Jeff would implement the plan because she no longer trusted her judgment, no longer felt that she could be trusted by others to . . .

Regina stopped and frowned. It suddenly occurred to her that something Robin had said about her trip to Minnesota was important, only she couldn't remember what it was. Something about . . . No, it was gone. But she'd made notes. She could review the notes and maybe that would spark a memory. Yes, that is what she would do. She would rest for moment. Then she would read the notes.

Only, moments later, when she turned away from the view, Regina had forgotten what she had planned to do.

CHAPTER FIFTY-THREE

Cyrus Benfield was a beanpole with curly white hair that seemed to want to fly off in all directions. In a prior life he'd been the lead guitar in a rock band called the Wooly Bullies and he'd never changed his hairstyle. That turned off enough potential employers to convince Benfield to hang out a shingle. The dot-commers didn't care about Cyrus's hairstyle or tattoos, and his firm, which now employed seventy-five attorneys, owned a good chunk of the dot-com business in Oregon.

Cyrus had served the firm representing Meredith Fenner with a notice that he wanted to depose her. Benfield had agreed to hold the deposition in Atlanta, where Meredith had moved, so she would not have to fly to Portland. Benfield had gone to law school with a partner at an Atlanta firm that occupied four floors at the top of an office building on Peachtree Street, and the partner had made a conference room available to the parties.

During the first hour and a half of the deposition, Benfield led Fenner through a series of background questions. Then he started asking about Meredith's time in Florida.

"Now, Miss Fenner, you lived for a while in Miami, where I understand you studied nursing?"

"I went to community college with the goal of obtaining a nursing degree."

"Well, that's very admirable. And I understand you still plan to pursue that dream."

"Yes."

"Did you know a woman named Alexis Cooper when you lived in Miami?"

Fenner hesitated for a second before answering. "I had a few friends in Florida, but that name doesn't ring a bell."

"So you never worked with Ms. Cooper?"

"I mean, I could have. I was a clerk in a large supermarket for a while. I didn't know all of the employees."

Benfield smiled at Fenner and nodded. "Yes, I can understand not knowing the employees at the supermarket. But I was thinking about the Miami Airport Marriott, say about five years ago. Did you ever work with Miss Cooper there?"

Fenner frowned. "I never worked at that hotel, so no."

Benfield pushed the mug shot of Allison Mason, aka Alexis Cooper, across the table.

"Maybe this will help."

Fenner studied the mug shot. When she looked at Benfield, she seemed puzzled.

"That's Allison Mason."

"Where is this going, Cyrus?" asked Benjamin Whitworth, Fenner's lawyer.

"We have some information that your client

knew Allison Mason in Miami when Mason was using the name Alexis Cooper. I just wanted to find out what your client thought."

"I'd like to talk to my client before we proceed," Whitworth said.

Benfield looked at his watch. "We've been at this for a while," he said. "Why don't we take a break."

"Sure," Whitworth replied.

Everyone stood up. Benfield stretched, then headed to a credenza where there were pastries and a coffeepot. Meredith spoke to her attorney in the hall for a few minutes. Then she headed to the ladies' room. To get there, she had to walk through the firm's waiting room. She was almost there when she noticed a man sitting on a sofa. He was watching her. When she got close enough to see him clearly, she stopped and stared. Then she turned around and walked the other way.

"Well?" Robin asked Daniel Prescott as soon as he got out of the elevator in the office building's lobby.

"I don't know."

"Best guess?" Jeff asked.

"It was five years ago and I only got a quick look at her just now. She did look spooked when our eyes met and she turned around and walked away. But I can't say one way or the other."

"Okay. I appreciate the honesty," Robin told

him. "We don't want you to say Fenner and Candi are the same person to please us."

"I get that," Prescott said. "So, what do you want me to do now?"

"The deposition will end sometime soon. I'd like you to wait here and try to get a better look. Mason's lawyer is going to signal us when Fenner leaves. Wait in front of the elevator bank. When she comes out, walk up to her and address her as Candi. See how she reacts."

The deposition ended a little after three and Benfield and Whitworth talked shop while Meredith waited outside the conference room. As soon as Whitworth and Meredith walked away, Benfield pulled out his cell phone and speed-dialed Robin.

"Okay, let's head out," Whitworth told his client.

"What happens now?" Fenner asked.

"We negotiate a settlement that will make you a very wealthy young woman."

Whitworth started toward the waiting area, but Fenner seemed reluctant to follow him.

"Is something wrong?" Whitworth asked.

"No. I . . . This brought back bad memories and I'm a little upset."

"That's understandable. But you can head back to your apartment now and let me work for you."

"Thanks," Fenner said as she walked down the

hall. When they got to the waiting room, the man wasn't sitting on the sofa.

Fenner and her lawyer talked as they went down in the elevator. The doors opened and Fenner found Daniel Prescott standing in front of her.

"Candi?" Prescott said.

Fenner was startled. Then she forced a smile. "You're mistaking me for someone else. My name is Meredith."

"Oh, I'm sorry. You look like someone I know."

Fenner turned away and forced herself to walk out of the building at a normal pace.

Robin and Jeff walked up to Prescott as soon as Fenner was out of sight.

"I'm still not sure," Prescott said.

CHAPTER FIFTY-FOUR

Robin tried to sleep, but she was too frustrated. She had been counting on Daniel Prescott to make a positive identification, but Prescott couldn't swear that Meredith and Candi were the same person, which made her wonder if her theory of the crime was completely wrong.

Robin tossed and turned until her eyes grew heavy. She had almost drifted off when a knock on her hotel door woke her. Robin swore and walked down the short hall as the knocking continued.

"Yes, what is it," she said.

"Mr. Prescott?"

Prescott had been given this room but the TV wasn't working, so Robin and Prescott had switched. Robin opened the door to explain that, when she saw a person in a hoodie and dark glasses holding a gun. The world slowed to a crawl and a voice in her head told her to move. Robin twisted away just as the gun fired. She felt a blast of hot air at the same time she threw her weight into the door. It smashed against a hand and the gun flew into the room.

Robin slammed the door shut and sagged against it. It dawned on her that she'd just been literally inches from being dead.

• • •

Jeff joined Robin in her hotel room shortly before someone knocked on her door. Robin left Jeff in the sitting area and opened the door for a heavyset white man and a muscular black woman. The white man flipped open his ID and the woman followed suit.

"You the person who called nine one one and asked for a homicide detective?" the man asked Robin.

"Yes, sir."

"Well, you got two of us. I'm Dennis Parks and this is Alicia Prince."

"My name is Robin Lockwood and someone just tried to kill me."

"Why would they do that?" Parks asked.

"Come in and I'll explain. It's complicated. And look out for the gun," Robin said as she pointed toward the floor. "I left it where it fell and I haven't touched it."

The detectives studied the gun for a moment. "You'd better start at the beginning," Prince said.

Robin told the Atlanta detectives about the Oregon case and her decision to switch rooms so Daniel Prescott could watch TV.

"So you think the shooter was after Prescott?"

"I'm sure of it. Meredith Fenner is the person who took the shot at me, but she was really after Prescott because he's the only person who can

352

prove that she and Allison Mason knew each other before they moved to Portland."

"Why are you so certain that Fenner tried to shoot you?" Detective Parks asked.

"I got a pretty good look at her just before she fired. And I'll bet you her prints are on that gun."

After the detectives talked to Prescott, they made a few calls to Oregon to verify Robin's story. Before they left, they asked her to go to police headquarters in the morning to give a detailed statement.

"You're pretty amazing," Jeff said when they were alone. "I don't know how you've stayed so calm after almost getting killed."

"I may look calm, but I was scared shitless."

"Well, you certainly handle stress well."

It suddenly dawned on Robin that she was alone in a hotel room with Jeff. She looked at him. He met her eyes for a moment. Then he looked away.

"I guess we should get some sleep," Jeff said.

They were inches apart.

"I'm still wound up," she said. "I don't know if I can get to sleep." Robin's throat was dry and her heart was beating rapidly. "Do you want to stay with me tonight?"

Jeff hesitated. For a moment, it looked like he might kiss her. Then the moment passed.

"I think your adrenaline is asking me to stay and I think we'd both regret anything we did. I'll see you in the morning."

Jeff walked out of the hotel room. Robin sat down on the couch and wondered if she should be relieved or disappointed that Jeff had been a gentleman. Then another thought occurred to her. She'd seen the scars on Jeff's face, but she had no idea about the damage to the rest of his body. Was he afraid of the way she would react when she saw him naked? Robin wanted to believe that it wouldn't matter to her, but she couldn't know how Jeff thought about himself and how he imagined she would react.

CHAPTER FIFTY-FIVE

Regina had a Town Car waiting for Jeff and Robin at Portland International Airport and had given instructions for the chauffeur to take them directly to her office. As soon as they were in Regina's office, Robin told her boss what had happened in Atlanta.

"Have they found Fenner?" Regina asked.

"No, but they found her prints on the gun, and there's an APB out for her," Robin said.

"Have you told Les Kreuger what's going on?" Regina asked, referring to Alex Mason's appellate lawyer.

Robin nodded. "I called him from Atlanta. He's going to set up a meeting with Kyle Bergland and the assistant attorney general who has Alex's case. He's hoping he can get Alex off death row. Les wants you and me at the meeting."

"Maybe only you should go," Regina said.

"Hey, boss, don't get gun-shy," Robin said. "Your brain is still working just fine, and we can use all the brainpower we can harness."

"How strong is the case against Fenner?" Regina asked.

"The attempted murder at the hotel is solid."

"What about Alex's case?"

"We don't have much," Robin said. "The police

sketch artist used a computer to put a blond wig on Meredith, and Prescott said she and Candi could be the same person, but he also said it's been five years since he saw Candi and he saw her for only a short time."

"So his ID is weak."

"Yes. If Meredith denies that she's Candi and Allison says she took someone else along, we don't have any way to prove Allison knew Meredith before they moved to Portland."

Regina's features went blank and she stared into space. Then she shook her head.

"What is it?" Jeff asked.

"There's something. I know there is, but I can't remember what." Regina's chin dropped to her chest. "I hate this. I hate it. I used to be so quick, and now . . . I hate it."

Jeff walked around Regina's desk and put a hand on her shoulder.

"It's okay. You'll remember. And if you don't, we'll figure it out. We're a team. If there's something there, we'll find it. Why don't you reread everything we've got on this case and try to figure out what's bugging you. And take notes so we'll know what you're thinking even if you can't remember."

"Do you think she really knows something?" Jeff asked Robin as soon as they left Regina's office.

"I don't know. She might have stumbled across

something she can't remember or it could be a fantasy. I'm going to work on the theory that she knows something of substance but can't recall what it is. So I'm going over everything again."

Rereading the Mason file brought no new revelations and Robin was ready to believe that there was no gem buried in the reports. A little after seven, her vision started to blur and her brain turned to mush. When she could read no more, she changed into the workout gear she kept in her office and ran home. The weather had changed from the mild, sunny days of summer to the gloomy days of Oregon's rainy season. Robin plowed through heavy, sloppy drops that splattered on her face and made the run very unpleasant. She was huffing and puffing during the last mile and a half and she vowed to get back on a regular schedule.

Robin staggered into her apartment, took off her wet clothes, showered, and microwaved some leftovers. Then she found an action movie on TV and fell asleep during a high-speed car chase. Her sleep was deep and was not invaded by revelatory dreams, and she was no closer to figuring out how to expose Allison Mason when she woke up in the morning.

CHAPTER FIFTY-SIX

Kyle Bergland met Regina, Robin, and Jeff in the waiting area of the Multnomah County district attorney's office and led them to a conference room where Les Krueger, Assistant Attorney General Diana Montgomery, and Carrie Anders were waiting.

"Did Fenner really try to shoot you?" Anders asked Robin.

"Most definitely."

Anders shook her head. "She played me for a fool."

"She played everybody," Robin said.

Montgomery, a slender woman with a pale complexion, short black hair, and lively blue eyes, was dressed in a gray jacket and skirt and a blue silk blouse. She had been invited to the meeting because she was representing the State in Alex Mason's appeal of his conviction and sentence of death. As soon as everyone was seated, the assistant AG looked at Regina.

"Spell it out for me."

"Robin has the best handle on the evidence," Regina said.

The offices of the Oregon attorney general and the Oregon Supreme Court were in the same block, and Montgomery had met Justice Cloud's former clerk several times.

"Tell me why I should let a convicted serial killer off of death row," Montgomery said to Robin.

"He was framed, Di. Allison Mason and Meredith Fenner set up Alex Mason so they could steal the bulk of his fortune through Fenner's lawsuit and Allison's divorce."

"And you're convinced of this because . . ."

Robin told Montgomery their theory about the women's plan to frame Alex Mason.

"But their plan hinged on no one finding out that Meredith and Allison had known each other before they moved to Portland. We think we can prove they did. Five years ago, Allison Mason was arrested for prostitution in Miami. She was working for an escort service and using the alias Alexis Cooper. Daniel Prescott, a salesman from Minneapolis, hired Allison through the service. Allison brought another woman for a threesome. This woman, who was not employed by the escort service, called herself Candi and had long blond hair, which Prescott thought was a wig.

"Recent events in Atlanta have convinced us that Fenner was the other woman in the threesome. Fenner is suing Alex Mason for torturing and kidnapping her. If she wins, she'll be a multimillionaire. She was deposed in Atlanta, where she's living. We asked Daniel Prescott to come to the office where the deposition was being taken to see if he could identify Fenner as the woman who went with Allison to his Miami hotel. He couldn't, even though he stood face-to-face with her, but Fenner didn't know that.

"Luckily for Prescott, the TV in his hotel room didn't work. He and I switched hotel rooms. Around midnight, Meredith came to Prescott's old room and asked for him. When I opened the door, she took a shot at me, but it went wide. I knocked the gun out of her hand and the Atlanta police found Fenner's prints on it. She got away, but I can't believe she won't be picked up soon."

"There still might be a problem with making a case against Allison," Montgomery said. "Even if Meredith implicates Allison, the confession of a codefendant isn't enough to get an indictment if it's not corroborated by other evidence, and we don't have any. If Allison denies she's involved, a smart lawyer will argue that Meredith acted alone and is falsely accusing Allison to escape from death row."

"Regardless of whether Allison can be prosecuted, it seems to me that there is enough evidence to send Alex Mason's case back to court," Les Krueger said.

"It certainly looks that way," Montgomery said, "but I'm going to have to talk this over with the big boss."

CHAPTER FIFTY-SEVEN

At 5,157 acres, Portland's Forest Park is the largest urban forest in the United States. With more than eighty miles of trails, fire lanes, and forest roads, the park lets visitors experience a true northwest forest without leaving the city limits of Portland. It also provides many isolated places where people who do not wish to be seen can meet.

The canopy constructed by the thick trees that grew over the narrow forest trail provided some cover, but heavy drops still spattered off of Allison's poncho. She hated the rain, but she'd considered the weather in Oregon to be a minor annoyance with which she had to cope while she put her plan into action. As Allison trudged toward the place where she'd told Meredith to wait, she thought about how rich she would be when her divorce was final. She would be able to live anywhere, and places where the sun always shone were at the very top of Allison's list.

One place she was seriously considering was the island where she and Meredith had stayed just before Allison moved to New York. Allison smiled as she flashed back on those sun-drenched afternoons and warm tropical nights where palm trees and crystal clear blue-green waters were always close at hand. The sultry weather had encouraged slow, steamy sex and the imbibing of exotic tropical drinks on the white-sand beach.

Of course, Meredith wouldn't be with her on that beach. Not after the stunt she'd pulled in Atlanta. And that thought brought Allison back to reality. The stupid bitch had almost ruined everything. At a minimum, she'd cost Allison the money Meredith would have gotten when her suit against Alex was settled. But those millions were the least of Allison's worries. Fenner was great in bed and had been perfect for the part of a pathetic, sympathy-inducing victim of torture, but she was not bright. Allison had weighed this drawback when she'd chosen her to play the part of Alex's third victim. Meredith's submissive nature and lack of a conscience had outweighed Allison's concerns about her IQ. Now Allison knew she'd made a mistake.

Meredith was waiting for her, huddled next to a towering fir. When she saw Allison, she rushed over to her and embraced her lover. Allison tolerated the embrace for a few moments, then pushed Meredith away.

"What happened in Atlanta?" Allison demanded.

"I'm sorry, Allison. I'm so sorry."

"It's too late for that now. Tell me what happened."

"They questioned me about my lawsuit in an office building. When I rode down in the elevator, that guy we fucked in Miami was waiting in the lobby. He called me Candi."

"What was he doing there?"

"They brought him."

"Who brought him?"

"Regina Barrister's associate. They must have figured out that I was with you in Miami. They asked if I knew you and they asked about the hotel where we did the threesome."

This was Allison's worst nightmare.

"I followed them to their hotel and got the guy's room number. I didn't know what to do. I wanted to call you, but you said I shouldn't ever do that because the cops could check our phone records."

"What did you do?"

Meredith couldn't meet Allison eyes, and she looked down at the muddy trail.

"He's the only one who could say we knew each other before Portland. He can wreck everything."

"What—did—you—do?"

"I couldn't think of any other way, so I went to his hotel room with my gun. Only he wasn't in his room. The associate was. She slammed the door on my wrist and the gun fell, but I got away."

"Thank God for that," Allison said.

"What should I do, Allison? I can't go to jail. I'd never make it in there."

"I'll never let that happen."

Meredith's eyes widened as she saw the knife in Allison's hand. She leaped to the side just as Allison stabbed at her. The rain had made the ground slippery and Allison slid forward. Meredith slammed both hands into Allison, who fell into the thick, solid trunk of an oak tree. Pain lanced through Allison's shoulder. She gritted her teeth and struggled to her feet. By the time she was standing, Meredith had disappeared into the mist.

CHAPTER FIFTY-EIGHT

Harry White sat on an uncomfortable plastic chair in the contact visiting room in the Multnomah County jail. When the door opened and Meredith walked in, Harry didn't feel a thing. His ability to feel had been destroyed the moment Carrie Anders told him that Meredith had been charged with attempted murder in Atlanta and was on the run.

Carrie had called again last night to tell Harry that Meredith had been picked up in California when she'd used a credit card to buy gas for a car she'd stolen. He was at the jail today because Carrie had asked him to negotiate a deal with Meredith before she got a lawyer, in the hopes that his connection with Meredith might carry some weight. Harry told her that he never wanted to see Meredith again and that there had never been a real connection. But Carrie persisted and appealed to him on behalf of Alex Mason, and he gave in.

Meredith was wearing an orange jumpsuit that was too big on her, but she still looked beautiful. The guard left them and Meredith sat down. Harry couldn't speak. He could only stare. Meredith smiled and looked at him with the eyes that had once filled him with desire.

"Hello Harry," Meredith said. "It's nice of you to visit. I've missed you."

"No you haven't." Harry smiled sadly. "You know, I really loved you, but now I know that the woman I fell in love with never existed. She would never have been able to torture those poor helpless women."

"And neither could I."

Harry shook his head. "I know what you and Allison did. You're monsters."

"If you believe that, why are you here?"

"To give you a chance to save your life. Agree to testify against Allison and you'll get life with the possibility of parole. Refuse and you'll take Alex Mason's place on death row."

"What could I say? I've never met Allison. I'm a victim, Harry. Just like those other poor girls. You saw me that first day. You saw how I'd been beaten and abused. How could anyone fake that?"

"Easily, if they had no conscience. So, what will it be? Death row or a chance at freedom?"

"In how many years, twenty, thirty? Think about it, Harry. The torture I went through in that cabin lasted less than a week. The torture I would suffer as an innocent prisoner would be a million times worse."

"That torment is what Alex Mason is experiencing, Meredith. If there's a shred of humanity left in you, please help him."

"Mason is a convicted serial killer who tortured me. Why would I want to help him?"

Harry wondered how he could have been so wrong about Meredith.

"You know you're going to prison in Georgia for attempted murder," Harry said as he stood up and rang for the guard. "Cooperate and we can work with the authorities in Georgia to get your sentence to run concurrent with a life sentence here. Think about the deal, but don't think too long. We're going to give Allison the same option. First come, first served."

The door opened. Harry turned his back on Meredith and started to leave. Then he stopped and turned around.

"Something has really bothered me," he said.

"What, Harry? Maybe I can help you."

"The scar on Mason's hand. Did Allison tell you about that or did you learn about it by reading the police reports I gave you?"

Meredith just smiled. Harry waited a beat. When it was clear that Meredith wasn't going to answer, he left the room. When the door closed behind him and he was alone, Harry's heart seized in his chest and it took all of his will to fight back tears.

CHAPTER FIFTY-NINE

The rain was still coming down a week after Allison's trip to Forest Park. She couldn't believe how stupid Meredith had been. What had she been thinking when she went to that hotel and tried to kill Daniel Prescott? Of course, thinking had never been Meredith's strong suit. If she'd been thinking when they had their threesome with Prescott, she would never have boosted his wallet and there wouldn't have been a reason to kill him.

Wondering about what Meredith would do next had Allison on edge. Meredith hadn't tried to call her, which didn't surprise her, since she'd tried to kill Meredith. Allison was hoping that Meredith had run to some small town where she could change her name and spend the rest of her life waiting tables in a bar.

The doorbell rang. Allison wasn't expecting anyone. She walked into the foyer and looked through the peephole. Kyle Bergland and the oafish detective whose name she could not recall were standing on her doorstep, huddled under their umbrellas. Allison fixed a welcoming smile on her face and opened the door.

"Good afternoon, Mr. Bergland. What can I do for you?"

Bergland smiled. "You could let us in before we drown."

Allison noticed that the detective wasn't smiling, but she laughed anyway. "Sure. Come on in."

Bergland stepped into the entryway and held the umbrella outside for a moment to shake off some of the water.

"What brings you out in this downpour?" Allison asked.

"A very serious situation, Mrs. Mason. Have you read about Meredith Fenner?"

"I have, and I can't believe she tried to shoot someone."

"She did, and it's the reason that she tried to murder Daniel Prescott that brings us here."

Allison looked puzzled. "I don't understand."

"Daniel Prescott, the man Fenner tried to kill, is the person you had sex with in Miami when you were working as an escort."

Allison's brow furrowed. "What possible reason would she have to kill him?"

"Only one we can think of," Bergland said. "You had a threesome with Prescott. If Fenner was the other woman in that threesome, it would mean that you knew her before you two moved to Portland and it would cast doubt on the charges against your husband."

"I still don't get it," Allison said.

"Let's cut the crap," Carrie Anders said. "You

and Fenner cooked up a scheme to steal Alex Mason's fortune, and it was working just fine until Fenner tried to kill Prescott. We're here to tell you that Fenner is in custody and she's made a deal; no lethal injection if she testifies about your part in the murders of Tonya Benson and Patricia Rawls."

Allison's mouth gaped open. "You think I . . . That's ridiculous. I've seen Miss Fenner on TV, but I've never met her and I had nothing to do with the death of those poor women."

"Fenner says she met you in Forest Park last week and you tried to kill her."

"That's absurd."

"Maybe, but before we go, we have something for you." Bergland held out an official document. "That's a subpoena. The court is holding a hearing on a motion for relief of judgment in your husband's case and you're going to be a witness."

Allison closed the door behind the detective and the prosecutor and walked back to the living room. Should she be worried? Allison poured a glass of Alex's very expensive single-malt liquor and stared out at the rain. Her divorce attorney had explained that criminal charges had no bearing on the way the proceeds of a divorce were distributed, so she'd come out with several million dollars even if Alex was released from prison and the cops suspected she was guilty of murder. And they could suspect away, because they would never be able to prove anything. If Meredith accused her of being involved in the Rawls and Benson murders, she'd say that Meredith was making up the story so she could cut a deal with the DA and escape the death penalty.

What about Prescott? She'd bet anything that he wasn't able to say that Meredith was with her in Miami. If he could, she'd be under arrest. No, she was safe and she'd soon be rich.

CHAPTER SIXTY

The guards led Alex Mason to the defense table, where Regina, Robin, and Les Krueger were waiting. Alex stood in front of Regina.

"Les explained everything you've done for me and I want to apologize for the hurtful things I said in Judge Herrera's chambers."

"No need for an apology. You had every right to be mad."

"I still shouldn't have said what I did."

"That's all behind us, Alex. Our job is to get you out of jail, and we should accomplish that today."

"Will you be representing me?"

Regina smiled. "No, Alex. I've learned my lesson. Robin and I will be at counsel table, but Les will handle the case. I want to be sure that you have competent counsel this time around."

The bailiff rapped the gavel and everyone stood when Judge Herrera took the bench.

"Mr. Kreuger, this is your motion, so tell me why we're here," the judge said as soon as she was seated.

Les Kreuger was a bear of a man, with a florid complexion, gray-streaked black hair, and a deep voice that had been trained for opera in his youth.

"We're here, Your Honor, because recent events have made it crystal clear that far from being the perpetrator of several hideous crimes, Alex Mason is as much a victim as Patricia Rawls and Tonya Benson."

"I'll make that decision after I hear your witnesses. Call your first one."

"We call Meredith Fenner, Your Honor."

A guard led Meredith out of the holding area. Les Krueger had bought her a conservative blue dress, which made her look like an angelic waif. Robin had to keep reminding herself that the woman who was taking the stand was a sadistic murderer.

"I still can't believe the way she played us," Robin said to Regina. "Fenner came across as a saint, but she's really a vampire."

Regina's mouth gaped open. "Oh my God," she gasped. "Halloween!"

"What?" Robin asked.

"I knew there was something," Regina said. Then she leaned toward Krueger and whispered in his ear.

"Mr. Krueger?" the judge asked.

"May I have one minute, Your Honor?"

Robin leaned over to hear the conversation. She missed most of it, but she did hear Regina say, "Send Meredith back to the jail and have Bergland ask her one question. If she gives the answer I think she will, we've got Allison."

Twenty minutes later, Kreuger said, "We call Allison Mason, Your Honor."

Allison entered the courtroom with Jacob Heller. She was wearing a dark dress and a pearl necklace and looked self-confident.

"Your Honor," Heller said, "Mrs. Mason received a subpoena commanding her to appear at this hearing. I'm accompanying her because we are not certain why she's been summoned and whether there may be Fifth Amendment considerations."

"Very well, Mr. Heller. Take a seat. If Mrs. Mason needs to consult you, I'll let her. Let's proceed."

"Mrs. Mason," Les Kreuger began as soon as the bailiff administered the oath, "did you testify in Alex Mason's criminal case?"

"Yes."

"During cross-examination by Miss Barrister, did you admit to being arrested for prostitution in Miami, Florida?"

"Yes."

"Now my understanding about this incident is that you were working for the Excelsior Escort service. Is that correct?"

"Yes."

"And they sent you to meet a man named Daniel Prescott at the Marriott."

"I don't remember the man's name, but that sounds right."

"Would it help if I told you that Mr. Prescott was shown your picture and positively identified you as the woman with whom he had sex at his hotel?"

"I'm not denying I worked as an escort. I just don't remember the gentleman's name. If Mr. Prescott said I was the person sent by the escort service, I probably was."

"And you took another woman along?"

"Yes, there was another woman with me."

"Who was not an employee of the service?"

"No."

"She was a friend?"

"No, she was only an acquaintance."

"Do you remember her name?"

"No, I didn't know her well."

"Could her professional name have been Candi, with an *i?*"

"It's been a while. I don't remember."

"Mr. Prescott said that the other woman told him her name was Candi and that the three of you engaged in some S and M sex."

"Yes."

"This was a game—role playing—much like the S and M game you and Mr. Mason played?"

"Yes."

"Now S and M role playing can get rough, so the partners have a safe word they say if they want to stop, don't they?"

"Yes."

Kreuger smiled. "As I understand it, you and Mr. Mason used a safe word, *pumpkin.*"

"Yes."

"Speaking of silly words, wasn't Candi a made-up name that Meredith Fenner used when she was part of your threesome with Daniel Prescott in Miami?"

"I've never met Miss Fenner, ever."

"Remember, you're under oath," Kreuger said.

"I remember quite well," Allison replied angrily.

"You're aware, are you not, that Miss Fenner tried to murder Mr. Prescott in Atlanta?"

"I only know what was in the newspaper."

"If Miss Fenner wasn't the person in your threesome with Mr. Prescott, what motive could she possibly have had to murder Mr. Prescott?" Kreuger asked.

"I have no idea. I don't know anything about that."

"No further questions," Krueger said. "And Mr. Mason calls Daniel Prescott."

Prescott testified about the ménage a trois at the Miami hotel and positively identified Allison Mason as one of the two women.

"You have seen Meredith Fenner on several occasions up close. Was she the woman who called herself Candi?" Krueger asked.

"I think she was, but I can't be certain. Candi had blond hair, which I think was a wig. I've seen an artist's sketch showing Miss Fenner with blond hair and you had me view her with a blond wig at the jail. I think Miss Fenner was the woman who accompanied Mrs. Mason, but this was a brief encounter, five years ago, and I'm not a hundred percent positive."

"When Mrs. Mason got to your hotel, did you agree to engage in S and M sex with her and the woman who accompanied her?"

"Yes."

"Was there an agreement to use *pumpkin* as your safety word if you felt that the sex was getting too rough?"

"Yes."

"Who suggested the word?"

"Mrs. Mason."

"Was Candi present when you agreed on the word?"

"No, she was in the bathroom."

"Did you ever use the word while engaged in your sex acts?"

"Yes."

"When did that happen?"

"Candi bit me. It hurt. I said, 'Pumpkin' and she apologized."

"So Candi knew the safe word?"

"That is correct."

"Thank you, Mr. Prescott. My next witness is Meredith Fenner."

"Miss Fenner," Krueger asked after a few preliminary questions about the deal she'd cut with the district attorney, "do you know Allison Mason?"

"I do."

"What is your relation to her?"

"We were lovers."

"How long had you and Mrs. Mason been romantically involved?"

"On and off for about five or six years."

"Please tell the judge how you met."

Meredith turned to Judge Herrera. "I was a waitress at a nightclub in Miami and I served her. We started talking and I went home with her after my shift."

"How was Mrs. Mason supporting herself in Miami?"

"Mostly temp work, but she did occasional jobs for an escort service."

"Did Mrs. Mason take you along on any of her assignments for the escort service?"

"Just once. I asked her if I could go because I was curious and I thought it would be fun."

"Who was the client?"

"Daniel Prescott."

"Where did you meet him?"

"At the Marriott by the airport."

"What happened at the hotel?"

"Mr. Prescott had arranged for only one girl, so Allison asked if he would mind if we did a threesome. He wanted to know if it would cost more. Allison told him a price and he agreed."

"Where were you when Mr. Prescott and Mrs. Mason testified today?"

"In the jail."

"Could you hear what they said?"

"No."

"Have you read the notes of Regina Barrister's interview with Alex Mason?"

"No."

"Have you read any reports of any interviews Mr. Prescott gave to Miss Barrister's associate Robin Lockwood?"

"No."

"Did Mrs. Mason have a talk with you about how to conduct S and M sex with a client before you met with Mr. Prescott?"

"We talked about it on the way to the hotel."

"Did she tell you that S and M could get rough and that she would give the client a safety word that he could say if he wanted to stop?"

"Yes."

"What was the safety word Mrs. Mason told her clients to use?"

"Pumpkin."

"During your sexual encounter with Mr. Prescott, did the sex get too rough at one point?"

"Yes."

"What did Mr. Prescott do?"

"He yelled 'Pumpkin' and I stopped what I was doing."

"Did you ever go on another job with Mrs. Mason?"

"No."

"Why?"

Meredith blushed and she looked charming. The innocence this monster radiated fascinated Robin.

"After we finished, Mr. Prescott went into the bathroom to take a shower and I stole his wallet. Allison didn't know. We went back to her apartment and had sex. I took the cash and left the wallet. She called the next day, really pissed. She said the cops had come to her apartment. They'd found the wallet and arrested her. She got lucky because Mr. Prescott didn't press charges, but she said she'd never take me on a job again."

"What happened to your relationship after that?"

"I made up with her and it was on again. We went on some vacations and hung out. Then Allison moved to New York. She asked me to go with her, but I was in school and I wanted to get my degree. We agreed to keep in touch."

"When was the next time you heard from her?"

"She called and said she had something big but couldn't discuss it over the phone. She paid for my ticket and I flew up."

"What did she tell you?"

"She said that she was working at a law firm and sleeping with one of the partners. He'd let it slip that they were defending a case that was a sure loser and would cost their client millions. The client was being sued by an Oregon law firm and the firm was sending Alex Mason to depose several witnesses. Her firm had done a background check on Mason and she learned about his divorce and other stuff about him.

"Allison told me she'd seduced Mason in New York and had a plan to fly to Portland so she could trick him into marrying her. She knew he was wealthy and he'd be worth a fortune when the lawsuit was settled and he got his attorney fees. She'd learned that her firm was going to drag out the settlement but would settle eventually. That gave her time to put her plan into action."

"Why did she call you?"

"She'd checked on Oregon divorce law and knew she wouldn't get all of Mason's money if she divorced him, so she had a plan to get it all."

"What part were you going to play in this plan?"

"We were going to kidnap and kill some prostitutes. Then I would pretend to be the third victim of the serial killer. Then we'd frame Mr. Mason and I'd sue for millions."

"You recently moved to Atlanta, did you not?"

"Yes."

"Were you deposed as part of your suit against Mr. Mason?"

"Yes."

"After the deposition, did Mr. Prescott confront you and call you 'Candi,' the name you used when you and Mrs. Mason had sex with him in Miami?"

"Yes."

"Later that day, did you go to Mr. Prescott's hotel and attempt to kill him?"

"Yes."

"Why?"

"I thought he could prove Allison and I knew each other before we moved to Portland, and that would have ruined our plan."

"When you were on the run, did you come to Portland?"

"Yes."

"Did you meet Mrs. Mason in Forest Park?"

"Yes."

"What happened in Forest Park?"

"Allison tried to kill me." Meredith laughed softly. "That's when I figured out that the romance was over."

"Your Honor," Les Krueger said when all the evidence was in, "the attorney general, the Multnomah County District Attorney's Office, and Mr. Mason join in asking you to set aside Mr. Mason's conviction and sentence of death. We believe we have established beyond any doubt that he is the victim of an evil plot cooked up by his wife and abetted by Meredith Fenner.

"Mrs. Mason denies any involvement in this plot, but she also denied ever knowing Miss Fenner before Mr. Mason was arrested. That is a lie. Mr. Prescott and Miss Fenner put them together in Miami. Furthermore, her own testimony condemns her.

"Mr. and Mrs. Mason played S and M games and she admitted that *pumpkin* was their safety word. Mr. Prescott testified that Mrs. Mason and he agreed in the Miami hotel that *pumpkin* would be the safety word. The only records of the safety word are in notes Miss Barrister took when she interviewed Mr. Mason and in the reports of Miss Barrister's associate Robin Lockwood, which Miss Fenner did not see, and in testimony today that Miss Fenner could not hear, but Miss Fenner knew that *pumpkin* was the safety word Allison Mason used in Miami and Portland.

"What are the odds of two strangers coming up independently with *pumpkin* as their safety word? No, Your Honor, Mrs. Mason and Meredith Fenner were lovers in Florida and coconspirators in Oregon."

"How did you figure out the 'pumpkin' thing?" Jeff asked Regina as soon as Alex Mason was led back to the jail so his release could be processed.

Regina laughed. "Robin called Meredith a vampire. That made me think of Halloween, which made me think of . . ."

"Pumpkins!" Jeff laughed.

"Exactly."

"Brilliant, boss."

"Yes, it was, wasn't it?" Regina said breaking into a smile.

Les Krueger walked over, and Jeff left to talk to Robin.

"Going back to the office?" Jeff asked.

"Yeah," Robin said.

Jeff noticed that Robin didn't look happy.

"Is anything wrong?"

"I'm a little sad."

"Why? Alex Mason is free and Allison's under arrest. What's sad about that?"

"I was thinking about Regina."

"Regina? She was amazing. Figuring out that deal with the safety word was brilliant."

"It was, Jeff. But she might have been brilliant for the last time, and that's why I'm sad."

CHAPTER SIXTY-ONE

On the evening Alex Mason became a free man, Stanley Cloud picked up Regina from her office and drove her to dinner at their favorite restaurant.

"Everyone is buzzing about the Mason case," he said as soon as she was in the car.

Regina smiled. "It took a while, but it ended well."

"I heard that your deduction about that safety word was the nail in Allison Mason's coffin. I'm really proud of you."

Regina beamed.

Cloud was quiet for a while, staring straight ahead and gathering his courage.

"Regina, I've made some decisions."

"Oh?" she asked warily.

The chief justice smiled. "You don't have to worry. They're good decisions. First, I'm divorcing Leslie. It's something I should have done a long time ago. I just didn't have the guts. I'm proud of you, Reggie, and I hate having to skulk around whenever we want to be together. It makes our relationship sordid, and it's not."

"You're not being realistic, Stanley. The medication Dr. Guest gives me isn't a cure. It's just part of a holding action. I'm going to be an entirely different person once the disease outworks the drugs. There'll come a time when I won't know who you are, and before that I won't be the Regina Barrister you fell in love with."

"I know that. And that leads me to my next decision. I talked to Dr. Guest and he gave me a rough time line. You still have several years where you can travel and enjoy life; when we can travel together. So I'm going to step down as chief justice—"

"No, Stanley . . ."

"It's not a sacrifice. It's something I want to do. All my life I've let my ambition rule me. I drove myself in high school so I could go to the best college. Then I worked without stop so I could get into the best law school. Then it was endless hours at my firm so I could make partner. All this time, life has been passing me by. I've been to Paris once. I've never been to Venice or China. I don't want to die with regrets."

Stanley paused and took a deep breath. "Look, Reggie, you're the love of my life and you always will be. We have a window where we can be together and see the world. We can go to Santorini and watch the sunsets. We can go to the Taj Mahal and Victoria Falls. I want to see these things with you while you can still enjoy them. I don't want to sit in an office doing the same thing I've been doing my whole life.

"I know this is a lot to take in. You don't have

to make a decision now. All you need to know is that I'll stand by you no matter what you decide and no matter how bad it gets."

Regina felt her cheeks grow hot. She tried to stop her tears, but she couldn't.

"Thank you," she managed to say.

"No, thank you, Regina. I was dead before I met you. You brought me back to life."

EPILOGUE

Robin was walking down the hall to talk to Jeff about a case when she heard the receptionist answer the phone with the words "Barrister, Berman, and Lockwood." She smiled as she always did when she heard the name Regina had put on the office door the day before she left on her around-the-world tour with Stanley Cloud.

Robin had a lot to smile about. In the eight months since Alex Mason had been cleared of all charges and Allison Mason had been convicted of murder and sent to death row, Robin's law practice had exploded. Regina had spread the word about Robin's part in solving Alex Mason's case. That, coupled with what Stanley Cloud had said about her ability as an appellate attorney, had brought major appeals and several serious felony cases into the office. Robin was still a little nervous about her skill as a courtroom attorney, but Mark and Jeff, and especially Regina, had been terrific mentors.

Another reason to smile was that she and Jeff were going to see a movie at the Portland Independent Film Festival after work. It wasn't an official date, but it also wasn't their first unofficial date since they'd returned from Atlanta.

Robin was almost at her office when the receptionist hailed her.

"There's a gentleman on the line," Susan said. "He's calling from the jail and he's just been arrested for murder. Do you want to take it?"

That smile on Robin's face spread out. "Sure. Put him through."

"Another day, another murder," she said as she headed for her office.

ACKNOWLEDGMENTS

I got the idea for this book when I read "Ready or Not, When Colleagues Experience Cognitive Decline," by Cliff Collins, in the November 2014 issue of the *Oregon State Bar Bulletin*. Douglas S. Querin and Mike Francis provided me with great insight into how dementia affects attorneys.

I am incredibly grateful to Dr. Jeffrey Kaye, the director of the Oregon Center for Aging and Technology and the director of the Layton Aging and Alzheimer's Disease Center at Oregon Health & Science University. He took valuable time away from his very important work to read *The Third Victim* so that my portrayal of Regina Barrister's battle with dementia would be accurate. Any inaccuracies are my fault entirely.

Thanks also to Robin Haggard, Daniel Margolin, Sohaye Lee, Andy Rome, and Dr. Karen Gunson, for helping me with my research.

Special thanks to Keith Kahla, for his terrific edits. The book you are reading is much, much better than the manuscript with which he started. Thanks also to my other coconspirators at St. Martin's: Alice Pfeifer, Hector DeJean, Carol Edwards, Ken Silver, and David Rotstein.

My deep appreciation to Jennifer Weltz, for helping me find a new and exciting home at St.

Martin's Press, and to Jean Naggar and everyone else at the Jean V. Naggar Literary Agency, for their decades of support.

Finally, I want to thank Melanie Nelson, who—as my dedication attests—has brought joy back into my life.

Books are produced in the United States using U.S.-based materials

Books are printed using a revolutionary new process called THINKtech™ that lowers energy usage by 70% and increases overall quality

Books are durable and flexible because of smythe-sewing

Paper is sourced using environmentally responsible foresting methods and the paper is acid-free

Center Point Large Print
600 Brooks Road / PO Box 1
Thorndike, ME 04986-0001 USA

(207) 568-3717

US & Canada:
1 800 929-9108
www.centerpointlargeprint.com